THE MORTAL ENEMY MURDER CLUB

GLORIA CHAO

PARK ROW BOOKS

PARK ROW BOOKS™

Recycling programs for this product may not exist in your area.

ISBN-13: 978-1-335-00190-0

The Mortal Enemy Murder Club

Park Row Books
22 Adelaide St. West, 41st Floor
Toronto, Ontario M5H 4E3, Canada
ParkRowBooks.com

HarperCollins Publishers
Macken House, 39/40 Mayor
Street Upper,
Dublin 1, D01 C9W8, Ireland
www.HarperCollins.com

Printed in U.S.A.

26 27 28 29 30 LBC 5 4 3 2 1

Praise for Gloria Chao's Hu Done It Mystery Series

The Mortal Enemy Murder Club

"Clever, twisty, heartfelt, and full of shenanigans. You won't stop laughing or gasping! I devoured this series."

—Wendi McLendon-Covey, star of *St. Denis Medical* and *The Goldbergs*, and cofounder of Strong Beach Productions

"Laugh-out-loud funny, balanced with just the right amount of warm and fuzzies. . . . I adore how Chao shows women showing up for one another at their glorious, messiest best."

—Bianca Marais, *USA TODAY* bestselling author of *A Most Puzzling Murder*

"Chao deftly keeps us guessing (and laughing) as the suspects—and the bodies—pile up. By the end, I was desperate to be in the club myself—with mortal enemies like these, who needs friends?"

—Birdie Horne, author of *Don't Cross Mo Ellery*

The Ex-Girlfriend Murder Club

"Cozy fans will devour this breezy, bloodstained ode to female friendship."

—*Publishers Weekly*

"A perfect blend of laugh-out-loud humor and clever mystery."

—*Library Journal*

"*The Ex-Girlfriend Murder Club* has it all: wacky shenanigans, heart-felt vulnerability, and a cleverly plotted murder."

—Mia P. Manansala, author of the bestselling Tita Rosie's Kitchen Mystery series

"A wildly funny, clever, and heartfelt debut."

—Laurie Elizabeth Flynn, *USA TODAY* bestselling author

Also by Gloria Chao

The Ex-Girlfriend Murder Club

Ex Marks the Spot

When You Wish Upon a Lantern

Rent a Boyfriend

Our Wayward Fate

American Panda

For Anthony, for making this and every
story better, including ours.

And for anyone who wishes to be part of the
Ex-Girlfriend Murder Club. You are.

Through the Looking Glass

Three Weeks into the Future

Harsh fluorescent lighting, a two-way mirror, an incessantly ticking clock—why was I here *again*?

And this time, I wasn't backed up by the Ex-Girlfriend Murder Club.

This time, we had to work with our most hated foe. Our most hostile adversary.

We had to become . . . the Mortal Enemy Murder Club.

I'd learned the universe wasn't against me, but that didn't mean other people weren't.

Kathryn's Fifth Law of Life (and Death), now proven: Karma's a bitch.

CHAPTER 1

Kathryn's First Law of Life: Because there's no luck in the world, you have to make everything happen for yourself, one step at a time.

And I'd taken so many steps recently I almost couldn't see the starting point.

Almost.

"Hi, Ma."

"Wei, Yushan, is you? You get package? Self-Himmylack machine because you single and I worry you choke with no one to help."

Every time my mother called, I was magically transported back to the start line. Why hadn't I told my mother about the extremely hot detective who'd already saved my life multiple times and was now around to give me the Heimlich if needed?

Because this was my *mother.* The one who thought her friend's son would make the best husband solely because he had family money and was a doctor. And the one who bought me a Life Alert and was still paying for the subscription even though I never told her that it had saved my life in a very different way than she'd intended (I did not fall and couldn't get up; I was being held hostage and couldn't get the fuck out). I couldn't bear to answer all the questions that would surely arise once she found out about Adrian. *He handsome? What he do for work? How much money he make? What his SAT score? Why you not introduce us?*

So in lieu of telling her anything, I just said, "I got the package—thanks, Mom—but you don't have to worry about me so much."

"Of course I worry! Do nothing but worry! Soon I will be just skin and bones!"

This was the perfect opportunity to tell her about Adrian, but I couldn't. I rationalized (lied?) to myself that we needed more time, a better setting, maybe an in-person talk. "Sorry, I have to go, I'm just getting to work."

"Ah, you at the lab already? Try and have a good day, yes, Yushan? I know it not perfect, but at least you still at Harvard."

And here was yet another way I was back at the starting line, facing a second can of worms I wasn't ready to open (obvious origin of idiom: bait for fishing; I love knowing where sayings come from). Why haven't I told her that I left my postdoc at Harvard? Because even though we'd made some progress in our relationship, I didn't think she'd approve of the new job. Not to mention, the actual quitting was so different from how I'd pictured it that it almost felt like it hadn't happened.

Months ago, instead of walking into the lab, clearing my throat confidently, and dropping the mic as planned, I had walked in with hunched shoulders, then made a noise like I was choking on my own spit.

Not a single head looked up from their work. Not even Johannes, the lab tech who'd had it out for me since day one. Maybe I wasn't even worth his time anymore. So I quietly shuffled to my bench to grab my few possessions—a notebook and pen, and the name tag on the lab coat. The coat wasn't even mine; it belonged to Harvard. But the name tag—I figured no one else would want that. *Kathryn Hu, PhD.* I remembered how it felt the day I got that. Like I'd succeeded. I'd chanted in my head, *Kathryn Who? PhD, that's Hu!* I was still a PhD, but once I stowed this name tag away, I'd become *Kathryn Who? There was a Kathryn here?*

I didn't speak to anyone. Then, later that day, I said goodbye via email, though I did end it with:

I think I'll be <u>in my element</u> in the new job.

6–92,
Kat

Six because the sixth element is carbon, C, and the ninety-second element is uranium, U.

No one responded.

Which, sadly, did not inspire much confidence to be myself in the new job. Which meant that now, several months in, I'd still barely said a word. But despite being in danger of losing my position, I couldn't help it. Just like I couldn't help my shoulders hunching now as I shuffled into the forensic lab where I was currently training—a.k.a. the job my parents didn't know about, and in the same department as my secret boyfriend.

My phone pinged, and I jumped, wondering if my mom could somehow see me through one of the many you're-single gadgets she'd sent that were now weighing down my keychain.

That not Harvard! How can you lie to your mama, after all I do for you? Send you gift, warm your lotion when you a baby, come to America with nothing so you can have better life!

But it wasn't her. Of course not. It was worse, in a different way.

An email, the fifth one of its kind.

Come join *Dish Gets Served*!

Are you a victim of the *Dish Served Hot* podcast? Did Mandy Thorne ruin your life? If so, you're not alone! Join us for a once-in-a-lifetime meetup to commiserate, vent, socialize . . . and maybe more. You don't have to go through this by yourself. We want to be there for you, and maybe also find a way to cancel her show. What better way to get revenge on the Queen of Revenge than to serve the dish right back to her, steaming hot?

I would be happy to never think about *Dish Served Hot* or Mandy Thorne ever again. Yes, I was a victim—Mandy tried to ruin my life—but I just wanted to move on. Find a way to completely forget that she dedicated an entire season of her much-too-popular revenge-story podcast to framing me for my ex-boyfriend's murder—which was yet another incident I wanted to move on from.

I'd unsubscribed multiple times from the Dish Gets Served email list, but they just kept popping back up in my inbox.

As I unsubscribed and deleted yet again, I heard, "Hu!"

"Who?" asked another CSI-in-training, Diane.

Every time.

"Me, that's Hu," I joked only to myself as I hurried to stuff my phone away.

But my boss, Gerard, was already stomping toward me. "What's rule number three here?"

"No phones," I answered dutifully.

Did I mention my boss hates me?

"And rule number one?" he asked the entire room. "The most important characteristic for a forensic chemist?"

"Integrity," answered his minions.

"Breaking rules is most definitely not a show of integrity." Gerard sniffed with condescension.

That logic seemed circular . . . He made the rules, and breaking the rule was breaking the rule was . . .

Gerard leaned closer to me, but only for show; his voice *rose* in volume to make sure everyone could hear. "You think you're real fancy, don't you?"

"No, no I don't," I answered honestly. How could I convey just how not fancy I felt all the time? "I'm regular ketchup, plain pants"—fancy ketchup is a real USDA designation for grade A ketchup and *fancy-pants* is an official term included in the dictionary—"and, um . . ." What was the opposite of black tie? "I'm white tie. No, wait! That's even more formal! I'm, uh, pajamas."

Gerard ignored everything I said and taunted, "Miss fancy-pants chemist coming here from Harvard, thinking you can do what we've all been training to do our entire lives."

I never fit in at Harvard, yet I somehow didn't fit in here *because* of Harvard. And I hadn't helped myself by taking—and passing, with flying colors—the certification exam early. I thought it would help Gerard's treatment of me, but ever since I got the exam results a week ago, his *fancy-pants* comments had only gotten worse. Unfortunately, I still had more hours to go to meet the certification training requirement, hours which now felt even longer thanks to Gerard.

Kathryn's Second Law of Life: There isn't a universe that's out to get you; turns out, life is just hard.

CHAPTER 2

"You're heeeeere!" Olivia ran up to me and squeezed me for so long I started to understand the appeal of a weighted blanket. "Thanks for coming."

"Are you kidding? I wouldn't miss it!"

When I first discovered that my ex, Tucker Jones, had been cheating on me—when I walked in, half naked, on him proposing to Olivia—I never would have guessed that we'd become the closest of friends. But now, I couldn't imagine my life without Olivia Valentina McCarthy, whose full name I first heard from Tucker's lips following the words *will you marry me*. (Not to mention, less than ten minutes later, I'd heard those very same words followed by *Kathryn Yushan Hu*.)

Olivia let go of me and promptly grabbed my hand, leading me into the theater. "Come sit at my table."

"It's your first night! Don't you want to try your act out on a stranger?"

"Of course not! That's terrifying. You'll clap and love me no matter what, right?"

"Do you even have to ask?"

We shared a smile as she pulled a chair out for me.

The Magic Lounge was aptly named, being more cozy lounge than theater, with tables throughout at different levels so that everyone could see the stage. The event began with appetizers and private shows for each table, followed by two headliner performances on the main stage. Tonight was Olivia's first table show after training for months.

When we—the Ex-Girlfriend Murder Club—had been trying to clear our names by figuring out who murdered our shared ex-boyfriend, we had called Olivia *Double-Oh-livia* for her 007 skills in picking locks, breaking into safes and laptops, and just being a badass in general. Skills she had learned from the private investigator she often worked with at her law firm, and maybe also from YouTube. "You never know when you might need to save your own ass," Olivia liked to say, and she had certainly saved my ass plenty of times. Sleight of hand was something she'd always wanted to add to her arsenal, and of course, if she was going to do it, she was going to go all out and become a full-blown paid magician, even if it was just a few nights a month. This exact personality trait was what made her so good at so many things, including her chosen expertise as a criminal defense attorney. I, on the other hand, would never be able to do what she was about to, mostly because I hated being the center of attention. I preferred hiding behind my chemicals and glassware.

A plate of sliders appeared on my table like magic—though not really, the waiter was just quiet and my eyes were on Olivia. But I was definitely in the right mood for tonight.

Olivia opened a new deck of cards and fanned them in front of me like a pro, which, after tonight, she technically was. "Pick a card."

Even though the line felt cliché, I'd never heard it from someone one-on-one. The excitement bubbled through me like carbon dioxide.

I grabbed a card from the middle.

"Look at it," she instructed. "You can show me. Okay, three of clubs. Do you want to keep this or switch?"

"Um . . . keep."

"Okay." She turned the card over, then gestured for me to open my hands, which I did. She placed the card face down in my left palm and instructed, "Hold that tight between your hands. Don't let anyone get to it."

"Who's coming for it?" I joked, but I of course clamped my right hand on top.

"Okay, so . . ." She squared the rest of the deck in her hands, then began to slowly flip the top card over.

"No! Is that the three of clubs?" I asked.

She finished the movement quicker to reveal a king of hearts. "No. That would have been cool, though. But here we have the king of hearts, which is symbolic. I don't currently have a king of hearts in my life. But you do."

I blushed thinking about Adrian, who was meeting me here soon, though he was running late due to a work emergency.

"Because of that, this"—Olivia flicked the king of hearts—"should be yours."

She turned the card face down, then waved it over my hand.

"No . . ." I said, the word just an exhale.

She grinned mischievously—the same grin right before she broke into a safe or laptop or condo—and then she pressed the card she was holding, the king of hearts, into the back of my hand that was clamped on top of the protected card. A second later, she turned her card face up to reveal it was now the three of clubs.

"That means . . ." She gestured for me to open my palms, and when I turned the card in between over, my mind was blown that it was the king of hearts. As my mouth dropped open, Olivia didn't seem to think much of it as she asked calmly, "Things still going well with McHottie, I assume?"

"Olivia!"

"What?"

"That was amazing! Like, just—holy shit."

"Okay, you don't have to patronize me."

"No, seriously, how'd you do that?" My fingers flipped the king of hearts back and forth, examining it for Hu (doesn't) know what.

Olivia smiled—wide, unabashed, and real—and my heart soared that I not only knew this smile but that it appeared often when we were together. Then she leaned close to me and whispered, "If I tell you, I'll have to kill you." But she couldn't even get through the whole sentence without giggling. "Just kidding, I'll teach you later—it's easy!"

She'd also been teaching me to pick locks, which I hadn't used in any other setting, but I felt cooler just being able to do it.

Olivia leaned back and shuffled the cards. "Now, for my next trick—"

Someone slipped into the seat beside me. I turned, ready to greet Adrian with a kiss on the cheek, but thank god I didn't because it was a stranger wearing a trench coat, a giant hat, and sunglasses.

"Oh, fun!" I exclaimed, turning so I was half facing Olivia and half facing the new arrival. "Another magician? Or your assistant?"

The newcomer's head was tilted down so I couldn't see their face beneath the hat. "Olivia McCarthy and Kathryn Hu?" a woman's voice whispered.

"Yeah?" I responded automatically before asking myself, *Why did she ask about Olivia's name?* And then I turned to see the confused look on Olivia's face.

Before I could scoot backward or run off, the person whipped their disguise off. The woman before me looked familiar, but I couldn't quite place her.

"Mandy?" Olivia said, her voice hesitant. "Mandy Thorne?"

"I need your help," Mandy said, her voice desperate. "Someone's trying to kill me."

CHAPTER 3

Kathryn's Third Law of Life: Well, shit, life does sometimes have a sense of humor.

Except Olivia and I weren't laughing. Because the irony of the situation was not lost on us. Mandy Thorne had tried to take down both Olivia and me for a murder we didn't commit and now had the gall to ask us for help?

Olivia spoke first. "Seriously, Mandy?"

I couldn't muster up any sarcasm. I couldn't even gloat. All I felt in Mandy's presence was ill.

Mandy looked at me as she said, "Kat, please."

"Don't call me that." My late ex-boyfriend (and also the ex of Olivia and our friend Elle) had been the first one to call me Kat, and now that nickname was reserved for close friends.

Mandy continued, "Y'all are the only ones who can help—" But I held a hand up, stopping her.

Had her fake Southern accent just become a habit or was she doubling down now that Elle—the missing third of the Ex-Girlfriend Murder Club—had exposed her lies?

Mandy's eyes filled with tears. "Kat—Kathryn, please. I know you're a good person. Help me." And suddenly, the Southern accent was gone. "My podcast has done good, exposing cheaters and liars and helping to empower women. But there are consequences, and they're biting me in the ass now!

Someone's stalking and threatening me. I mean, I've always gotten hate mail, but this is different, I can feel it. I've been seeing the same person everywhere, and I think they know where I live. And it's ramping up. The messages, the language, how often I'm seeing them. This is serious. You have to believe me—"

"Why should we believe a single thing you say?" Olivia asked.

"Why on gods' shit-ass earth would I lie about something like this?" Mandy retorted.

"So you wouldn't lie about that, but you would lie about a real murder just for ratings." Olivia began looking around. "Where are the cameras? The microphones?"

I knew Olivia was partly joking, but anything was possible with Mandy. I ran my fingers along the bottom of the table just in case.

Just chewed gum, yuck.

Mandy shook her head frantically. "No recording devices! I swear to gods! Can't you see this from my point of view for a sec? It was hard enough for me to come here."

I couldn't hold it in anymore. "Hard for *you*? You're the one who made shit up just to throw us under the bus!"

"One of you did do it!" she threw back.

Olivia and I glanced at each other. It had been a while since Tucker's murder was solved, but neither of us had fully wrapped our minds around what had happened. How could we? It was a topic we avoided at all costs.

"And you got your revenge on me!" Mandy continued, no doubt referencing how Elle—writing as Lassy McBush—had taken Mandy down by exposing her shitty journalism and fake curated persona. But that was just a reminder that we couldn't trust Mandy. What if this was all some elaborate scheme to serve the dish right back to us? Since she couldn't get to Elle, maybe she had set her sights on Olivia and me.

"I'm the victim in all this!" Mandy yelled, making this even easier for us.

Olivia pointed at the door. "Get out."

Audience members had begun turning our way.

Mandy dropped to the floor on her knees. "Please. I'm begging you. You're my last hope." She swallowed hard. "No one believes me."

"And you thought we would?" Olivia's head swiveled again, searching for security this time.

But just as Olivia raised an arm to wave someone over, Mandy did the last thing I would've guessed.

"I shit in the Love Hut."

Olivia and I both whipped our heads toward her.

"What?" I couldn't have heard that right.

"I took a shit in the hut, okay? The bathrooms were unbelievably stinky—not at all what you'd think for a hit reality show—and I thought there weren't any cameras in that corner, and . . . I did it, okay?"

Whether or not Mandy Thorne had taken a dump inside the Love Hut she shared with twenty other contestants had been a hot debate the last few years, with Mandy vehemently denying it despite what we all saw on our too-high-resolution screens.

"Do you believe me now?"

Olivia laughed. "You really think that would be enough to change our minds about you? All it does is remind us how much of a liar you are! You've been doubling down on that *Love Hut* lie even though *we all saw you do it*. You're clearly capable of lying about anything!"

Desperate, Mandy grabbed the edge of my shirt, and I leaped back on instinct. But she held tight, pulling me closer.

Before she could say anything, though, a strong arm wrapped around my side and a tanned hand swiftly removed Mandy's fist from my shirt. "Everything okay here?" Adrian was using his authoritative cop voice, which sounded calm and collected, but his strong grip around my waist signaled he was anything but.

"Kat, you *owe* me this," Mandy blurted. "This mess? Is your fault! All three of you! Especially Elle—no, *Lassy McBush*. Her articles, the disastrous episodes, all that shit with your ex—it fucked over me and my podcast. Everyone was up in arms after your story came out. So these death threats, the danger I'm in, whatever blood gets spilled—it's on your hands!"

"Mandy . . ." I didn't even know what she was asking of me. Just because we'd solved Tucker's murder, just because we had once been the Ex-Girlfriend Murder Club . . .

"Don't listen to her," Olivia said. "She's delusional."

And in a flash, the desperation on Mandy's face was replaced by anger. "Well, if you two aren't going to help me, maybe I should just seduce Kat's man here to get *him* to help me, just like she did—"

"Time to go," Adrian said, his arm leaving my waist to lead Mandy out.

Mandy swiveled her head to yell back at me over her shoulder. "If anything happens to me, Kat, it'll be on you! I swear to gods—"

The doors cut off the rest of her sentence.

Of all the words she could've said . . .

Those were the last words Tucker Jones ever said to me. Right before he was murdered.

• • • •

"Kat, don't," Olivia said as soon as Adrian and Mandy disappeared from view.

"Don't what? I'm not going to do anything."

"She's scum. Human garbage. A walking dumpster fire. She doesn't deserve our help. You know this is all made up just for ratings. *Again*."

"Of course." Olivia was 100 percent right. Everything about Mandy sucked. Even when she was begging us for help just now, she couldn't refrain from saying horrible things like that seduction comment. Though . . . Adrian's captain was still giving him flack for our getting together, and I sort of saw how it looked from the outside.

"Don't you agree?" Olivia asked Adrian as soon as he returned. "Mandy is bad news bears?" (Origin derived from a movie of the same name.)

Adrian frowned. "Agreed."

"Whoa there, calm down, Detective," Olivia teased. "No need to fly off the handle."

"Call me Adrian, please," he insisted. "And I said I agree."

"Adrian agrees with utmost enthusiasm," Olivia said, throwing an arm around his shoulders. He stiffened but didn't remove it. She threw her other arm around me. "So we'll leave it alone and enjoy our night?"

I nodded. "We'll leave it alone."

• • • •

As much as I wanted to, I couldn't get Mandy out of my head that night. And not just because she'd managed to slip a handwritten note into my purse before she left (had she been learning sleight of hand, too?).

Please, Kat. I'm innocent. I know you know that in your gut. Please help me.

But the bigger reason I couldn't get Mandy out of my head was that even though I had been trying to for the past few months, I hadn't really moved on. Hadn't forgotten. Neither had Olivia, really, given that she hadn't been on a single date and spent every moment at work taking on difficult cases where she was the only one who believed the client. And even though she never said so out loud, I think she still saw Adrian as the detective who almost put us away, as evidenced by her still calling him *Detective*.

I couldn't talk to Olivia or Adrian about my nagging thoughts about Mandy, so how could I figure out if Mandy was telling the truth? If someone truly was trying to kill Mandy Thorne, maybe it would help to talk to a real murderer.

And it just so happened that I knew one.

CHAPTER 4

"Kitty Kat, my darling, you look well."

"Elle, hi." She would always be Elle to me, not Lauren. Because Lauren was the one who'd murdered Tucker. Elle was the one who'd turned herself in to save Olivia and me.

It didn't make any sense. I wasn't sure it was supposed to.

Elle hesitated. "I'm so happy to see you, but . . . you shouldn't be here."

I hadn't been able to bring myself to visit since she'd been put away—and I wasn't sure whether it was out of fear, denial, or a combination of both—and until this moment, it hadn't crossed my mind that maybe she didn't want me here.

"Would you like me to leave?" I asked, not sure what was going through her head.

Uncharacteristically, she couldn't meet my eye through the glass separating us. "You shouldn't want to see me after what I did. And I don't deserve to see you."

"Don't say that," I found myself saying.

"The only thing I deserve is what I got—to be in here. So don't look so sad. I'm exactly where I belong."

"Elle . . ."

Finally, she looked at me. "I can never make it up."

"What you did to us?"

"And . . . what I did."

In that moment, I realized one of the big pieces I couldn't reconcile wasn't just Elle and Lauren, but whether it was just Elle or Elle and Lauren that had regrets. Had she turned herself in just to save Olivia and me, or was it more than that? Did she only regret framing us, or all of it?

And right now, Elle was answering that. She regretted it all, including the murder. And she wasn't asking for forgiveness. She was asking for damnation.

I'd been staying away because it had all felt too overwhelming, but Elle wasn't asking me to understand, to forgive, to absolve. And that epiphany was freeing. Because this was massively complicated, and maybe we didn't have to unravel and dissect it. Maybe it would never make sense.

But maybe we could still move forward.

With that realization, I found my words. "I'm here to see my friend Elle. Who isn't doing great, but maybe I can lift her spirits a little. At the very least, she looks great."

Elle's surprised eyes rose to meet mine, and in the span of a few seconds, she seemed to go on an emotional roller coaster. But by the end of it, she found her way back to a slice of her old self. "Well, how many people do you know who can pull off orange as well as I do?"

I grinned. "Just you, Elle. Just you."

Through the glass, we shared a smile, one that conveyed more than we could with our words.

"So where's your partner in crime?" she asked.

I noticed she didn't say *our*, but I pushed past it. "She, um, doesn't know I'm here."

"You need to hold onto each other."

I knew what she meant, but it also wasn't that easy. So I changed the subject. "There's been an interesting development I thought you'd want to hear about."

She sat up straighter, pressing the phone harder into her ear. "Was I right?"

Had she predicted Mandy would fear for her life and come to us for help? That certainly hadn't been on my Bingo card.

"McHotStuff was an eleven-out-of-ten lay, wasn't he? Those grunts are annoying day to day but must be such a turn-on in the bedroom. And his hands, they're *enormous*—"

"No!" My face went from zero to fire-engine red in a hot second.

"No? I could've sworn he would've been all about your pleasure, all gruff and masculine on the outside but then a softy just for you on the inside. And speaking of inside—"

"I meant no, I don't want to talk about it."

Elle leaned forward, her face just inches from the glass. "Kathryn Yushan Hu. I am locked up for the rest of my life. You will not deny me this one small pleasure, emphasis on *pleasure*."

That was the only way she could've made me fold. Attempts to make a deal had not panned out for Elle, and she was in here for life without parole.

"Maybe you were right," I forced out. "About some of those things. Okay, most. Though I like his grunts—in all settings."

"And?"

"And it's good. Better than good. The best I've ever, you know, had."

"Annnd . . ."

"What else do you want from me?" My face must have been the color of blood itself by this point.

She pouted. The contrast of her puppy dog eyes with her prison jumpsuit was too much, so I threw her a bone, pun intended (likely dog origin).

"I never knew what it could be like with someone I feel so safe with. Or how hot it could be with someone I know can protect me. And someone with . . . big hands . . ." I almost choked on the words as they came out. "But that's not even what I love most about our relationship. It's how he's my best friend, the one I want to share everything with, the one who's just *there* for me, always." I paused. "That's cheesy." Not to mention horrible that I was telling this to someone in Elle's position. "And despite all that, I'm still self-sabotaging. I haven't told my parents about him yet."

"Why not?"

"Because! They're impossible!"

"Could be worse," Elle muttered under her breath.

"Sorry. Have your parents visited at all?"

"Of course not. They're so ashamed of me. As they should be."

"I'm sorry—"

Elle silenced me with a wave of her hand. "Anyway, you said you had some juicy gossip for me? A *development*?"

This wasn't the way I'd wanted to move on from Adrian's big hands, but I would take it. "Mandy Thorne came to us asking for help from the Ex-Girlfriend—from Olivia and me."

Elle laughed. "Yeah, good catch. She definitely doesn't want the Ex-Girlfriend Murder Club to help. She'd murder me before she'd ask me for help."

"Mandy thinks someone's trying to kill her. Olivia thinks it's all part of a greater plan for her to mess with us, but I can't help but think . . . what if it's true? What if she's really in danger? I mean, there are plenty of people who have good reason to hate her, and I just thought maybe you would . . . maybe you could . . ." I didn't know how to finish that sentence.

"Relax, Kat. I get it. You want to get into the head of a murderer, which you couldn't be further from. And of course I'm the perfect person to ask. Not to mention, I—er, well, Lassy McBush knows Mandy Thorne better than most. Honestly, given what Mandy's done to others, I wouldn't be surprised if someone really were after her. But I would be less surprised to discover she's doing this for ratings. Get Queen Victoria and Queen Elizabeth—well, I was Elizabeth, but you know what I mean—to help solve her own threat of murder? Hell, even I would listen to that."

I nodded. "That makes a lot of sense. And it's the most likely explanation." But even as I said those words, I couldn't ignore the niggling doubt in my gut.

Elle sighed, seeing right through me. "You believe her, don't you? And you're going to help."

"I don't know yet." I paused, then vocalized what had been bothering me the most. "Mandy said that if anything happens to her, it'll be my fault—"

"This is not on you. And neither was Tucker's death. Obviously."

I didn't respond. I wanted to believe Elle, but I just couldn't seem to get there.

"Kat, you're too trusting. Too kind." I didn't want to be reminded of just how trusting I'd been to give Tucker my heart. "I know Mandy. And you can't trust her. Please protect yourself."

I'd been struggling with that part of me ever since Tucker blew up everything I thought I knew. And her words were a kick straight to my Achilles' heel. "It's not all bad to give people the benefit of the doubt," I argued.

Elle bit her lip, hesitating before saying, "Be careful, Kat. Mandy and I—we're not all that different. I understand her on a level you never could. And I'm telling you, she's dangerous."

"I'll be careful, okay?" I leaned forward. "But for the record, I gave you the benefit of the doubt, and I don't regret it. I was right about you, Elle Watson."

Elle's eyes filled with tears. "I'm not sure you were, Kat. But it means more than you can ever know that you believed in me. Don't feel bad for me. Like I said, I deserve to be here for what I did. I'm very sorry. To you, to Olivia, to Tucker, to the universe."

"You don't have to—"

"I do. I'm sorry, Kat. Truly."

I placed an outstretched palm against the glass. Elle returned the gesture, a lone tear spilling over.

A moment later, she was gone. Taken back to her cell by an armed guard.

Even if I was right, she couldn't escape karma. Was that same karma now here for Mandy?

Kathryn's Fourth Law of Life: Sometimes you get served what you deserve.

CHAPTER 5

"You put the what where now?"

I giggled. For someone who was used to high-pressure situations, Adrian could get surprisingly flustered over something as small as eating a new food.

"Here, let me." I gingerly picked up a soup dumpling with my chopsticks, plopped it into his Asian soup spoon, then topped it with ginger strips soaked in black vinegar. "You can nibble the top and slurp out some of the soup first, or you can eat it whole—"

Adrian popped the entire dumpling into his mouth. His eyes widened as he chewed slowly, savoring the mix of flavors swirling over his tongue. A second later, he swallowed and let out a low groan.

Damn you, Elle, I thought as my mind filled with *un*savory thoughts at his noises.

Adrian was a bread-and-butter kind of guy, much too literally—he kept a loaf of bread and free packets of butter in his desk for his lunches because "it's easier" and "what's better than two of life's staples?"

Well, soup dumplings, for starters.

He put his hand over mine as he said, "You're something else." Three simple words from a simple bread-and-butter man, but they meant so much more coming from him.

"Because I introduced you to soup dumplings? Hate to break it to you, but there are millions of people in the world who know how delicious they are." I still didn't know how to take a compliment.

He chuckled. Then he took my hand in his. "You make me see the world in a different way. A better way. You'll be a terrific forensic scientist." He said it so confidently, like it was fact, and I wished that I—and my boss—could see me that way. "Everything still going well there?"

"Mm-hmm," I mumbled, grateful for the soup dumpling in my mouth, and not just because it was delicious.

I wanted to talk to him about my issues with Gerard, my fears, my insecurities. But it felt complicated with him in the same department. And maybe I was scared for him to lose some of that confidence in me because it was all that was keeping me from running away from the job in defeat.

"Everything good at work for you?" I asked, trying to shift the focus.

Adrian cleared his throat. "I got a new partner today."

That . . . was almost as surprising as Mandy showing up at Olivia's magic show. After his previous partner took a bribe and skipped town, Adrian had been closed off to new partners. Until now, apparently.

The topic was so sensitive I didn't want to spook him. Carefully, I asked, "So what's this new partner like?"

"Trustworthy, I believe."

"That's great. What makes you think that?" I knew it took a lot to gain Adrian's trust, and it likely took more than usual in this instance, given his history with partners.

"I once thought Ricky was a yes-man. Content to be in the background. No guts, no opinions. But then, recently, he was the only one who didn't follow the pack. Everyone else thought this case was open-and-shut, black-and-white, but not him. It was a B and E at a bakery, and everyone thought it was the owner's rival, a bakery down the street, but Ricky saw an inconsistency. It was too convenient, a perfect bow on top, and the high-tech security system just happened to malfunction during the break-in. He worked the case until it was solved. And I helped him."

"Annnd?" I prompted.

Adrian grinned, his signature but elusive dimple appearing. "And the owner did it. Both for the insurance money and to frame his rival in revenge."

Nothing made Adrian shine more than solving a case, especially a difficult one. And even though his description of Ricky had started off negative, it finished in the most affectionate way possible for my grumpy detective.

"I'm happy for you," I said as I placed a hand on his forearm—his quite muscly forearm, I couldn't help noticing every time. "Feels like everything's coming together, doesn't it?"

"Actually . . ." Adrian cleared his throat again, but this one was different. It was hesitant. Nervous. "Kat, I want to ask you something."

I put my utensils down.

"My parents are coming to town in a few months, and I want to introduce them to you. If you want."

This was sweet. Exciting. Monumental. But all I could feel was my palms growing clammy. Because how could I meet his parents when mine didn't even know about him? And even though this was all I'd wanted with my ex, Tucker, all I could think about now was how Tucker had lied and told me his parents were in Canada when really they were already dead, maybe from heartbreak after he'd stolen their money and ran off.

"That's so nice!" I forced out. "Um, how are you going to

explain how we met?" It was one of the many reasons I didn't know how to tell my parents.

"With the truth." He said it like it was so obvious.

"Right. Of course." Why would anyone consider any other possibility?

His eyes softened as his mouth curved up on one side. "Our situation was unique, of course, but all the more reason I fell for you so quick. Who else in the world, when accused of murder, would become determined to solve the case herself? And then have so much compassion for the guilty party—not to mention *trust*, even after what you'd just gone through with your ex—that you let Elle decide her own fate. No one else would have done that. So why wouldn't I want to introduce you—the real you—to my parents?"

"That . . . is so sweet." Why couldn't I see myself the way he saw me? I hesitated before adding, "What if that's why Mandy came to me?" Because I was the only one dumb enough—I mean, compassionate enough—to believe and help her?

Adrian frowned. "The why doesn't matter. Mandy Thorne is bad news. Especially when it comes to you. For your safety, I agree with Olivia—stay away."

I shoved a soup dumpling in my mouth, which muffled my next two words. "Of course."

• • • •

When I returned home, I was greeted by another package from my mom.

Just perfect.

Groaning, I brought it inside and opened it. Then I called my mom immediately.

"Mom!"

"Wei, Yushan? Is you? You get package I send?"

"Why did you send me something that's made for toddlers?"

"How you know is for toddler? I take package off."

"Because it's called Helicopter Mom! And it's supposed to go on your wrist and looks like it'd only fit two of my fingers."

"Aiyah, Yushan, your fingers not that fat. You can fit at least three fingers in there—aim higher! And do you not see? I change it. Make into keychain for you."

Because my keychain needed yet another thing. "Mom! Why did you get me this?"

"Has flashlight *and* alarm. You replace other alarm I get you. This better."

That . . . actually was better. Before, I wouldn't have wanted to give her the satisfaction, but I reminded myself I was trying to improve our relationship. "Okay, thanks, Mom."

I bit my tongue to avoid asking for more age-appropriate gifts in the future.

"You put on keychain and send picture as proof. I give you to keep you safe, because you single."

That only reminded me about all my lies of omission.

Should I just tell her? Rip the Band-Aid off?

"Mom . . ."

"Is flashlight helpful in lab? You use for research?"

"Actually, I changed jobs. I'm working in a forensic lab now. So in some ways the flashlight is fitting—I'm sort of a detective, though I'm still in the lab doing chemistry."

"What? Yushan! How you make this change without talking to me and Baba?" Without moving the phone away from her mouth, she called out, "Baba! Get on phone now!"

My parents were the only people I knew that still had a landline.

"Wei, Yushan, that you?"

"Yushan detective now!" my mother yelled into the phone even though they were probably right next to each other.

"Eigh? Detective? Why?"

As they quibbled amongst themselves and I heard *business school* and *dermatology* thrown out over and over—*You so good at reading those invoices, what happen? Dermatology is best, just pop pimples and collect piles of money, and you not even try to apply to medical school yet!*—it became crystal clear.

I couldn't tell them about Adrian. And I couldn't tell Adrian that while he wanted to introduce me to his parents, I couldn't even tell mine he existed.

CHAPTER 6

Even though Olivia and Adrian had warned me away, Adrian's words had also unknowingly pushed me right through Mandy's front door. That person he wanted to introduce to his parents? The one he fell for? She wouldn't be able to sleep at night if something did happen to Mandy after she'd begged me for help.

And I couldn't get the words out of my head. *If anything happens to me, it'll be on you.* They haunted me in both Mandy's voice and Tucker's.

So that's how I found myself in Mandy's ridiculously over-the-top recording studio in her ridiculously over-the-top mansion. Also, as a side note, had she bought this with podcast money? OnlyFans?

"Can we go somewhere else?" I asked, my eyeballs ping-ponging around the studio. The padded soundproof walls were creeping me out.

"Why? This is perfect. No one else can hear us."

That . . . made me feel worse.

She seemed to know what I was thinking, because her face fell. "Why're you here if you don't trust me?"

That was a fantastic question. Part of it was that I was scared she *was* up to some grand diabolical plan, and I wanted to stay ahead of it instead of behind. But I couldn't tell her that.

When I didn't answer, she just sighed, stood, and led me out of the recording studio, through a grand foyer, then into a living room with a massive white couch. Why did only rich people seem to own white couches?

"Happy?"

Not in the least, but I was ready to get started now. And the first thing was . . .

"We can't tell the police about my helping you." Not yet, anyway. I didn't want to worry Adrian. I would loop him in once I knew more. Once I knew how deep I would or wouldn't be going.

Mandy waggled an eyebrow. "Ooh-la-la, trouble in paradise?"

I ignored her. "We also can't tell Olivia."

"Why the hell not?"

Because she hates you. Because she thinks you're human toxic waste and everything you touch is cursed—which, Olivia wasn't wrong. Mandy Thorne was the same woman who'd made money from other people's pain and vengeance, who'd encouraged retaliation, who'd tried to ruin the lives of the Ex-Girlfriend Murder Club with lies just for ratings.

To get Mandy to drop it, I channeled Elle and snapped, "Do you want my help or not?"

Instead of flinching, Mandy's mouth curved up in a sly smile. "I didn't realize this Kat had claws. Guess we don't need Olivia after all. She's gone. Dead to us. Buh-bye!"

I exhaled loudly. Maybe I wouldn't survive this for another reason that I should have foreseen—Mandy was going to annoy me to death.

Retrieving my notepad and pen, I tried to focus. "Tell me why you think someone is coming after you."

"Because they are. Duh."

I flipped the notepad closed. This was too hard.

"Jeez, is Detective Broody rubbing off on you?" Mandy

rolled her eyes. "Fine, we'll skip the foreplay. I've been getting death threats, okay?"

I opened the notebook again.

But then she said, "I'll share the messages with you, but can you also get your boyfriend to help me? Maybe over pillow talk or with whatever you did to get him to help you?"

This time I stood. I didn't have to put up with this; I was here out of kindness. I'd just taken a step when Mandy said—so softly I almost didn't hear—"I'm scared, okay? And maybe a little embarrassed. It's hard to talk about all this."

She reached into her pocket and retrieved her phone. After a few taps, she unexpectedly handed it to me.

<@DownWithMandy>
You motherfucking piece of shit.

<@ThorneInYourAss>
Try again

You ruined my life. You ruined so many lives. You should be burning in hell.

Ok. Buh-bye.

If you ignore me you're going to regret it. I'm going to make you pay.

Not just you but everyone you know and love.

That's what you did to me. You took everything from me! My job, my relationships, my health, my sanity, my life. Now I'm going to do the same to you.

You think you can frighten me?

You think I'm scared of you?

I eat assholes like you for breakfast.

You're a whore.

You wish you could have me.

I'm gonna sic my lawyers on you before you can blink.

If I ever find you, I'll cut your throat.

Not if I cut yours first.

I'd like to see you try.

You won't have to wait long.

Bring it, motherfucker.

Okay, this was bad.

"Who do you think this is?" I asked.

"Hell if I know. Why d'you think I need you?"

I glanced at the messages again. "You have no idea who this is, you believe they're trying to kill you, and your first instinct was to threaten to cut their throat?"

"The best way to combat stuff like this is to fight back. You ever see a red panda? They're small—like me, I'm petite, tiny—and when they feel threatened, they stand on their hind legs and raise their arms to appear bigger. It's foolproof: threaten the predator back until they go away."

I tamped down my first thought—that this was the exact strategy of Ray Underwood, the loan shark who had kidnapped me, wanting to make sure he punished the ones who owed him money (or in my case, their loved ones) to scare other clients into paying. Instead I said, "That cannot be the best strategy."

"Hey, what do you know? I get a lot of threats!"

"Then why are you particularly scared of these ones?" I

didn't mean for that to come out so emotionless, but it was the scientist part of me talking—analyzing data, presenting facts as they come.

"Because of *this*, Kath-ryn," she said, emphasizing each syllable in my name like I was a child being scolded. Little did she know that for me, it was *Yu-shan*, not *Kath-ryn*.

Mandy tapped on her phone and showed me her text messages.

Unlike the DMs, the texts contained no words, just photos. The first—her walking to her car in a parking lot somewhere. The second—her, through a window. In her home. In the very room we were sitting in. And at the edge of the photo was a knife clearly clutched in the hand of the photographer.

A chill crept down my neck like I was suddenly being watched. Which, maybe we were.

This was a terrible idea. I shouldn't have come here.

But also, maybe Mandy wasn't lying.

"Alright," I said reluctantly. "I'll look into it."

"What're you going to do?"

Even though I did have a plan in mind, I didn't divulge it. Even if Mandy was telling the truth, it didn't make her trustworthy.

"Just lie low for a while, okay?" I told her. "Keep your head down . . . and don't do anything stupid."

Now, if I could just follow my own advice.

Final Reminder:
You don't want to miss *Dish Gets Served*!

On the fence? We promise you won't regret coming. This is your one chance to meet with other like-minded *Dish Served Hot* victims. There is something for everyone here. Want revenge? Want to vent? Want to just socialize with others in a fun setting over delicious food and drink? Join us!

Please note location change below.

CHAPTER 7

Even though everyone in my life was telling me to leave it alone, even though my own gut was telling me this stunk to high heaven of lies, shadiness, and the worst person I knew, there was a perfectly easy way to look into Mandy's claims. It had been showing up in my email again and again, no matter what I did. And while I knew now that there was no universe sending me messages or controlling things, how much could it hurt to take a peek at the Dish Gets Served meeting and see if I could locate the person trying to serve Mandy Thorne the hottest revenge dish of all?

I just hoped I wasn't in over my head or walking into a trap. Though, couldn't just being aware of those possibilities be seen as growth?

I would never tell my mother this, but as I headed out the door, I made sure my Life Alert was on my keychain.

• • • •

The Live in Our Bubble boba café across town was already in utter chaos when I arrived ten minutes before the start time listed in the email. Hordes of bodies were weaving around each other with no clear direction, only confusion and clashing.

My eye was immediately drawn to someone dressed up as

fire, literal fire, with flames licking up the sides of her body and sticking out from her head. Even her face was painted red, orange, and yellow.

And beside her was a sexy firefighter.

What was this, Comic-Con?

But that made up only a small part of the chaos. Because upon further inspection, there wasn't just a mass of people here. It was actually two separate masses squaring off and shouting at each other.

"Down with Mandy!" one of the groups cried. I couldn't help noticing that phrase matched the username of the person behind the threats. Had that person started the chant? Had they organized this event? Maybe figuring out who was behind all this would lead me to the culprit.

"Mandy's our queen!" the second mass yelled from the other side of the café, surprising me.

"Lassy McBush is queen!" hollered someone . . . *in a blond wig.* She was also wearing the very same outfit Elle had been photographed in for the news story that had gone viral—fuchsia crop top, leather pants, and stilettos.

I instinctually started toward her. I knew it wasn't actually Elle, but I wanted it to be her so badly I couldn't help feeling drawn to this impersonator.

But I didn't get far before I was swarmed.

"Join us, Dish Gets Served, in taking down the podcast," the girl in front of me said urgently, handing me a flyer. Her hair was a stunning purple ombré I'd always coveted but was too chicken to try. (Origin: the behavior of hens being perceived as easily frightened; poor chickens.)

"No, join *us*, Always Hot, to support Mandy and get her the acclaim she deserves," said another girl as she pushed past Purple Ombré to get to me.

Apparently, the Dish Gets Served meeting had been infiltrated, and not just by my recon mission. And with a name like *Always Hot*, the firefighter and flame costumes I'd seen earlier now made more sense.

"Which side are you on?" the Always Hot Mandy Supporter demanded, her green eyes and nose ring glinting in the light.

"Dish Gets Served," I answered immediately, both for my mission and as my honest answer.

The Dish Gets Served girl smiled. The Always Hot one shoved her flyer in my face urgently as she said, "I don't think you understand just how much Mandy has helped some of us—"

"Don't." The single syllable came out of my mouth short, curt, and hot.

There were a million reasons why coming here was a bad idea, yet I'd just discovered a new one—I was mixed up in this more than I wanted to be, and it was bringing up quite the slew of emotions.

Probably reading into the pain on my face, the Mandy Supporter asked, "Who are you?"

Yes, I wanted to answer. *I am Hu*. But that would be funny only to me.

"Um, you okay?" the Dish Gets Served girl asked. I was taking too long to answer and acting like the social pariah I perennially was, even when I wasn't undercover.

Well, was I undercover? Or was it better to be myself since I really was a victim of the podcast?

Adrian's deep voice filled my head. *And the most important thing is . . .*

And then I heard Olivia saying, *Come on, Kat, use your head! You're the brains, too.*

They were right. I had to protect myself. Even though I was the heart of the Ex-Girlfriend Murder Club, I was here by myself, so I had to be the brains and guts, too. And I was investigating a potential murder threat, which was dangerous enough without using my real identity.

I grabbed the first name that popped into my head. "I'm Lauren." Maybe I shouldn't have used that. Too late now, though.

"No, I meant, what episode were you? On the podcast," the Always Hot girl clarified.

But before I could answer—and thank god, because I didn't know what I was going to say—someone else entered behind me chanting "Let's goooooo! *Dish! Gets! Served!*" which was apparently worse than whatever had been written on my face, because the Always Hot girl turned her attention to him.

The Dish Gets Served representative put a hand on my shoulder. "I'm Penelope." *Penelope with the purple hair,* I thought as a mnemonic device. "And you're not alone here, Lauren. Mandy ruined so many lives"—the same wording from the threatening messages: coincidence or clue?—"but together, we can do something."

"What kind of something?" I pressed, hoping for more. "I'm up for *anything.*" I was trying to imply violence and murder with that last word in the hopes of getting her to admit to something, but coming from me, it somehow sounded like I was up for silly-stringing Mandy's house.

Or something sexual, I heard Elle joke in my ear.

Penelope pointed to the flyer in my hand. "Cancel the show, of course. That would be the ultimate victory!"

She didn't seem to be hiding ulterior motives, but I'd been around the murder block enough to know to suspect everyone. (Obvious origin about walking around a city block and observing the world.)

"What did Mandy do to you?" I asked.

Penelope's cheeks puffed out as she exhaled. "Well, Lauren, I sadly had the worst one on the show."

This sounded promising. I just had to keep her talking. "I'm sorry to hear that. Which episode?"

"My boyfriend thought I was cheating on him—which I *wasn't*, by the way—and he was evil. Truly evil. He not only hatched a plan but *waited* to execute it."

"The monster!"

"I know, right? Cruel much?"

"So what did he do?" This had to be worse than pulling teeth (that saying dates back to the 1830s, chosen for the vivid imagery evoked). Was she reluctant because of how heinous it was? Could she be the one threatening Mandy?

Finally, Penelope revealed, "After he broke up with me—again, for no reason; I wasn't cheating—I kept using his Netflix account." I nodded, encouraging her. "And then—you won't believe this—he waited until the release day of the series finale of *Murder in Copenhagen* to change his password!"

I kept waiting, but she seemed to be done. "Oh. Um . . ."

"The series finale! Of *Murder in Copenhagen*! Only the show that the whole world was watching! The entire internet was talking about it and spoiled it for me! The biggest reveal of all time—the protagonist of *eleven seasons* had done it and had been lying to us for over a decade—and I didn't get to watch it. I must be the only person in the world to have missed the reveal live, other than those living under a rock."

I apparently lived under a rock. Also, was she kidding? She thought her situation was the *worst one on the show*? As someone who had been framed for murder, there was about to be a murder in this café. A murder of my sanity and patience. And maybe I also momentarily imagined releasing frogs #1, 2, and 4 in her home despite all I'd learned.

"Did you organize this?" I asked.

Penelope shook her head.

"Do you know who did?"

"For all intensive purposes, didn't we all kind of organize this?"

Well, no, but now all I could think about was the malapropism she'd just used where she misstated the saying *for all intents and purposes*.

Before I could respond, someone walked in with a giant *Always Hot* sandwich board, which caused many of the Dish Gets Served folks, including Penelope, to run toward the door and chant, "Down with Mandy!"

I didn't belong here, no matter what Mandy had done to me. This atmosphere, the hate in the air—all I wanted was to be away from this.

Right then, my gaze was pulled away by a particularly aggressive man approaching those with Dish Gets Served signs. Whatever he was saying was causing his audience to inch away and look for an escape. Somehow, he was instigating even more conflict—and among both groups, I noticed, as an Always Hot Mandy Supporter yelled at him.

And with that, I was reminded why I was here—precisely because of all this hate.

I started to make a beeline for the aggressive guy, but I was intercepted. A man in his late thirties stepped into my path and introduced himself. "I'm Asher." Somehow that name seemed to fit him and his messy ash-brown hair.

"Lauren." Might as well be consistent in case Penelope and Asher found themselves talking about me. "What did Mandy do to you?"

"I had a fight with my neighbor over our shared fence and then I woke up to a mysterious white powder on my lawn."

"Oh god," I couldn't help saying.

"Oh, just you wait. Turns out it was instant mashed potatoes. When the sprinklers went off . . . poof! Lawn full of mashed potatoes."

I bit my lip to keep from chuckling. It was terrible, of course, but there was a reason *Dish Served Hot* had become popular (though the revenge was normally more justified).

"Go ahead, laugh," Asher said, his voice devoid of humor. "All it did was ruin my lawn and trigger several HOA fines."

"Oh. Sorry," I said sincerely.

"I'm just messin' wit you," Asher said with a grin, waving his hand. "It was actually pretty funny. Ingenious, really. After that, I had no choice but to laugh, and then we made up. Figured out the fence, split the HOA fines, and we're good now."

"So which side are you on here?" I asked, gesturing to the crowds on opposing sides of the café.

Asher shrugged. "I was just curious what this meeting was. Didn't think it'd be so . . . whatever this is. I came for the mixer part. So are you single, Lauren? What's your connection to the podcast?"

I suddenly blanked. I didn't want to answer either of those questions, but I also couldn't think of a good way to escape without being weird and drawing even more attention.

Was it better to make something up about my podcast connection and hope he'd assume I was talking about an episode he hadn't listened to? And then I remembered—the show was anonymous. So I could claim to be anyone. But then a new problem arose. I suddenly couldn't think of any episode details.

"Horse dildos!" I blurted out.

Goddamnit, Kat. When would I stop doing that? At least it was a good answer. The horse dildo episode would forever be seared into my brain thanks to it being the first episode I ever listened to, and the only episode I played the Tucker-Jones-Can-Go-Fuck-Himself drinking game to with Olivia and Elle a million years ago. That was also the day we wished Tucker

Jones dead—metaphorically. Or so I had thought. I hadn't realized one of us had wished it for real.

Asher's eyebrow rose—maybe a little lasciviously. I definitely should not have mentioned dildos to the guy who just asked if I was single.

"Um, the episode with the horse dildos. That's my connection."

His brow furrowed in confusion. "You're the one who did all the horse stuff to her ex?"

Wait, that would make me team Always Hot, because the girl from that episode, code name Genevieve, had been grateful to Mandy for giving her the revenge idea. And I needed to be team Dish Gets Served to keep consistent with what I'd told the other two girls, and to relate to the potential murderer.

"I'm the, uh, secretary. The one who the guy had been cheating with—though of course I didn't know about his girlfriend"—even when I was pretending, I couldn't bring myself to be a cheater like Tucker—"and I got the aftermath of everything that Genevieve did. Can you imagine kissing someone who has horse piss in his beard, on his face, and in his clothes and hair? And *her* piss? That humidifier sprayed that shit—or well, pee—*everywhere.* He smelled like a bar bathroom at the end of the night. And I *kissed* that. On the mouth." *Okay, take it down a notch.*

Asher frowned. Had I talked too much? I always did this when I was lying—overexplained, talked five minutes past when I should have shut up.

But then he said something that made my heart drop to my knees.

"That girl over there claims *she's* the secretary from the horse dildo episode."

That . . . was the worst possible consequence of my lie, was it not?

I'd moved on from my previous hypotheses about the universe having it out for me, but at times like these, I couldn't help but wonder if I had indeed been onto something.

I turned slowly, waiting to look destiny in her dark, angry, accusatory eyes. Only to look into dark, *amused*, accusatory eyes.

Olivia's eyes.

What was she doing here?

"I know her," I said to Asher without taking my eyes off Olivia. "She thinks she's being funny, pretending to be me."

And off I marched.

CHAPTER 8

I was over-the-moon relieved that Olivia was here. The brains of the Ex-Girlfriend Murder Club.

But Olivia was not as jazzed as I was.

"Why didn't you tell me you were coming here?" she asked.

"I didn't want to drag you into something you didn't want to be a part of. Why didn't *you* tell *me*?" I said, trying to turn it around on her even though she obviously came because she knew I'd be here.

It was so obvious she didn't even bother answering. Instead, she said, "Mandy is chaos and lies and bad motives rolled into one. She's the devil incarnate. She doesn't care about anyone but herself."

Olivia was right. I couldn't refute any of that.

"And everything around this is so suspicious," she continued. "Isn't the timing of this meeting too coincidental? And what about the invites that continued to come no matter how many times you unsubscribed?"

I hadn't told her that was happening to me, which meant it must have happened to her, too. Which meant, yes, she was correct. This was all super suspicious.

"Okay," I said. "We'll go. I'm sorry for making us come here."

What had I been thinking, anyway? Olivia was right—we

had no idea what Mandy could be up to, and she'd given us no reason to give her the benefit of the doubt.

But just as we were about to head to the exit, we couldn't. Several men in black suits and with earpieces streamed in, walling off the door on either side.

What in the world was happening now?

I glanced at Olivia, apologizing with my eyes for getting us into yet another mess. When would I learn? This was why I wasn't the brains. This was why people shouldn't just blindly follow their heart without thinking things through.

The person who walked through the door next was not at all who I was expecting.

A middle-aged woman in a pantsuit.

Olivia's mouth opened in surprise. "That's . . ."

"The governor," I finished, equally surprised.

"Hello, hello!" the governor said, waving as she entered. She remained in the doorway, blocking everyone's path. "I heard there was a meeting gathering here about *Dish Served Hot*, and I just wanted to stop by to say that just like you, I'm a Mandy Thorne fan! She is a feminist, empowering women everywhere to stand up for themselves and take action!"

Half the room began booing, and the governor's surprised eyebrows signaled that she truly had no idea what she had walked in on.

"Now, of course," she continued smoothly, "I understand why some of you aren't fans, and isn't that what's great about this country? Here we are, to discuss our differences, and what's right for one person isn't necessarily right for another." The crowd appeared to shrink as they closed in subtly around her. She checked her watch. "I have another engagement to be at. I just wanted to stop by briefly. Lovely to see you all, don't forget to vote!"

As quickly as she had appeared, she disappeared, her security making sure no one followed.

With that, the bubble burst and the crowd erupted in chatter.

"What the hell was that?"

"I heard somewhere that Mandy had connections to the governor."

"Spineless. Just spineless."

"Who told her this was a meeting in support of Mandy?"

"It *is* in support of Mandy! Al-ways Hot, Al-ways Hot!"

Now that the doorway was clear again, I planned a pathway through the bodies and took my first step.

But Olivia caught my arm. "Kat . . ."

I looked back at her. "Yeah?"

"This is a terrible idea."

I nodded. "You've already convinced me. Struck gold—struck sewer? Since it's a bad idea?"

She didn't smile. Whatever she was thinking, it was serious.

I turned to face her. "What is it?"

"If the governor is a fan . . ." She paused.

"I know. I'm as surprised as you are."

Olivia shook her head. "No, I'm saying, if the governor is a fan, she's the one person who can pardon criminals."

"Oh. *Oh.*" I was silent for a moment as the information sank in.

"And maybe if we help Mandy . . ."

My voice was small as I said, "She might help us."

"Now, I'm not saying that Elle doesn't deserve—"

"I know, Liv. I know." Maybe I knew even better than she did, given my recent conversation with Elle in prison.

"I'm just saying, it's her only option not to spend the rest of her life . . ." Olivia took a breath. "Maybe at some point . . . I just . . ."

I closed the distance between us and pulled her into a hug. "If there's a chance, we take it." I was fully committed now. "For the Ex-Girlfriend Murder Club."

Olivia nodded. "For the Ex-Girlfriend Murder Club."

And this time, even though we were down an arm (er—gut?), we were older and wiser.

"Let the investigation begin."

CHAPTER 9

"How dare you show your face here!" screamed a girl with a blond pixie cut as she pushed a guy straight into us, knocking me over and Olivia to her knees.

Okay, maybe we were just older. No wise owls here, even though my last name is the sound they make. (Though, in reality, owls are not the brightest; the phrase was derived from Greek and Roman mythology.)

Olivia and I had been following the drama, going to where there seemed to be the most tension, and that came with a price—bruised knees.

As I helped Olivia to her feet and the fight continued, I noticed the guy being yelled at had familiar ash-brown hair.

Asher.

Only, the fight didn't make sense based on what he'd said to me earlier.

"You conniving little piece of shit," the girl seethed. "Are you here playing your sick little games?"

Asher had claimed he and his neighbor were on good terms now. Had he been lying about that? Or had he been a repeat guest and this was about a different episode connected to him?

And, of course, this was the guy who had hit on me. I attracted the walking—*dancing*—red flags, didn't I? What did that say about Adrian?

No time for that can of worms.

A crowd was forming around them, supporters and detractors alike. Purple Penelope went up to the pixie-cut girl.

"You good?"

"Wha—" The girl who had been yelling at Asher swiveled her head to take in the bodies encircling them, and her rage extinguished in an instant. "All good. Just—a misunderstanding."

Asher turned and ran, getting swallowed by the crowd.

Before I could surge forward to talk to the pixie-cut girl, she turned and bolted in the opposite direction from where Asher had gone.

Super suspicious, on all fronts.

I contemplated chasing after one or both of them, but another situation seemed to be developing behind us.

"Wyatt? Is that you?" a girl said.

I tugged on Olivia's sleeve and we turned to eavesdrop as Wyatt responded, "Isla? I'm surprised to see you here."

"Are you here for the . . . thingy?" Isla asked. "Did I mess you up that much with what I did?"

"I could care less about whatever all this is," Wyatt said, and I forced myself to ignore the malapropism that actually gave the saying the opposite meaning. "This is my boba spot."

"Oh, right, I forgot you lived near here. But, wait. I thought you didn't like boba."

He scratched the back of his head. "That was just when we met. But after, because you loved it and I regretted how . . . I mean, because of you, I would . . . I just like it now."

There was a brief pause where I thought Isla was softening, but that wasn't exactly it. "Why do you have to do that? You're so sweet sometimes and then other times, you do shit like ask me for an open relationship one week after you agree to be exclusive. And you couldn't have just had boba with me when we were together?"

"Do I, like a group of pandas, regret some of my decisions?" Wyatt said.

Isla laughed. "Yes, because together, they're an embarrassment."

Okay, I could and did care less about the previous malapropism after that word-play joke, which was completely up my alley. I loved weird collective nouns for groups of animals. A fluffle of bunnies, a prickle of hedgehogs, a destruction of feral cats.

Wyatt tilted his head to one side. "Didn't you get the last laugh anyway?"

She chuckled. "You know, I thought so, but I didn't."

"Oh, right. I heard you got fired."

"That was a huge misunderstanding! But they didn't believe me! I didn't do what they said—I wouldn't have—"

"Is that why you're here?" he asked, gesturing to the Dish Gets Served signs.

Isla sighed. "No. That was another lifetime ago—doesn't matter anymore."

There was a brief pause. Then Wyatt said, "I got your apology."

"Good. I am sorry, you know," Isla said, then added a small smile, which Wyatt returned.

After another beat, Isla said, "Guess we helped each other grow, huh?"

I wondered if maybe there would be a reconciliation here—and from the hopeful look in Wyatt's eyes, I wasn't the only one—but whatever else had gone down between them seemed to have been too much.

"I'll see you around, yeah?" Isla said.

Wyatt winked. "Not if I see you first."

They shared one last smile, wistful and full of history.

Olivia's and my eyes followed Isla as she left Wyatt behind

and exited the café. Maybe their conversation had been the closure she needed to move on.

"How many of them do you think came here hoping for reconciliation?" I asked Olivia, my gaze flashing to Wyatt.

"Um, at least more than one." Olivia pointed to a couple making out against the wall.

They broke apart just long enough for one of them to say, "No one fights with me like you do, Henry!"

Then they were back at it, their mouths and bodies fused to each other and the wall.

A match made in heaven? Or hell.

"Is it odd that so many former couples are here?" Olivia asked.

"I mean, not really. Romantic relationships had the most heated revenge"—as I was well aware—"so they're probably the ones most passionate about the podcast."

"No, I mean, how did they all know about this, on both sides? Who organized this event? Who formed these groups?"

"I was wondering the same thing," I said, my hope rising. Olivia's suspicions only supported my hypothesis further, that finding the organizer would lead to Mandy's aggressor. "Let's go down that rabbit hole."

Maybe we were older *and* wiser after all.

"So you and I received emails about the Dish Gets Served meeting," Olivia said, getting the ball rolling.

I nodded. "Mine went to my Harvard account, which is the only public one, though not for much longer." I figured they'd be taking away that email address any day now. "Did yours go to your personal or work email? Or maybe the account you created to contact Mandy from?"

Olivia straightened. "It went to my work one, which is public, but I hadn't thought to check the fake account." She pulled her phone out and typed for a few seconds. "It went to that one, too."

"Who even knew you had that?" I asked.

"And who knew about our connection to the podcast?"

Suddenly, her eyes widened. Then they ignited with fury.

A second later, I caught on. "No."

But her clenched teeth said *yes*.

Goddamnit.

We looked at each other, then both began scanning the room. And our eyes landed on our target at the same exact moment.

CHAPTER 10

My insides were ablaze as Olivia and I marched up to the target—which was, fittingly, the girl in flames.

"You have five seconds to tell us what's going on," Olivia hissed as she grabbed a red-and-yellow elbow and led us to a corner away from other people.

I didn't fully believe it was her until I heard her voice.

"Well, mighty nice of you both to show up."

Mandy fucking Thorne. Who else? She was the only one with all of these people's contact information, including the governor. She was the organizer. Meaning, we had no idea what was real and what she was up to.

"I thought changing this to a boba shop would entice you," Mandy added, winking at me. "As would a visit from my friend in a high place."

I should have known. There is no universe. Meaning, I should have realized that *someone* had been controlling things. Just like last time, when Elle had been the one in charge of my destiny, not Lady Luck. But this time was so much worse. Because the puppeteer was *Mandy Thorne*, devil incarnate, the lying *Love Hut* shitter.

My stomach churned and I worried I might be sick.

"Who's that?" Olivia asked, jutting her chin toward the firefighter waving her sign a few feet away, her back to us.

"Someone who fits the theme and knows how to dress well," Mandy answered.

"She's not with you?"

Mandy shook her head.

"And how can we believe anything coming out of your mouth?" Olivia asked. "You lied."

Mandy shook her head even more vehemently. "I never lied. You never asked me about Dish Gets Served or who organized it—"

"And if we had, you would've told us?"

"I never even got a chance to!" Mandy exclaimed. "You wouldn't listen!"

She had a chance to tell me when I was at her place, but I didn't want to bring up our private talk in front of Olivia, so I let it go.

Olivia narrowed her eyes at Mandy. "What's your game here?"

"To not get killed!" Mandy reached into her purse and pulled out a plastic baggie.

Olivia and I both gasped and took a step back.

"This was left *inside* my front door last night."

Olivia and I looked at each other.

Then Olivia sighed, the weary sigh of someone who had been through too much. Under her breath, she asked me, "We have to, don't we?"

I nodded.

As much as I didn't want to admit it, Olivia and I couldn't do this alone. We needed Mandy. To solve this, to help Elle.

So for Elle, we had to do this. We had to team up with our sworn enemy.

We had to become . . . the Mortal Enemy Murder Club.

CHAPTER 11

I held my breath as I examined the baggie. Even though the contents were fully encased, the CSI-in-training part of me still felt like I should be wearing gloves.

"Did you touch this with your bare hands?" I asked Mandy.

"I'm not a fucking idiot. I've watched crime shows. I put gloves on before I bagged it."

Inside the clear Ziploc, there was a large chef's knife covered in blood. And the blood looked real. The color, the consistency. I opened the top briefly. The smell.

Who the blood belonged to was certainly an important question and perhaps a lead, but there was nothing I could do to answer that right now.

"Do you see it?" Mandy asked.

"The blood?" Olivia said, looking appalled at Mandy for thinking me so incompetent.

"No, dummy," Mandy said with an eye roll.

"The fingerprints," I said, angling the knife so it would catch the light in a favorable way.

If Mandy was telling the truth about putting gloves on, that raised several questions. Why would the person who placed this be so careless? Or were the fingerprints a part of it? Maybe this person wanted Mandy to know who was threatening her, and why. Or maybe there was a bigger picture we couldn't see.

"So let's do this," Mandy said.

"Do what?" I asked.

"This!" She gestured around her at all the bodies milling about.

"Talk to them?" Olivia asked. "We have been."

"No," Mandy said, exasperated. "*This.*" She gestured to the people again, but then also to the knife. More specifically, to the fingerprints on the handle.

She couldn't mean . . . "Are you saying you want us to get the fingerprints of everyone here to compare to the knife?"

"Duh."

"We are not doing that," I said as Olivia nodded in agreement.

"Then why the hell did I ask you two to come here?"

It was like Mandy was trying to make this as difficult as possible.

For Elle, I reminded myself.

"We're going to go talk to more people," I said. "You're welcome to do whatever you like."

I channeled the guts of the Ex-Girlfriend Murder Club as I turned and melted back into the crowd, Olivia by my side. Even though Mandy certainly embodied that title in her own way, I did not want to see what she would push us to do.

CHAPTER 12

"Don't you know who I am?" a girl with glamorous beachy waves was yelling at Olivia and me.

Our first mark was not the friendliest, which unfortunately meant we could be onto something.

"I'm sure I'll know you once I hear about your connection to the podcast," Olivia said sweetly.

"I'm *the* victim of *Dish Served Hot*," the girl claimed, puffing her chest out. "I'm the GOAT, but actually the WOAT, because it's the worst of all time."

Apparently, everyone here thought they had the worst of it. Even if they'd only missed a series finale. Which made me wonder, was I also narcissistic for thinking I had one of the worst ones? Or was being framed for murder pretty far up there? Was this girl like the last one, blowing things out of proportion, or was she a potential suspect?

Just then, the ball of flames sauntered up to us. *Mortal Enemy Murder Club*, I tried to remind myself, though I couldn't help thinking about the million ways Mandy's presence could derail us.

I ignored her as I tried to guess the girl's podcast episode. "Were you the one whose cheating photos got posted to your business website? Oh! Or the one whose life savings were donated to Scientology thanks to her sister?"

"Or the one who Mandy wrongly framed for murder?" Olivia said with a glint in her eyes.

Mandy glowered at her.

The girl was suddenly scrutinizing us like . . . well, like one of us was dressed up as fire.

"Why are you wearing that?" she asked Mandy.

"Because she's just as passionate as you are," Olivia said dismissively. "I'm sorry you had to dance with the spawn of Satan." I wouldn't have been surprised if Mandy's head broke out in real flames beside me. "So what was it like for you?"

"What do you think? How about I come over and rub ghost pepper seeds all over your vibrator?" Oh, shit. That was way worse than the series finale girl. But still, *the worst* of all time? "He knew what he was doing. Invisible fucking fire. I was out of commission for weeks."

Olivia must have remembered this girl's episode because her eyes widened, then narrowed. "Didn't you put Tabasco in his Fleshlight first?"

"Of course I did! To get back at him for trying to steal my dog!"

"Wasn't the dog both of yours? And the breakup a result of you cheating on him?" Olivia asked. She would of course have little sympathy for the cheater.

"Who the hell are you, remembering all these details?"

Someone with an eidetic memory, I kept to myself. And thank god for it. These details would help.

"Here, you seem thirsty," Mandy said, producing a glass of water from god knew where—somewhere inside her costume. "This'll calm you down."

The girl smacked the water away as she stormed off. Mandy only just managed not to drop it.

"You didn't even try for the fingerprint!" Mandy hissed.

Then the human ball of flames blazed after the girl, the glass outstretched and water spilling over the sides.

With Mandy gone, I asked Olivia, "Who was the podcast guest in that girl's case?"

"Super rare double guest. Girl went on first, thinking she was so awesome for the Fleshlight bit, then he got back at her and made sure to rub it in even further by coming on the show, too. That one was big, with the two of them getting into it online and people taking sides on social media. A live, interactive AITA, if you will." She searched briefly on her phone. "Gia and Russ. Unique case where we have their real names since they were fighting publicly, too."

"If it became so public, maybe that's why one or both of them are mad at Mandy," I suggested. "Not sure it's enough to lead to murder, but maybe it led to threats?"

Olivia sighed. "I hate to say it, but if Mandy does manage to get a fingerprint, we *could* compare it to the knife . . ."

"I know, but most of the people here have a reason to hate her. We can't feasibly trick all of them into drinking water. And besides, do we have enough glasses? How do we even keep them all straight?"

Olivia pursed her mouth to one side. "We don't have to get *everyone*. We could just get a few that are extra sus."

Both of our gazes immediately went to Asher. (I also made a mental note to find that aggressive guy, who I currently didn't have eyes on.)

Olivia ticked her chin in Asher's direction. "If we were to, say, get him to pass over a used glass or something, could you . . . ?"

I definitely could. I actually had a fingerprint-dusting kit and a pair of gloves in my purse, having come from work, but even if I didn't, I could've MacGyver-ed (MacGalver-ed?) it with makeup powder and tape.

"If I do the fingerprinting, you have to do the flirting," I said.

Olivia grinned. "Deal."

It was nice seeing her excited about flirting for the first time since Tucker. Maybe there was some additional good that would be a byproduct of all this.

• • • •

"Hey there. All the good pickup lines are taken, but it seems like you aren't."

Was Olivia rusty or had she never needed to be good at flirting because of her looks? Not that I was one to talk—I probably would've said something like, *Hey, Big Boy, I could rehydrate your complex carbs like that lawn sprinkler did*, which was somehow both too nerdy and too sexual at the same time.

Luckily, Olivia was so gorgeous that Asher did not seem to care. And he certainly didn't notice me hovering behind her.

"For you, I'm not taken regardless of the situation."

Gross. But at least it was working.

"Give me your number?" Olivia said, though it came out more like a sexy demand than a question.

Asher couldn't get his hands on Olivia's phone fast enough. Her phone that we'd intentionally removed from its case.

When he handed it back, Olivia was careful to only touch the corners.

"I'll call you," she lied. Then she headed back to me and deposited the phone into my gloved hands.

Double score. Not only had we gotten his fingerprints, but if he gave us the right phone number, we'd have a way to contact him, too, and without giving him Olivia's info.

"I should've used sleight of hand to get it," Olivia said as I got to work with the fingerprint tape.

"That would've been more complicated." If she'd swiped

something from him, she'd have needed to put it back after I lifted the print.

"More complicated but more fun."

"Fine, next time you can use sleight of hand."

Her spirits lifted. "Okay, who's the next target?"

"Next time after today," I clarified.

She pouted. "No fun."

"What're you talking about? This is plenty fun—we're away from mortal enemy number one." (Origin: Al Capone being labeled "Public Enemy No. 1" by the Chicago Crime Commission.)

Suddenly, as if the universe had heard me (not that there was a universe), from the other side of the café, a scream pierced the air.

CHAPTER 13

"You give that back!" a raven-haired woman was yelling. *At the human ball of fire.*

This couldn't be good.

"Why do you want my glass? You can't possibly work here dressed like that! And why are you holding two other glasses?"

The woman reached forward and knocked the glasses in Mandy's hands to the floor, shattering one of them.

Mandy screeched, then yelled, "My gods, what's wrong with you?"

The entire room went silent.

"It's Mandy!" someone cried, pointing at her.

Mandy's voice was already recognizable, especially to this room, and the *my gods* only sealed it. (Origin: the historical practice of using a wax seal on an official document.)

"No, no, I'm just imitating her," Mandy said frantically, backing up. "Because she's my goddess! Always Hot forever, am I right? Mandy's our queen!"

A crowd rushed toward her as another group stood in front of her defensively.

Shit, this was going to get messy fast.

But one man was quicker than the rest, pushing through

arms and legs and torsos to get right in front of Mandy. He was clutching the drink in his hand so tightly I thought it might explode into a million pieces.

"It's you," he said, seemingly looking straight through the red, orange, and yellow paint.

And as he said those two words, my brain repeated them back, but to him.

It's you. It was the aggressive man from earlier. But, apparently, even more aggressive now.

I didn't think it was possible, but he gripped his glass even tighter. "I've been throwing darts at your face for months; I'd recognize you anywhere. Do you have any idea what you've done to me?"

Was this our guy? I'd targeted him earlier for a reason, and now he was giving us even more cause for suspicion.

"Fellow scorned victims!" he called out to the room, his words slurring seemingly from emotion. "We need to take Mandy Thorne down! Make her pay! Who's with me?"

Half the room cheered.

He took a few shallow breaths, swaying slightly—maybe he wasn't just emotional but also drunk?—then yelled, "She took everything from me—my job, relationships, friends, family, my fucking *health*." He gestured toward his midsection, and I couldn't help but notice that his swaying, difficulty breathing, swollen eyes, and scaly patches of skin did seem to point to some health issues. Maybe that was what explained his behavior. "That fucking bitch deserves to burn in hell!"

He threw a fist in the air and let out a primal scream, and the other Dish Gets Served members joined in.

His words eerily resemble those of @DownWithMandy, I thought as I glanced at Olivia. From the look she gave me, we were already on the same page.

As the chants built, Olivia and I tried to make our way to

Mandy. Unfortunately, the crowd was too strong. We could only watch from several feet away.

But Mandy Red Panda Thorne didn't need us. "Whatever happened, given what my show's about, you deserved it," she yelled.

He turned his attention to her, his focus a frightening intensity. "I deserved to lose everything?"

"Not my problem."

His hand clenched into a tight fist. "It's about to be."

The entire room was now silent, watching.

Mandy took a step closer to him. "Yeah? What're you gonna do about it, huh? You don't have the guts. You're just a small man crying over your own mistakes."

A creepy smile filled his face. "You don't even know what's coming for you. Everything's already in motion. You're going the fuck down, and everything that's about to happen, you deserve. And I will watch with pleasure. I wonder, when it all goes up in flames, will you question what you've done?"

"I'm only wondering how someone cared about you enough to even want to get revenge on you."

"The fucking audacity you have."

Mandy put a hand to her ear. "What? Don't mumble your words. Let me really have it."

"I said, you fucking bitch. How dare you show your face to me. Do you know what I'm going to do to you?"

Mandy dropped her hand. "That's not what you said."

"Then you heard me just fine when I said THE FUCKING AUDACITY! You won't be so confident in a few days! I'll be the one left laughing as I fucking gut you!"

Mandy rose up, figuratively and literally by raising her arms over her head threateningly. "Don't you fucking dare! I will kill you, you hear me? I'll kill you!"

At that, the entire room erupted. The man charged for Mandy but lost his balance and fell forward into the sexy firefighter. Arms shot out and pulled Mandy into the safety of the Always Hot folks. As everyone moved, Olivia also jumped into action, surging forward into the crowd toward Mandy. I tried to keep up but couldn't.

As I pushed through, trying to follow her bobbing head, yells volleyed back and forth between the two groups. Things were on the brink of turning physical.

Just as I caught up to Olivia, someone near us lost their footing and bumped into someone else. Of course, that led to pushing. Then shoving. Then utter chaos.

Olivia grabbed my hand and we forced our way through the throngs of people toward the edge of the room where it was less crowded.

"You were right!" I called out to her. "We shouldn't have come here!"

At the same time, she exclaimed, "I did it! I got it!"

"Got what?"

Her eyes gleaming, she held up a glass. *His* glass, I realized. The one that luckily hadn't exploded into a million pieces. We had done it. Solved the mystery of who was trying to kill Mandy and got his fingerprints to compare to the knife. We were steps away from closing this case.

Quickly, I retrieved my kit, then lifted the print before anything could happen to it. Just as I finished, the commotion reached an all-time high.

"What's going on—" Olivia started, but she was cut off as the crowd suddenly parted like the Red Sea, bodies spilling away from the center and toward the walls.

We were swept up by the wave, Olivia's and my hands forced apart, and it took all my energy to keep up with the pumping legs beside me so I wouldn't get pulled under. Thank god I got the fingerprint when I did, because I lost the glass and tore my gloves in the melee.

Once there was a giant gaping hole in the center of the room, I understood.

Nothing will empty a space faster than vomit. Someone had thrown up, and everyone had surged away from it immediately.

And with that, the riot was dispelled. A swell of bodies flooded out the front door while those closest to the epicenter frantically tried to clean themselves up.

I'd lost Olivia in the frenzy, and as I looked for her, I realized there was actually a more pressing concern: the aggressive guy could be making his move on Mandy this very second. What better timing than to use the pandemonium as cover? Though it did seem stupid to attack her after an entire room had just witnessed him threatening her. But he seemed unhinged, so driven by his hatred that he couldn't see logic, reason, or what was in his best interest.

I had to find Mandy, quick, before it was too late.

But no matter where I turned, I couldn't spot the flames anywhere, even though they were practically red flashing arrows pointing to her.

Though, if I couldn't find her, maybe that guy wouldn't be able to, either?

I tried to find him instead. He was wearing normal clothes—jeans and a plain gray T-shirt, if I recalled correctly, a little ratty with some holes—and he didn't possess any distinguishing features like glasses or birthmarks or a hat. I tried to find his balding head of brown hair, but that was like trying to find Waldo (originally Wally, but US publishers changed it).

What if I couldn't find either of them because the angry guy was going after Mandy right this second?

Someone grabbed my arm, and I turned around, my heart beating in my ears.

But it wasn't Mandy or Olivia. It also wasn't the angry guy, which would have been scary but at least helpful. This person was just unwanted.

"Asher, what?" I said. There was no time for pleasantries.

"Do you know where your hot friend is?"

Not that I wanted him to still be hitting on me, but maybe I felt offended at how fast he'd forgotten me.

"No, but if you see her, please let me know—"

Suddenly, a collision near the door led to punches thrown, then bodies thrown.

Forgetting Asher—who did not seem to care about helping me to safety—I tried to think fast. I couldn't go out the front now—meaning neither could Mandy, the angry guy, or Olivia if they weren't already out of here—so maybe the best course of action was to find a place to hide until the worst of this passed.

With my sights set on the restrooms in the back, I bobbed and weaved as chaos rained down around me. Some people were still yelling at each other, some were screaming from utter alarm, and some were snatching pudding cups and mochi donuts from the counter, the poor employees outnumbered and overwhelmed.

When I reached the bathroom corridor, a few people were entering and exiting, but it was already calmer than the rest of the café.

Might as well check for Mandy, Olivia, and the angry guy.

I poked my head into the women's bathroom—no luck. A few people were hiding out in the stalls, but I could tell from their pant legs and shoes that they weren't my targets.

Back in the corridor, I hesitated outside the men's room. But I had to be the guts here. Elle wasn't coming to save me—not even the imposter Elle—and without Olivia (who I hoped was okay), it was up to me.

Reminding myself this could be life or death, I marched

into the men's bathroom as if I belonged there. And I nearly bumped into an almost naked guy at the sink washing vomit off his pants and shirt.

"Oh! I'm so sorry!"

He instinctively tried to cover himself with his clothes, only to flick the vomit *onto his face.* And from the extreme disgust that appeared on his now puke-speckled face, it didn't seem to be his vomit.

"Sorry!" I had to make it up to him somehow. "Can I buy you a drink?" Then I realized that seemed like I was coming on to him. "Or dessert!" That made it worse. "I mean, I'm just sorry!" I pulled out a five-dollar bill and threw it at him. Now it seemed like I was paying him for the peep show. "Fuck!"

This was going well. So well. At least I hadn't seen a ball of flames or Olivia's ballet flats in there.

I exited and turned toward the family restroom at the end of the hallway. The last place to check, and also a great hiding spot for Mandy, Olivia, and me if it was empty.

The door was unlocked. Success. Everything was going according to plan.

I'd just have to text Olivia and tell her to find Mandy and come meet me here—

I screamed. The second bloody-murder scream of my life.

Because there was a limp body on the floor. Sprawled. Unmoving.

Again, familiar.

CHAPTER 14

I couldn't stop screaming.

Once, twice, over and over.

This time, I knew better. I didn't run for the body. I couldn't get my DNA on it, couldn't be found standing over it.

I shouldn't even be here. This was the *second* body I'd found.

Someone entered the bathroom behind me. And also screamed.

I turned and saw purple-ombré hair. Penelope. And Penelope was no longer smirking or chanting or playing victim. She was just screaming. And that bone-chilling, feel-it-in-my-marrows scream switched something in me. From old Kat to new Kat, CSI-in-training.

So when Penelope started toward the body, I automatically grabbed her arm and pulled her back. Then pulled her out of the bathroom.

Then I retrieved my phone from my pocket. And called a number I both desperately wanted to dial and simultaneously wanted to avoid.

"Adrian? Something's happened. And I need your help."

CHAPTER 15

None of this made sense.

The man who had screamed at Mandy, wanted revenge, and thrown darts at her face for months, the man who *Mandy had just threatened to kill*, was dead. Sprawled forward on the bathroom floor, head turned to one side, a knife sticking out of his back.

Not just any knife.

The same. Exact. Knife that Mandy had shown Olivia and me earlier in the baggie.

Or I assumed it was the same. The part I could see was the identical size and shape. But now there was more blood on it. So much more.

And the blood was not just on the knife. It was spreading out beneath him. So much so that he'd been able to use it to write two letters, *A-S*, the meaning of which was lost on me. I assumed he hadn't gotten a chance to finish whatever he was trying to convey.

I was so sure that we had found him, the person out for Mandy's blood. But it was his blood that had been spilled instead. How had we been led so astray? How had the situation flipped so impossibly upside down?

Upside down, just like my stomach was right now.

But I had to hold it together. Someone else had already

vomited today, and I couldn't contaminate the crime scene any further, especially now that I was on my way to becoming a CSI, now that I was supposed to know better because this wasn't my first murder rodeo (that saying, minus the *murder*, became popular after Vern Gosdin's 1990 song "This Ain't My First Rodeo").

I texted Olivia:

Where are you?

I managed to get outside. U?

Thank god she was okay.

Instead of telling her what had happened or where I was, I just told her:

You have to clear the café. And find Mandy.

Her response came immediately:

I'll try.

I stood guard outside the family bathroom, yelling at people who entered the corridor with, unfortunately, the first thing that popped into my head.

"There's diarrhea everywhere!"

On the plus side, everyone who stepped foot in the hallway pivoted on their heel and booked it out of there. I certainly would've in their shoes.

Between *diarrhea* yellings, I also checked on Penelope, who had paled about five shades.

"Take a few deep breaths," I told her.

She shook her head. I wasn't sure if she was just disoriented or didn't want to inhale the scent of the dead body, but it didn't smell yet. That would come from the putrescine, cadaverine, hydrogen sulfide (which I knew way too much about for my own liking, thanks to Tucker's murder), and hundreds of other gases and chemicals released by bacteria breaking down tissue and organs over time—much more time than had passed here.

Which was, what? When did I last see him? It couldn't have been more than fifteen minutes ago. I had rare insight into this case, having been here, so I should recall as much as I could, and combining that with my CSI and murder-solving skills, maybe I'd be able to figure this out after all. Maybe Mandy was right to come to me. Maybe I could finally convince my boss that I deserved a place in the forensic lab.

• • • •

"What are *you* doing here?"

That . . . was not what I was hoping to hear out of my boss's mouth.

Of course Gerard was the first one here on the scene. Like my Third Law says, life apparently has a sense of humor, which was quite annoying for me right now.

"I can help you!" I declared desperately.

Gerard's face twisted into disapproving-lecturer mode. "What's rule number one?"

"But this doesn't have anything to do with integrity," I argued.

"You are sticking your nose where it doesn't belong, yet again. Our job is to be in the background, to use science and stick to the facts. We should be more computer than human, but better than computers because we not only analyze data but fill in the blanks. We use every tool at our disposal *except* emotion. Now, can you honestly tell me you can do that here?"

I refused to respond. Because the straight, honest answer was *no, I couldn't*, but wasn't that exactly the reason why I was useful here? No one knew this case and its players better than me. It was exactly why, just a few minutes ago, I'd been thinking this was my chance to prove myself. But Gerard saw those exact same qualities as the reason why I didn't belong.

Gerard looked down his nose at me as he said, "You have no idea what you're doing. And you don't make any effort to learn. Move out of the way." He opened the bathroom door, not even a hint of shock when he spotted the dead body. How many had he seen before he got to this point? Did I ever want to get there? "You checked to make sure the victim is deceased?"

"Oh, um, no, but that's because—"

Gerard held a hand up to stop me, then shut his eyes as if he was exhausted by my stupidity. Snapping on gloves, he went into the bathroom.

Just before the door swung shut, I saw him checking for a pulse.

Well, I would have done that, too, if I'd had another pair of gloves to replace the ones that had torn. This didn't mean I wasn't cut out to be a CSI. Did it?

I tapped my foot, unsure whether I should stay out here or go in and hope Gerard was preoccupied enough not to yell at me.

Just as I was about to make my move, I heard them. Sirens, outside. The mayhem in the rest of the café had been dying down—likely thanks to whatever Olivia had done—and with the sirens, it completely shifted. Instead of yelling at each other, everyone started yelling exclamations like *oh shit!* Then all that could be heard were rapid footsteps stampeding toward the exit.

Then, relative silence. A few people left behind were still clamoring and hustling, but compared to earlier, this was almost meditative.

And finally, Adrian appeared in the bathroom corridor, his

broad shoulders, towering height, and heady scent filling the space.

My knight in shining trench coat.

Suddenly feeling like everything was going to be okay, I ran to him. And he caught me. My rock, my sturdy Birch tree that was always there, always standing even in the worst storms.

Wondering why I hadn't just told him from the start, this man who would go to the ends of the earth to protect me, I folded. Collapsed in on myself like a dying star.

And as I knew he would, he held me up. Supported me completely, his warm strong arms enveloping me in safety.

Despite the dead body nearby, despite Gerard peeking out of the bathroom, spotting me in Adrian's arms and looking at me with disgust like I was a squished bug beneath his shoe, and despite the fear and adrenaline that had been flooding my system just moments before, all I could think and feel was a single word.

Home.

CHAPTER 16

Harsh fluorescent lighting, a two-way mirror, an incessantly ticking clock.

It was another interrogation, but oh-so different from the last one. Because this time, Adrian couldn't be the one to interrogate me. Conflict of interest. So even though he had brought me a blanket, water, and a chocolate bar (again, so different from last time), he had to leave me in there alone—waiting, stewing, being driven up the wall by the bright lights and *tick-tick-tick*ing.

"Kathryn Hu?"

"That's me." *That's Hu*, I didn't add.

"I'm Ricky, Birch's—um, Adrian's—partner."

"Nice to meet you. I've heard good things."

He sprawled out in the chair opposite me, relaxed. "You don't have to lie to me—I'm assuming he partnered with me because it was me or Itchy Ike, who, no matter how many times we've told him, just has to scratch his butt, even when he has gloves on and is examining a crime scene. I mean, he turns his own pants into a crime scene, getting everything from blood to feces on them. Can you imagine being that itchy? He hasn't been allowed in the field for five years now."

I couldn't help chuckling. I also couldn't help noticing how Ricky seemed to be the complete opposite of Adrian. But maybe that was why they worked. Friendly cop, grumpy cop. Though I guess in my current situation, it was just friendly cop.

"So are you okay?" he asked. "Tell me what happened."

I ran through it, starting from when Mandy showed up at the Magic Lounge, all the way to the interrogation room now. And Ricky nodded through everything, taking copious notes and only stopping to clarify certain details or ask for my thoughts on Mandy (my answer: who knows with her?). He didn't react much, but I did notice his impressed eyebrows when I mentioned Olivia's sleight of hand skills and her job as a criminal defense attorney. Old worries returned, and I hoped he wasn't suspecting her because of her Double-Oh-livia-ness. But it wouldn't help for me to blurt out, *She's innocent! I promise!* Especially when last time, one of our friend group hadn't been.

Maybe Olivia could charm Ricky into not suspecting her.

Once I finished my recounting, I waited, unsure what angle he was going to take. But his next question still surprised me.

"So who do you suspect?"

"Uh, do you ask all your suspects that?" Maybe this was some sort of test.

He peered at me curiously. "You think I was interrogating you?"

"I mean . . ." I gestured around us to indicate that we were in the interrogation room.

"If you think that's how I do interrogations, maybe *I* should be partnered with Ike."

I let out a short laugh.

"Kat, I was just getting your statement." He raised an eyebrow. "Unless I *should* be treating you like a suspect?"

My palms immediately filled with sweat, the pink cupcakes resurfacing—the physical representation of my tendency to look guilty even when I wasn't. In elementary school, when someone ate Jenny's birthday cupcakes before they were passed out, my ears and face turned so cupcake-pink during questioning that I was still blamed even after Jason vomited pink frosting all over the carpet.

But Ricky grinned and said, "I'm just messing with ya."

I forced out a *ha!* but somehow it made me sound more guilty. So I just clamped my mouth shut as he said, "You're Birch's girl," as if that meant everything.

I couldn't help wondering if Ricky knew I'd been a prime suspect in Tucker's death. And that Birch himself had suspected me for a while. And that their captain still treated me like I was somehow involved.

"Plus, yours and Olivia's statements matched," he added.

So he had already interviewed her. I wasn't sure if Ricky or Adrian would have handled that, but maybe there was a slight conflict between Adrian and Olivia as well now.

"I just have one last question, and it's serious." Ricky leaned toward me as I tried and failed to repress every pink-cupcake reaction. "How do you get Birch to do anything other than grunt?"

The sudden surge of relief exited my body as a too-loud chuckle.

I was embarrassed, but Ricky just smiled as he stood. "Do you need a ride home? I could spare Birch for an hour or so, though we have a long to-do list. He'll be here for a while tonight, unfortunately."

"I'll be okay," I told Ricky, immediately thinking about how I also had a to-do list to tackle and my own partner to search for.

Ricky led me out of the room and into the sea of their to-do list. It seemed they had managed to bring in a good chunk of the people from the café, which meant the precinct was teeming with unhappy, worked-up folks. And they were worked up without even knowing that someone had died. The screaming back at the café after I (and Penelope) had discovered the body had been absorbed by the rest of the uproar, and thank god, because I couldn't imagine what it would be like once that news got out. People were already yelling and fighting as it was. Not to mention, it was better for Adrian and Ricky's investigation if the news wasn't widespread yet.

My partner found me first, running up and pulling me into a hug. And that same single word came back.

Home. Olivia and Adrian both felt more like home to me than my apartment.

When we pulled apart, Ricky straightened his spine. And Olivia? Well, she *flipped her hair.* I'd never seen her do that before, and suddenly I was looking at Ricky in a new light. He was early thirties, lean and fit, with dark hair and green eyes.

Maybe Ricky's arched eyebrows when I was talking about Olivia weren't due to interest in her as a suspect but just plain interest. And maybe that interest was reciprocated.

I wondered how their non-interrogation had gone. Even with my limited interaction with Ricky, I could almost hear the banter and flirting between the two of them.

Ricky opened his mouth to say something but was called away by the captain, who gave me a dirty look.

Olivia watched him leave. I nudged her elbow with mine, but she quickly pretended she was just looking at the crowd around us.

"So . . ." Olivia said, switching gears. "Are you thinking what I'm thinking?"

We were, unfortunately, in this now, and it had turned personal with me discovering the body. Again.

"Hell yeah," I said, channeling Elle.

It was time to go undercover.

CHAPTER 17

To be consistent, my cover story was already set—I was the secretary from the horse dildo episode. And Olivia was going to be the wronged girl from the episode, the horse (dildo) whisperer. She could say she'd lied about being the secretary to Asher and a few others just to get on my nerves. We just hoped to god the real horse dildo guests weren't here.

"We need names, too," Olivia said under her breath to me.

"I, uh, might already be Lauren."

She closed her eyes for a second, then laughed. "I think Elle would be flattered."

"And you?"

Her eyes twinkled.

• • • •

"Hi, I'm Nancy."

As in Nancy Drew. Best fake name ever. This was Double-Oh-livia's world and I was just stumbling around in it (origin: Dean Martin talking about Frank Sinatra). Case in point, Olivia had said that if I wasn't already Lauren, she would've called me Velma after *Scooby-Doo*, which was kind of apt for me. I always felt slightly invisible, underappreciated, and also like I couldn't fully see until I put the right lenses on.

The first girl we targeted in the waiting room—chosen

because she was the only one who seemed to be keeping to herself—just looked at Olivia warily, as in *how dare you deign to talk to me*, before returning to her phone screen.

I was really tired of all the shit with these podcast people.

But just as I was about to follow up—and maybe lose my own shit—Ricky called her name. *Shira Templeton.* I pulled up my Notes app and added her name to the running list I had, which already included Asher, the no-name pixie-cut girl who'd been yelling at him, Penelope, the WOAT Gia, Wyatt, Isla, Henry who was apparently the best at fighting and also making up, and the no-name girl he was making out with. I hoped Ricky wasn't just blowing smoke about his interrogation techniques and would get something out of someone here. (*Blowing smoke*'s origin: smoke screens.)

"Ice queen, am I right?" said an all-too-familiar voice from behind me.

"Hi, Asher," Olivia said with a sigh.

As much as I didn't have the patience for him right now, I did have an important question for him. "You lied," I said, turning around to face him. "Why?"

"What are you talking about? And if anyone lied, it was the two of you. You *both* said you were the secretary from the horse episode—"

"She is," Olivia interjected. "I'm code name Genevieve, the one who went on the show. I was just—"

"And you're still lying," Asher said, smirking.

I narrowed my eyes at him. "How do you know?"

"Pro tip—you just admitted you *were* lying by asking how I knew."

"I did not. I was merely asking you why you think I'm lying." He was clearly working us as much as we were working him.

The annoying smirk grew. "Because I know Juliette, the *real* secretary."

That . . . we couldn't refute. We couldn't call his bluff.

The smugness was radiating off him. "So? Why're you lying?"

"None of your business," Olivia stated.

He leaned toward her. "I'll show you mine if you show me yours."

She recoiled. But she also put our mission first, saying, "How can I be sure you'll show me yours?"

"Guess you'll just have to trust me."

That was probably the worst thing a guy like Asher could say to two women who had dated Tucker.

"Fine," I said, jumping in. "Why be yourself when you can be someone else? We were all wronged by Mandy, but some people have better stories than others."

Asher cocked an eyebrow. "Well, then, what's your real story?"

"What's yours?" I countered.

"I can be whoever you want me to be." He winked at Olivia.

We weren't getting anywhere, even with him interested in one of us.

"I want you to be the guy who answers our questions," Olivia said. When he didn't offer up any more information, she changed direction and asked, "Did you know that guy who was yelling threats?"

"Who, Eugene? He's harmless."

"Didn't sound harmless to me," I said as the horrible words *I'll be the one left laughing as I fucking gut you* rang in my ears.

Asher waved a hand. "He's all talk. I'm sure he wouldn't harm a fly."

"How do you know him?" Olivia asked. And it was a great question. For all we knew, Asher was just a compulsive liar uttering made-up names and facts.

"He was going around talking to everyone today. And I'd spoken to him online before. He's upset about what happened to him—like most everyone else here—but he just needs to get it out of his system, complain to like-minded individuals, have a few drinks or whatever so he can sleep at night."

I couldn't wrap my mind around how confidently Asher spoke about this, but maybe he'd never had a friend turn out to be a murderer. "And it doesn't concern you that he's still this mad and can't sleep most nights?"

"Is it because *you* relate to that kind of emotion?" Olivia pressed.

"Jesus, ladies," Asher said, frowning. "You two are not at all who I thought you were. And I don't just mean because you've been lying to me from the start. Whatever you're after, it's not here. And I don't think you should come to any of our meetings again in the future."

Just then, yells that could only be described as hysterical broke out from across the precinct. My first thought was that the pixie-cut girl who'd yelled at Asher had spotted him and was coming over for round two, but it was so much worse than that.

It was Penelope. And she was still reeling from the body she'd stumbled in on.

"They're not telling you everything!" Penelope was screaming. "Someone DIED! In the café! Do you hear me?"

She'd just exited the captain's office, and the door opened to reveal the face that still haunted my nightmares. And somehow, the captain's glaring face found me immediately. How was this my fault?

Penelope pointed at me. "And *she* told me to just breathe, like it was no big deal!"

Okay, maybe that was a little my fault.

"There was blood! And a kn—"

"That's enough," the captain said, her voice cutting through the hysterics like a, well, like a knife.

The captain motioned Penelope back into her office, shutting the door just as the entire room exploded in an uproar.

If I thought it was commotion before, we were in full-blown turmoil now.

CHAPTER 18

Five minutes later, I realized I needed to embody Velma and view this situation through a new lens.

Because while, yes, everyone was yelling and fighting and screaming in fear and anger and confusion . . . *jinkies*, there was a silver lining: The yelling and fighting and screaming were now focused on the very topic we were investigating.

"Who do you think it was?"

"The victim? I bet it was Mandy! Poor thing was really getting it before she disappeared into thin air."

"She deserved it! And anything else that might've come her way!"

I turned in the direction of the last comment to see it had been said by WOAT Gia. Into the notes it went.

Soon, people began taking stock of who was there and who was missing, with whispers of possible names being floated out.

"Was it Kendra?"

"No, she's over there."

"Where's Barrett?"

"Has anyone seen Shira?"

The whispers continued until someone—I wish I saw who—stumbled onto the truth, and it began to spread.

"Where's Eugene?"

"Who's that?"

"Eugene Maxwell. The angry guy. The one who was screaming at Mandy."

"That guy? He was walking around that event trying to rile everyone up. Guess he succeeded."

"His real goal was to hurt Mandy, though."

That was the one. Olivia and I had been sitting in complete silence, not wanting to move a muscle so we could hear every word, but that was exactly the type of information we'd been waiting for. And now, we had to follow up.

"I got the same impression," Olivia said, running over to the guy who'd said that, me on her heels. "What makes you think he wanted to hurt her?"

The man was young—maybe eighteen or nineteen—wearing an oversized hoodie and jeans. "I dunno, just, like, the shit he was saying."

"Like what?"

"That he wanted to buy her an ice-cream cone, what do you think?" The others around him laughed.

"I'm Nancy," Olivia said.

"I'm not interested."

"Did Eugene say *how* he wanted to hurt her?" Olivia asked.

"What are you, a cop?" said Not Interested.

"Do I look like a cop?"

A few police officers milling about turned to look at her.

"Not that there's anything wrong with that," Olivia added quickly.

We were starting to stick out in the crowd, meaning our recon might be coming to a natural end.

But as the others began turning away from us, a woman who had been hanging in the back motioned Olivia over, her dark brown eyes flashing with fear behind her bright red spectacles—trendy spectacles I would have admired any other day, but today they only reminded me of the scene on the bathroom floor I was desperately trying to forget.

"Did Eugene creep you out, too?" the woman asked.

Olivia nodded. No lie there. "I'm Nancy, and this is Lauren."

"Yasmin, nice to meet you." She smiled, but it was tight on the edges.

"What did Eugene do to you?" Olivia asked.

The reluctant smile slipped off her face. "I was angry at Mandy—because of her show, my brother made my parents write me out of their will—but I just wanted her evil podcast to be off the air and for her to know what she'd done to us. But Eugene had somehow figured out who I was and wouldn't leave me alone at the café, bragging about how he was going to make her pay, and how I could join him if I wanted. He said something about messages and . . ." She hesitated, looking around the station and pausing on several uniformed officers nearby.

Olivia and I leaned in closer.

"He talked about a knife. And poison. Something about how he's a scientist and can make it look natural." This must've been why I saw everyone inching away from Eugene earlier. "It was . . . pretty scary. He had this look in his eye . . ." She trailed off, and it was worse leaving it up to our imaginations.

Eugene must have been the one threatening Mandy. And it didn't seem to be just talk. The messages and knife we knew about. But poison? That was new.

"What did you do?" Olivia asked Yasmin.

"I pretended like I wasn't creeped out because I was terrified of him. You don't want to be on the wrong side of someone like that, you know? But I'm scared if anyone overheard us, they'll think I look suspicious or something, like I was encouraging him. But I was just trying to save myself! Did he say similar stuff to you?"

Olivia shook her head. "We didn't get that far."

"Consider yourself lucky." Yasmin chewed on her lower lip. "Do you think something happened to Mandy? Do you think he might have . . ." She couldn't finish the sentence. "I should've said something sooner."

I didn't want Yasmin to rack herself with guilt, but I also didn't want to divulge too much. Also, I hadn't seen Mandy yet, so I honestly didn't know if she was okay.

When I couldn't find any words, Olivia replied, "I think Mandy can take care of herself."

Upon hearing that, Yasmin's shoulders lowered from her ears. "You're right. I mean, shit, girl can hold her own, no? I wouldn't have expected that out of someone so small, though I guess knowing her personality, maybe I should have, but seeing her in person, I just didn't think she had that in her. I was just as scared of her as I was of Eugene. Actually, now that I think about it, you don't think she was the one who—I mean, she wouldn't be capable of doing something like *that*, would she? Though I guess if she felt threatened . . ."

I grabbed Olivia's arm so suddenly and desperately she let out a small gasp. "We have to find Mandy," I whispered to her.

We had to find that red panda.

CHAPTER 19

Mandy Thorne had managed to disappear into the crowd during the commotion by shedding the flames on her costume, but she was eventually picked up by an officer while running away from the scene of the crime, dressed in only a skintight black unitard.

This was still her state of dress as she sat across from Olivia and me in the interrogation room. While the harsh fluorescent lighting, two-way mirror, and incessantly ticking clock were the same, for the first time Olivia and I were in charge.

"Why were you running?" I asked Mandy.

"Why wouldn't I be running? The café was filled with people who want me dead!"

"People that *you* put there before showing up willingly," Olivia pointed out.

"In disguise! I was completely invisible! Well, not invisible—I looked fucking fire, and I'm not talking about what I was dressed as—"

"Mandy," I said, trying to get her to focus. "Where were you after the fight with Eugene Maxwell?"

"Who?"

"The man who you got into the . . . row . . . with. Eugene."

Mandy's mouth twisted in a sneer. "Oh, that horrible guy. I don't know, that's when all hell broke loose. Thanks to him, everyone was coming after me, but luckily some of those Always Hot angels saved me. Stripped off the flames, then provided cover and got me to the door. Once I was out of the café, I ran. I was waiting for—I mean, I was hoping someone would pick me up. And the police did."

Mandy glanced at the two-way glass, then back at us. "What's with the questions? I requested you two because I thought you'd be on my side, but you're just doing the interrogating for them."

Mandy had refused to speak to Adrian and Ricky, saying she'd only talk to Olivia and me, hence why we were allowed in here now—with Adrian and Ricky watching, of course.

As far as I was concerned, though, I was not on Mandy's side, not when all the evidence was pointing to her.

Channeling Adrian, I ignored her question and asked, "Where did you go after you, you know . . ." I couldn't say the words out loud, not when I knew what had happened.

"Threatened to kill Eugene Maxwell," Olivia filled in.

"You keep talking about him like I should know him," Mandy said. "Wait . . . How do you know his name?"

"Mandy!" I burst out, tired of her bullshit, which was uncharacteristically making me the bad cop instead of Olivia. "Did you or did you not red-panda Eugene Maxwell?"

Mandy puffed her chest out. "Of course I did! You saw me. The entire place saw me. And it worked, did it not? I'm telling you, red panda—always a triumph. Don't let anyone walk all over you."

The entire place saw me? "Are you talking about—"

"When I yelled at him. Shut him down. Owned that shit. I raised my paws and roared right back and neutralized the threat before he could do anything."

I still didn't know if she was talking about yelling at him or murdering him.

"Don't underestimate the power of words," Mandy said. "No one understands that better than me, award-winning podcast host."

So, did she truly not know what happened to Eugene? Or was she acting? It was in her bio:

> Mandy Thorne: influencer; podcast creator, host, and star; OnlyFans superstar; best contestant on reality dating show *Love Hut*; actor.

But she couldn't be *this* good of an actor. I knew she wasn't—I'd seen snippets of *Bikini Babe Rebels 4* on her website. And Mandy being ignorant of Eugene's fate made a lot more sense than her striding in here and confessing—proudly—to murder.

"Mandy, where's the knife?" I asked, hoping to get to the bottom of everything another way.

"What knife? Oh, *the* knife. Oh, shit, my purse! I don't have it!"

Okay, now *this* was acting. *Bikini Babe Rebels 4* style.

"Where is it?" I asked calmly.

"I told you, I don't know. I had it, and then I didn't."

I wasn't sure what else to do, so I glanced at the two-way glass where Adrian was watching, but before he or I could do anything, Olivia lost it.

"A man is fucking dead, Mandy! Killed by the knife last seen in your possession! Right after you screamed *I will kill you!* in his face to a room full of witnesses!"

I froze, thinking Adrian would burst in, but he didn't. Which maybe made sense—the information was already out there and we couldn't take it back. Might as well watch Mandy's reaction to it.

When Olivia looked at me, I knew what she was thinking—how this was what Elle's freedom depended on, and she couldn't take it anymore. But I focused on Mandy, trying to read what was going on underneath.

"Oh gods," Mandy said, the blood draining from her face. "He's . . . dead? And the knife? Oh gods . . ."

"So where is your purse?" Olivia asked.

"I—I don't have it! This is—oh shit. You have to believe me. I swear, gods as my witnesses, on the success and ratings of my podcast, on my life and the life of everyone I know and love, I didn't do this. You truly think I'm capable of *murder*?"

Neither Olivia nor I spoke.

"Fuck, *that's* what you think of me?" Her chin trembled. If she was acting, this was not *Bikini Babe Rebels 4* acting. This was Golden Globes and Oscar–level acting.

Her next words were so soft I could barely make them out. "I think I'm being framed."

Kathryn's Fifth Law of Life (and Death): Karma's a bitch.

CHAPTER 20

"I object!" yelled a female voice as a blur of black and yellow flew into the interrogation room.

"What the—" Olivia said just as the blur tripped and tumbled into Mandy's lap.

"There you are!" Mandy said. "Where the hell have you been?"

Ricky ran in, but since he was too late to stop the intruder, he hung back by the door.

"Are you a lawyer?" Olivia asked.

As the woman straightened up, Olivia and I both gasped.

The sexy firefighter.

"Who are you?" Olivia demanded.

"Jocelyn?" the firefighter said, her name coming out more as a question than a statement.

"She's not my lawyer," Mandy said, "but Olivia has a point. I don't want to say anything else until I have one."

She looked at Olivia expectantly, but Olivia gave her an over-my-dead-body look (maybe not the best choice of phrase for this particular occasion).

"Jocelyn, who are you?" Olivia asked again.

"I just told you . . ." Jocelyn said, genuinely confused.

"I mean, who are you to Mandy?"

"She's my assistant," Mandy said with a wave of her hand.

"Jesus, Mandy!" Olivia exploded. "How can you expect us to believe you when you won't stop lying to us? You claimed at the café you didn't know her!"

"We were undercover!" Mandy argued. "And she was dressed as a firefighter—of course we knew each other. We came together in a fucking couples costume, didn't we?"

Olivia let out a strained groan, but Mandy ignored it as she said, "Joce, can you tell the hot detective where my purse is? It's pretty goddamn important."

"Your purse?" Jocelyn blinked twice. "I thought you had it."

"No, I gave it to you!" Mandy's voice was getting hysterical. "Gods, Joce, you've always been incompetent, and I usually let it slide, but now it's really going to fuck me! How could you let this happen? And I told you to pick me up outside the café!"

Tears formed in Jocelyn's eyes.

Adrian strode in and made a beeline for her.

"Ms. . . ." Adrian paused, waiting for Jocelyn to fill in the blank, and I was momentarily taken back to when he used the exact same tactic on me (which I avoided several times).

But unlike me, Jocelyn sniffled, then answered, "Morningstar."

"Ms. Morningstar, if you could give us a moment with Ms. Thorne, we'll have some questions for you after."

Ricky led Jocelyn out.

I exchanged a glance with Olivia, then hurried after them.

Maybe Jocelyn would talk to me if we were alone, especially since Mandy trusted me.

"Are you okay?" I asked her.

Catching on, Ricky slowed, then turned, leaving me to walk her back to the waiting room.

Jocelyn sniffled but nodded. "Do you think—did I really mess things up?"

"It'll be okay," I lied, mostly because I didn't know what else to say. "You don't remember where the purse went?"

Jocelyn shook her head. "I put it down at some point—I was holding so many things. I didn't mean to. I just—I don't know why this happens. I swear I try. But it's just never good enough."

That I related to. I led her to a chair and sat beside her.

"How long have you been Mandy's assistant?"

"Three years," she said.

"And you like it?" I asked while wondering how anyone could possibly stand being with Mandy for more than twenty minutes.

"It's not just about liking the job, which I do. I owe everything to Mandy. When we met, I couldn't get hired anywhere, and she gave me a chance solely based on my having been from her hometown." In middle-of-nowhere Idaho instead of the South as Mandy had initially claimed—a truth uncovered by Lassy McBush. "We didn't know each other—I'm quite a bit younger than her—but she really understood my desire to get out of there and make it on my own. And now I'm a part of everything. Her brand, her show, her empire. I never imagined this when I left home."

"You wanted to get out?" I asked.

"It's just such a small town without much to offer. Nothing like this." Jocelyn gestured around, then realized she was in a precinct and dropped her hands. "I mean, getting to come to a big city was everything I dreamed of."

"Do you still have family back home?"

"My parents have passed."

"I'm so sorry," I said. "That must have been hard. Were you close?"

"Yes. They had me when they were older, though, so I was prepared to maybe lose them earlier. But it was still a shock when it happened. I still feel like a piece of me is missing, you know?"

"Was that partly why you left?" I asked.

Jocelyn nodded. "And why I'm so grateful to Mandy. I came here with nothing and no one."

"It sounds like she can be tough sometimes, though."

"Well . . . I've messed up more than I should," Jocelyn admitted, her gaze dropping to her shoes.

"In what way?"

"Getting her coffee order wrong; accidentally deleting part of a podcast recording; not replying to her OnlyFans clients fast—or sexy—enough; getting the wrong gift for her aunt—I should have remembered she was allergic to nuts . . ."

"Those sound like part of the learning curve for the job," I said sympathetically, even though all I could think was, *Mandy makes Jocelyn message her OnlyFans clients?* That sounded like a job from hell.

"Mandy's been good to me," she insisted. Then, hesitantly, she asked, "Is . . . Mandy in trouble? I swear she didn't have the purse. That was my fault."

"I believe you," I said. "Can you tell me, is Mandy ever different around you? Different than how she is with other people?"

I couldn't stop wondering if Mandy's acting skills were better than we thought, and whether everything, even *Bikini Babe Rebels 4*, was part of the whole Mandy Thorne persona.

"Mandy Thorne is exactly who she projects," Jocelyn stated. "She's honest, unabashed, and confident. It's why she's become who she's become. Why she's a good reality TV personality."

I found that hard to believe—how could Mandy function if she was always like that?—but maybe that truly was her. Or maybe she was just that method of an actor, staying in character even around her assistant.

Jocelyn seemed done with this conversation, shifting impatiently in her seat, so I thanked her for her time and then got her some water.

When I returned to the interrogation room, Mandy was miming zipping her lips shut to Adrian, who was sitting across from her while Olivia paced behind him.

"Ms. Thorne. We are simply trying to get a better understanding of what exactly went down earlier."

Mandy shrugged her shoulders.

Adrian leaned forward. "Do the letters *A-S* mean anything to you?"

Despite her previous threat of silence, Mandy's curiosity got the best of her. "*A-S*? What does that have to do with anything?"

I put a hand on the wall to steady myself. Because with those two letters, the crime scene I'd been trying desperately to block out appeared before me again.

I could see every pained line and curve, right next to the victim's body, next to his outstretched index finger, written in his own bright red blood . . .

I was going to be sick.

Noticing my wobbly legs and shallow breaths, Adrian strode over in three large steps, put his arm around me, and led me out the door. Olivia followed close behind.

"Hey! You're just leaving? For reals? What the fuck does *A-S* mean?" Mandy called after us. "I want a lawyer! Tell my assistant to call one!"

CHAPTER 21

Adrian helped me to his desk and covered me with a blanket.

"Better?" he said, more of a statement than a question.

Even though my legs still felt like jelly, I nodded.

"You should go home," he said gently. "Do you think maybe . . ." He glanced at Olivia, and she nodded immediately. She wouldn't leave me alone.

He leaned down and kissed my forehead tenderly. "Call me if you need anything. And . . . be careful."

I knew he meant the first part, but the second only reminded me how much we still hadn't talked about, how I'd looked into this behind his back, and how he knew I was probably going to keep looking.

"I will," I promised, telling myself I would do better for both our sakes, but he was already walking away.

• • • •

Back at Olivia's townhome, I couldn't get the *A-S* out of my head.

"I think we need to put on our sleuthing hats," I said.

Olivia's eyes lit up. "Oh? Should I go out and get us a couple of deerstalker caps?"

"Actually, funny story. The deerstalker Sherlock hat was

never mentioned in any of the books. That and the iconic cape came later in an illustrated edition."

Olivia grinned mischievously. "Well, since it's not even the official hat of Sherlock Holmes according to Sir Arthur Conan Doyle, then we can improvise, can we not?"

I beamed. "The game is afoot."

As I sat down at Olivia's dining room table, she disappeared into her bedroom, then reappeared with a cloche hat on her head and a trendy beanie in her hand for me.

Our official sleuthing hats. The cloche worked surprisingly well for Olivia, making her look classic and chic. As I pulled my beanie on, I worried I looked like a Smurf.

"So," I said as Olivia retrieved her laptop and turned it on. "The *A-S*."

"The *A-S*."

"It's not just two letters," I said. "It's everything. It's the last thing Eugene tried to communicate. And if I were him, with only moments left, what I would try to do is—"

"Identify my killer," Olivia said.

"Exactly. And he didn't write *M-T* or *M-A*. So as much as the evidence points to Mandy, as much as I don't know what to believe with her, this piece of evidence is making me wonder if she's telling the truth that she's being framed."

Olivia sighed. "Yeah. That's a good point."

"And with *A-S*," I continued, pulling up my Notes list of the people we'd met today. "The most obvious person that points to is—"

"Asher," Olivia said with a gasp.

I nodded. "Eugene could have started to write *Asher* but didn't finish."

"What do you think Asher's motive could've been?" Olivia asked.

"Let's figure that out."

Unfortunately, we didn't have a last name for Asher (and he'd put himself into Olivia's phone as *The Best You'll Ever Have*). So even with Double-Oh-livia at the keyboard, without a full name, we couldn't come up with much, hitting dead end after dead end (origin: 1850s, about drainpipes with no outlet leading to "dead" unflowing water).

"Why don't we call Adrian?" Olivia suggested. "I'm sure he has intel that would help."

"What do we know about Asher?" I said instead of answering her question (I wasn't ready to confront that particular can of worms yet). "Wait, what about the neighbor and mashed potatoes? We could find his *Dish Served Hot* episode!"

Olivia's cloche hat bobbed up and down. "Great idea."

Thanks to the unique details involved, it didn't take us long to locate it. I couldn't help wondering if the sleuthing hats had somehow helped, too. Regardless, it meant we didn't need to call Adrian.

I breathed a sigh of relief as Olivia pulled up the episode and pressed Play.

Dish Served Hot Podcast Transcript– Episode 22

[Podcast theme song plays, sung by creator, host, and star Mandy Thorne]

MANDY THORNE: Hello, my lovely Thornies! Today is a special day because *you* get a dish! And *you* get a dish! And *you* get a dish! Of steaming hot, boiling revenge. Better than Oprah, am I right?

And today is an especially fun episode. It is my honor to introduce to you . . . Mister Rogers.

MISTER ROGERS: Hello, neighbor.

MANDY: Hello. Though giving you that name is a bit ironic, since you are basically the opposite of everything he represented.

MISTER ROGERS: [laughing] Won't you be my neighbor?

MANDY: Definitely, definitely not.

MISTER ROGERS: I promise, if you were my neighbor, Mandy, things would have gone much differently.

MANDY: Is that so?

MISTER ROGERS: Very much so.

MANDY: So you wouldn't have destroyed my property?

MISTER ROGERS: [laughs] When you put it like that . . .

MANDY: Well, how would you put it? Why don't you tell our listeners what happened?

MISTER ROGERS: Okay, look, guys. I think we all know how home ownership can be stressful, and if there's a disagreement about property lines, it can get messy, right? And trust me, my neighbor is no picnic. Well, maybe one infested with angry ants. He just would not let anything go. First, he claimed the peach tree that was straddling the property line. Then he yelled at me when I picked up a peach that had fallen onto what was clearly *my* side. He wanted me to, what, chuck it back over? So that errant peach was the beginning of the fence.

MANDY: Oh, no.

MISTER ROGERS: Oh, yes. The goddamn fence. He just had to put one up that was huge and disgusting and an eyesore. And it made both of our yards feel claustrophobic. So I asked to have a discussion about it. Then another one when he proved to be a stubborn ass. And after twenty tries, I might have just gone to the HOA about it. But instead of taking it down like they ordered, he *added* to it—and horribly, might I add? Just nailing more and more boards on it—repulsive. And the part that was closest to my house? Five slats, with the middle one sticking up so it looked like a hand flipping me the bird. So what was I to do? And then I realized, that was exactly the right question I should be asking myself. What *could* I do?

MANDY: Oooh, yes, what could you do, Mister Rogers?

MISTER ROGERS: The obvious answer was to destroy the fence. But then I thought, why not be a little more creative? Why not go after more than just the fence?

MANDY: The peach tree?

MISTER ROGERS: Too small.

MANDY: His house?

MISTER ROGERS: Too difficult to access.

MANDY: His yard?

MISTER ROGERS: Exactly. I executed the perfect plan. I bought all the instant mashed potatoes my grocery store had—which is one of the cheapest food items you can get, by the way; I'm just a genius—and in the middle of the night, I scaled the fence and covered his lawn. May have also broken off the "middle finger" in the process. The next morning, when the sprinklers went off . . . poof! Lawn full of mashed potatoes.

MANDY: Devious! And as you said, ingenious. Cheap, simple, but creative and devilish.

MISTER ROGERS: Thank you, thank you. And, sorry to the real Mister Rogers. I did love you as a kid. But you didn't live next to my psycho neighbor, or else you would've been preaching revenge instead of kindness.

MANDY: I'm sure the real Mister Rogers would understand. So is everything copacetic with the neighbor now?

MISTER ROGERS: Of course not. He's pissed as hell. But if he comes after me, I'm already brainstorming my next move.

MANDY: Then we'll have to have you back on. Maybe your neighbor, too.

MISTER ROGERS: Hah! That'd be a first—rival guests on the podcast. I welcome it!

MANDY: Thanks, Mister Rogers. And let this episode be a reminder to you Thornies to follow the real Mister Rogers's advice and *look for the helpers*—anger, pettiness, and revenge.

CHAPTER 22

Most of Asher's story seemed to check out with what we heard on the podcast. Except . . .

"The girl with the pixie cut is not Mister Rogers," I said to Olivia.

"Agreed. We need to figure out who she is and why she's so mad at Asher."

"It's also weird that Asher used the same exact words from the episode when he was talking to me." *When the sprinklers went off . . . poof! Lawn full of mashed potatoes.* Not the most unique phrasing, but the *poof!* had been memorable. "He also said that he and the neighbor had a laugh, then split the HOA fines, which doesn't seem the most likely based on how Mister Rogers was talking about it." Though we didn't have proof that it didn't happen.

"You know, I think I can track down more information based on what we heard. This case has enough bizarre details that maybe we can use them . . ." Olivia trailed off, her fingers already flying on her keyboard.

I got up to retrieve a snack to both energize us and also give Olivia some space, but before I'd even reached the kitchen, Double-Oh-livia came through.

"Got it!" she called out.

I hurried back. "What'd you find?"

"Records of their official complaints, which got so bad a civil suit was filed, which is why it became public. And the mashed potatoes, fence, peach tree—they're all in here."

"And?" I said, sitting back down beside her.

"And Asher was lying about *everything*."

Olivia turned her screen toward me, and I gasped.

The two people on the screen—Mister Rogers and his neighbor—were *not* Asher. By name nor by image. They were two middle-aged men, neither of whom we recognized.

"I knew it!" I exclaimed. "I knew Asher was lying! I just didn't know he lied about it *all*. So who is he? And what was he doing at the Dish Gets Served meeting?"

"I don't know. I do have an idea how we can find out . . ."

I waited, knowing there was a *but* coming.

After a pause, Olivia said, "But you're not going to like it."

I chuckled softly. "Would it even be us if I did?"

CHAPTER 23

"I knew you'd call sooner or later," said Asher as soon as he entered the diner across town and saw Olivia and me standing there. "And *both* of you are here. Does this mean . . . ?" He waggled an eyebrow.

Ew. As if I would jump in bed with a human red flag. Well, I wouldn't do it knowingly.

"Why are you so—"

"Charming?" he finished for me. He turned to Olivia. "You find me charming, don't you? Or else you wouldn't have called?" He stepped forward, his arms out, and Olivia let him hug her. She even let him linger an extra second, though she did give me a brief pucker of disgust.

Once we were in a booth, with Olivia and me on one side and Asher on the other, I started in on my list of questions.

"So who are you?"

"Asher, at your service." He doffed an imaginary cap.

"Why did you lie about being the mashed potato victim of Mister Rogers?"

"I didn't. Why would I do that?"

Of course he wasn't going to give us anything.

"How well did you know Eugene?"

"I already told you everything I knew about him." He was cool as a cucumber (origin: 1732 John Gay poem).

"Who was that girl with the pixie cut at the café, and why did she say you were playing sick little games?"

"A bitter ex, talking about games from the bedroom—you'll of course understand that I choose to respect her privacy about the matter."

I didn't believe a word out of his mouth.

Tired of my questions, Asher glanced in Olivia's direction. This entire time, she'd been scrolling on the phone in her hand, her eyes locked on the screen.

"What, I'm not interesting enough for you?" Asher said.

"Oh, you are," Olivia said, still not looking up from the phone. "You know what's especially interesting?"

"What?" I asked, playing along.

"Asher really is so popular, isn't he? He seems to know everyone who's ever crossed paths with *Dish Served Hot*."

"He *did* seem to know everyone," I said, intrigued. "Eugene, Juliette the secretary, the girl with the pixie cut . . ."

Asher shrugged. "What can I say? I'm a likable guy. People gravitate toward me."

"I don't think that's it," Olivia said. And finally, she looked up from the phone. "At least, that's not the story your text messages tell."

"Wait—Is that—" Asher patted his pockets. "When did you take my phone?"

Double-Oh-livia wouldn't have let creepy Asher give her a lingering hug without some sleight-of-hand comeuppance.

"Give that back!" Asher yelled, reaching.

But Olivia extended her arm away.

"How'd you get past the lock screen?" he asked.

I'd made a resin fingerprint in the lab using the print we'd lifted from him back at the café—which made me feel pretty Double-Hu-Seven myself—but he didn't need to know that.

"So how does Asher know everyone?" I asked Olivia, ignoring him.

"It's not because he was on the podcast—which, I'm guessing you weren't. At all." Asher didn't react, so Olivia continued. "It's ironic you're claiming to *just be likable* when you're probably the most hated person associated with *Dish Served Hot*. You might even be giving Mandy Thorne a run for her money."

I couldn't take the suspense anymore. "What did he do?"

"He's been figuring out which person belongs to which episode and extorting them with the threat of publicly posting their identities."

Shit, I had not been expecting that. I knew Asher was shady, lewd, and a liar, but blackmail? Suddenly the *sick little games* comment made sense. The poor girl with the pixie cut was a victim of his blackmail.

But blackmail was not the same as murder. I looked at Olivia with a question in my eyes. She subtly shook her head, signaling that there was no evidence on his phone of him murdering Eugene. I sighed, disappointed to have hit a dead end.

Asher crossed his arms over his chest. "So what the hell do you want from me?"

Olivia threw his phone back at him. "Stop blackmailing people."

"Or else what? You'll tell the police? What would you even say, that you ambushed me, stole my phone, broke into it, and saw the evidence? Not only is what you did illegal, but everything will be gone within the hour anyway."

"It'll be an anonymous tip. And you may delete the evidence, but I'm sure the people you're blackmailing will corroborate the story, especially that girl you pissed off from the café."

The fear in Asher's face told us what we needed to know. We'd been just unhinged enough that he wasn't sure what we were capable of. And hopefully that would be enough to keep him in line.

Olivia and I stood at the same time. And she sealed the deal by leaning forward and whispering ominously, “We’ll be watching you.”

We left a stunned Asher holding his phone by two fingers and looking at it as if it were now bugged.

Outside the diner, Olivia exhaled. “Goddamn Asher.”

“Goddamn freaking Asher,” I repeated in agreement. “You didn’t actually bug his phone, did you?”

“I wish I had, but I hadn’t prepared for that.”

“So why don’t you think he was the one who killed Eugene?” I asked.

“Asher did message Eugene trying to blackmail him, but Eugene wrote back welcoming him to tell the world. Which is in line with what we saw—Eugene himself was shouting it from the rooftops, how Mandy screwed him over and how much he hated her. Then Eugene started texting Asher about poison and his expertise—the same stuff he told Yasmin at the boba café—and *he* scared *Asher* away.”

Maybe Eugene scared Asher so much that Asher wanted to take him out for his own safety?

“Did Eugene threaten to expose Asher?” I asked.

“Not that I saw.”

Murder seemed like a big leap, then.

After a beat, I said, “You’re sure it’s not him?”

“Sure enough to pursue other avenues for now.”

“Okay.”

“So what avenue is next?” Olivia asked.

I thought for a moment. “Well, I have an idea. Because my gut is telling me we’re not seeing the whole picture.”

Which meant, it was time to talk to *our* guts. The one who knew exactly how to think like a murderer.

I wasn’t sure if Olivia was ready yet, but it was time. Time to get the Ex-Girlfriend Murder Club back together.

CHAPTER 24

"Kitty Kat! Double-Oh! My loves!"

Elle placed a palm on her side of the glass partition over where mine was already waiting. A second later, Olivia's hand joined ours.

"Elle . . ."

I had told Olivia about my previous visit with Elle on the ride here, but since this was her first time visiting, I knew they needed to have their own moment, too.

"I wasn't sure you'd want me to come," Olivia said.

Elle paused, no doubt thinking about all the complicated emotions at play, and eventually, she said, "I'm glad you're here."

Olivia chewed on her bottom lip. "Even though I led you astray, thinking that your compliance could help you get a deal?"

I hadn't realized that that piece of it had been weighing on Olivia. Neither had Elle, apparently.

"Liv, the only reason I wouldn't want you here is because I'm not worthy of your friendship. You helped me so much more than I deserved. And I will never forget your kindness."

Olivia hadn't been allowed to represent Elle because her role in the case made it a conflict of interest, but one of her colleagues from her firm had. And Olivia had done whatever she could from the sidelines.

"I'm sorry I didn't come see you sooner," Olivia said.

"Nonsense!" Elle blinked a tear away. "So, what does bring you two here? I hope it's something juicy. Either gossip or some more fun stories?" She winked at me.

"Mandy Thorne looks guilty of murder," Olivia said.

"She claims she's being framed," I added.

Elle's eyes widened. Then, she burst into laughter. "It's just so fucking perfect, isn't it?" She switched to Alanis Morissette's raspy mezzo-soprano voice and, of course, altered the lyrics as she sang, "It's like a fucking thunderstorm on your wedding day." Then she returned to her own voice as she said, "Though Tuck and I had a sunny, warm day. It was everything that came after that that was the thunderstorm."

"Um, hello?" Olivia said. "You're forgetting the most apt line here. Meeting the perfect man, then meeting his beautiful but also deviously brilliant wife?"

"It always bothered me that in 'Ironic,' there are examples that aren't actually ironic," I said. "The lyrics mostly describe coincidences, inconveniences, or bad luck—not events contrary to expectation."

Elle beamed. "There's my girl."

"*Our* girl," Olivia amended.

I blushed. "It's not a saying, but—"

"It's still totally, completely Kat Hu," Elle said.

"Who? Me, I'm Kat," I joked.

Elle laughed. "Also very you."

It felt like old times, joking around and being ourselves even in the face of danger, because life was full of sadness—I mean, look where we were meeting—but the only way to get through was to lean on your loved ones and find pockets of laughter where you could. And often, the darker the situation, the more emotional release you needed.

"Seriously, though," Elle said. "How fucking turned are

these tables?" (Board game origin where if you turned the table, the person who was winning had to now play from the losing position.)

"I know! Mandy Thorne tried and almost succeeded in framing us—well, mostly you, Kat," Olivia amended as she looked at me, "for a murder you didn't commit, and now has the gall to ask us for help?"

"Well, technically I was the one truly framing you," Elle said quietly. "I'm still really sorry."

The Ex-Girlfriend Murder Club was back, but not without a caveat.

"Bygones," I said with a wave of the hand.

Olivia moved on swiftly, filling Elle in on the details of the case—the threats, the Dish Gets Served meeting, the fight, the knife, the lies, the red panda–ing . . .

Elle turned to me. "So what's holding you back?"

"How did you know there was something?"

"Because you wouldn't be here otherwise. You would've just let your hunny book Mandy and never looked back." Elle steepled her fingers. "So what's the evidence that someone might be framing her?"

I shifted in my seat. "It just feels . . . too easy. Too neat." Then I told her about the *A-S*. "I mean, it doesn't negate the evidence pointing at her, but it's significant enough that we should figure out what it means."

"Well, what do you think it means?" Elle asked.

"I think it's a way to identify the killer. Maybe the killer's name has the letters *A* and *S* in it. Even among the people we met, though, that leads to so many possibilities: Asher—though we think we've ruled him out at this point. Shira, which begins with an *S* and ends with an *a*. Isla, has both letters in it. Gia and Russ, one ends in an *a* and the other in an *s*. Why are there so many? I guess *A* and *S* are really common letters . . ."

I was off in my own world for a second, and when I looked up, Elle and Olivia were exchanging a wary glance.

"What?" I asked.

Elle leaned forward. "Babes, if the victim was trying to identify his killer as Shira or Gia and Russ, the last letters he'd start with are *A* and *S*."

I sighed. "I know. I just . . . want to make sure I think through every possibility."

Elle peered at me. "Or maybe you're getting hung up on the *A-S* being short for another name because of . . . me?"

It hadn't crossed my mind before she said it, but maybe she was right. Even though we had eventually figured out that Elle was short for Lauren, it bothered me that I hadn't seen it sooner, especially knowing Tucker's tendency toward nicknames.

"It's because it's the best clue we have," I only partially lied. "And it could be something."

"It could be," Elle agreed. "But it's not the only possibility."

"If Mandy didn't do it, there are too many suspects," Olivia grumbled.

"A wild-goose chase," Elle said before she and Olivia turned to look at me expectantly.

"In the sixteenth century, there were horse races where riders had to follow an erratic lead horse similarly to how wild geese have to follow their leader while in formation. It was likely popularized by Shakespeare using it in *Romeo and Juliet*."

I was relieved I already knew the origin of that one since we couldn't bring our phones in here.

"Well," Elle said. "A long list of suspects is nothing for you girls. You've been there before and came out triumphant."

But there were so many more suspects than last time, and everything was more muddled.

So I asked Elle the main question I came here to ask. "Do you think Mandy did it?"

Elle tilted her head to one side. "Do *you*?"

"I *am* worried Mandy did this—either as self-defense or a spur-of-the-moment red panda breaking point. I'm also worried that this is some elaborate plan of hers to get back at us. Why else would she have come to us—her mortal enemies—in the first place? Though that wouldn't make much sense, either—we did solve the previous case."

Elle rubbed her chin. "I agree with you—I wouldn't be shocked if Mandy did this. She *has* been sending Lassy McBush death threats. But criminal mastermind? I'm not sure she has it in her, though we all know she'd do anything for her podcast. And all of this—including her coming to you—could be for ratings, fame, listeners, a viral story. It's not that different from what she did to us. So the biggest question is, how far would she actually go?"

We paused to contemplate that, and I wasn't the only one who shuddered.

"It still doesn't make complete sense, though," I said. "Could something as negative as being accused of murder lead to a boost in ratings?"

"Uh, *yeah*," Elle said. "No press is bad press. I actually have some news of my own. I got a book deal."

Olivia smacked the counter. "Shut up!"

"For real?" I asked.

Elle nodded. "Memoir. And I've been getting so much correspondence from people that my agent suggested creating a website to answer them all."

"Like Dear Abby?"

"More like, *Dear Murderer, answer these way too personal questions*. But I don't really have anything better to do."

"Congrats on the book deal. That's really great," Olivia said.

"Yeah. It's great. I just wish it didn't take this for me to get it." Elle smiled wistfully. "So! We're all agreed: Mandy is the worst. But if you think something's not quite right, there's a reason. So figure out why."

"Easier said than done," I said, thinking back to the unending list of suspects.

"Well, instead of starting with Mandy or the people who were in the room, you should start with a more definitive source. And the one thing you know for sure is who the victim is. So start with him. Trace his interactions with Mandy, figure out who else he knew in that room, and go from there."

We were back. Not exactly as before, but Elle was still the one making us see things clearly and pushing us forward. Though this time, her guidance wasn't just part of her master plan to get away with murder.

The guards began moving toward us. Our time was almost up.

"Now I have a question," Elle said, turning to Olivia. "I know why Kat agreed to help Mandy, but why did you?"

Olivia glanced at me, and we had a silent back-and-forth in a split second. We didn't want to get Elle's hopes up this early about the governor.

"She admitted she took the shit in the hut," Olivia said.

Elle burst out laughing. "No shit! Well, confirmed shit, huh? I never thought we'd see the day where she'd admit that. I mean, yeah, that would shake me up, too. I am just eating this shit up—oh, god, that's horrible wording, isn't it? Or is it perfect?"

Elle was still laughing as they took her away, and as much as my heart hurt, I was glad we could give her at least that.

CHAPTER 25

We'd just sat down at Olivia's dining room table to a feast of Chinese takeout, with the cloche hat and beanie atop our heads, when Olivia announced, "Got Eugene's LinkedIn."

"That was fast," I said, reluctantly dragging my attention away from the scallion pancake in front of me.

"Graduated from Harvard, and then, oh, again from Harvard with his PhD, and worked as a medical researcher in a large biotech company. Although if I recall correctly, he said—screamed—at Mandy that he lost his job. And though his LinkedIn claims he still works there, according to the company's website, he doesn't."

"We should reach out to his former coworkers and see if any of them are willing to talk," I suggested.

Olivia nodded.

"Great start," I said, feeling hopeful.

But thirty minutes in, that hope was gone. Because while we'd found Eugene's LinkedIn page quickly, we hadn't found much else.

Olivia sighed. "Can you just ask your man for some intel?" We had finished most of the food and were now sitting in her dining room on the verge of literally scratching our heads (likely a biology origin: a self-soothing behavior that's instinctual when we feel confused or overwhelmed).

"I don't think it's a good time," I said, thinking about all the things Adrian and I hadn't talked about yet. And he was so by the book, I wasn't sure my requests would get us anywhere.

"You'd think now that you're in literal bed with the investigator, it'd be easier."

"Maybe you can get in bed with Ricky and see where that gets us," I teased.

That shut her up. Though I would've preferred if she wanted to talk about it, but she didn't seem ready yet.

"It's okay for you to like someone," I said gently.

"I don't even know him!"

"You have to start somewhere. And him being Adrian's partner is a good start."

She knew Birch's history and what it meant that Ricky was his partner, but that only seemed to irritate her more, maybe because of the added pressure that he could actually be a good match.

"Well," Olivia said, getting up from the table and grabbing the No Name body pillow shaped like a muscular dude's arm and torso. "It's all a moot point because I already have a man."

My mom had sent me No Name, of course, but I'd brought it to Olivia's after Adrian and I started dating because it was too weird to explain. The only downside was that Cinny Junior (my bunny that Tucker had gifted me as a bribe to talk to him one last time) had grown weirdly attached to it, and I felt bad separating them.

"You know, this is strangely comforting," Olivia said as she snuggled No Name (so christened because the only other name I could think of at the time was *Detective Birch*, pre–us dating).

"Not as comforting as the real thing," I said, thinking of Adrian's warm strong arms—the place I felt most safe and secure.

"Yeah, well, I prefer Mr. Inanimate. Can't talk back, can't forget my name, can't cheat."

I wished I knew what to say. But I knew how she felt, and I knew not to rush her.

Turning back to the notebook in front of me, I flipped to a new page. "Since we can't find anything else on Eugene . . ."

"No, Kat. No."

"We need to listen to *Dish Served Hot* episodes."

Olivia hugged No Name tighter. "Haven't we suffered enough already?"

"Who said police work isn't tedious? They just don't show you that stuff on TV. You think I walk into the room and spot the one hair we need? I have to test a million other things and I'm lucky if we do find something. You know that better than anyone, don't you, Olivia Valentina McCarthy, Esquire?"

Olivia groaned. "But at least at work, I'm helping people who aren't Mandy Thorne." Especially now that she was taking on more pro bono clients claiming to be falsely convicted.

"We're not doing this for Mandy," I said quietly, thinking about where we'd just come from.

"Okay, okay, you've struck oil. Snake oil, in this case," she muttered as she pulled up *Dish Served Hot*.

As curmudgeonly as she sounded, I knew Olivia forming a malaphor was a good sign. When we were first getting to know each other and she found out about my love of idiom origins, she learned about malaphors—the blending of two different sayings to create a humorous expression—just for me, and now it had become our thing.

"We opened this can of worms," I tell her. "Now let's go lie in it."

She beamed.

• • • •

Because the *Dish Served Hot* guests were anonymous with fake names, our task was quite arduous. We were not only trying to locate Eugene's episode, but we were also trying to match episodes to the people we'd met at the boba café.

Too many revenge stories later, I finally had something. "Jinkies!" I exclaimed, channeling my inner Velma.

Olivia ripped her earbuds out. "Thank god. I need a break. How did I ever like this show?"

"Is it hard to listen to because you can't stand Mandy's voice or words or lies, or because the pranks seem petty and childish now?"

"Both," Olivia grumbled. "So, did you find Eugene's episode?"

"No, but do you remember that couple from the boba café we thought might get back together?"

"Yeah," Olivia said slowly, thinking. "They talked about how they helped each other grow. Was it . . . Isla and . . ."

"Wyatt," I supplied. "I remembered him because he talked about an embarrassment of pandas."

Olivia smiled. "That totally sounds like your kind of thing."

"So Isla mentioned that Wyatt asked her for an open relationship a week after they agreed to be exclusive. And from that, I found their episode. Which is so much more of a doozy than I would've guessed, given their conversation."

Olivia leaned forward. "Do tell."

"Episode seventy-three," I said, writing that down in my notes. "After Wyatt asks for an open relationship, Isla is so pissed she gets revenge by swapping the contacts in his phone so that the new girls he's texting are now actually his mom's and stepmom's numbers, and he ends up sending dick pics to both of them."

Olivia's jaw dropped. "What."

"I know, right?"

"I would die if that happened to me."

"No kidding." I couldn't even think about that possibility.

My parents would lock me in their house for the rest of time. "Maybe time really can heal all wounds?"

A brief silence descended, during which Olivia was no doubt thinking about Tucker because her eyes kept flicking to the lamp in the corner that they'd bought together. Slowly, she and I were replacing the items in her townhome that she'd gotten from him or with him. We'd replaced her couch, but not the lamp, curtains, or clock yet.

"Or maybe his family is much more chill than ours," Olivia said lightly, forcing her eyes away from the lamp.

"Or maybe if they can get over all that, including her getting fired because of the podcast episode—"

"Or maybe she's just putting on a front for everyone because it's also exhausting to be angry about it. Maybe she's just numb."

We weren't just talking about Isla anymore. "Liv—"

"Put a star next to that episode just in case. We'll make a list of all the revenge that was bad enough to serve as motive for going after Mandy."

I was about to tell her that meant we'd be putting stars next to most episodes, but Olivia barreled on. "Isla and Wyatt's episode reminds me of one I listened to. Episode fourteen. The guest's ex-girlfriend sent him a picture of her having sex with her new beau, so he forwarded the photo to her dad."

"Yikes." I couldn't help thinking about how serious that relationship must have been for him to have the girl's father in his contacts.

"And here's one that gets two stars for extra-unhinged," Olivia said. "Episode forty-five. The girl found out her very serious live-in boyfriend was cheating on her, so for revenge, she sleeps with the guy's dad."

"That is . . . dedication. Just like episode fifty-two. He cheats, so she takes all his stuff and leaves him a scavenger hunt, with his PlayStation being in the place they first kissed, his laptop being where they celebrated their first anniversary—"

Olivia laughed. "Almost all my exes would fail that spectacularly. Except maybe Tucker. He might have aced it because he needed spotless notes just to keep track of all his girlfriends."

"Tucker wasn't worth that amount of time, in my opinion, even for revenge."

"I'm glad that's how you feel *now*. I mean, back then, you stole frogs and labeled their legs."

"I did, didn't I?" Luckily, it felt like that Kat existed a million years ago. But maybe this was a reminder that Olivia had to come around on her own time, and if being numb and putting up a front was what she needed at the moment, then I should support that part of the process.

Olivia gestured to her notes as she said, "At least you never felt like stealing your ex's pilot uniform to keep him from working; taking an ad out in the paper to announce his baby with his mistress and signing it *his soon-to-be ex-wife*; or rubbing Tabasco on the inside of his Fleshlight—that was clearly Gia from the café, by the way."

"Well . . . no. Mostly because Tucker wasn't a pilot, I wasn't his wife, and he had *so* many women he didn't need a Fleshlight."

Olivia laughed, and each deep, genuine *ha* went straight to my heart and lifted it higher.

Kathryn's Sixth Law of Life: Time *can* heal even the worst wounds, but you have to be patient.

• • • •

Our break did wonders because as we went back to listening, Olivia was smiling and chuckling softly.

As Olivia and I split the last crab Rangoon and she let out a particularly loud chortle, I suddenly looked up at her.

"Thanks," she said.

My eyebrows rose in surprise.

"For turning my attitude around—" she started to say, but then she understood the look on my face. "Wait. Did you . . . ?"

I nodded. "I think I found it."

Olivia waved her hands frantically. "Show me!"

I switched from earbuds to speaker, went back to the beginning, and we listened to the episode together.

Dish Served Hot Podcast Transcript–Episode 36

[Podcast theme song plays, sung by creator, host, and star Mandy Thorne]

MANDY THORNE: Welcome, welcome, my lovely Thornies, to another fantastic episode of *Dish Served Hot*, where we only serve revenge up steaming, bubbling hot—just like our tea. Cold is for losers, am I right? Gotta dole that shit out while we're still feeling red-hot anger!

And today's guest is no exception. This revenge is so juicy I laid down a plastic sheet—but don't worry, I'm not Dexter. If I ever murdered someone, it would be with poison—the hardest to trace back! And so easy to do if you think about it. And not messy at all.

Anyhoo, are y'all ready? Please meet Angela Martin—and that code name was very intentional, giving you a hint of what's to come.

Thanks for joining us today, Angela!

ANGELA: Mandy, girl, you are my hero! I know you must hear that a lot.

MANDY: Never gets old, though. Feel free to tell me again.

ANGELA: [laughs] You're my hero, truly. This awful, horrible, unspeakable thing happened to me, and without you and your show, I might have spontaneously combusted from all the festering rage!

MANDY: Don't worry. Me and my soon-to-be award-winning podcast will always be here for all y'all. Now, tell the Thornie family what happened.

ANGELA: Well . . . [deep breath] I thought I'd met the one. And I know people say that shit all the time, but, I'm telling you, this was different. The connection, the heat, the *passion*—woof! It was out of this fucking world! I mean, I like to think of myself as a lady, but when he and I were in a room together, I couldn't keep my clothes on! He had that kind of raw animal magnetism, you know? So of course I couldn't resist . . . even though we worked together.

MANDY: Uh-oh.

ANGELA: I know, I know, messy, right? But did you hear me about the raw animal magnetism? When I was with him, I didn't care about anything else! And we were colleagues at the same level, but our research didn't overlap much—though I will say it's pretty ironic he worked on cancer drugs when he was a fucking cancer, and I worked in vaccines, i.e., prevention, but couldn't prevent this clusterfuck—so, anyway, I figured it wasn't *that* bad. And we weren't technically breaking any rules in the beginning. The only rule is to disclose any relationships to HR, and we weren't there . . . yet.

MANDY: So did it become a relationship? How long were you together?

ANGELA: Ugh, at the time it felt like forever wouldn't be enough, and now I can't believe I was in it for as long as I was. We'd been hooking up for six months before it became official and he asked me to be his girlfriend. I was ecstatic!

MANDY: So did you tell HR?

ANGELA: So here's the thing.

MANDY: Oh no, not *the thing*.

ANGELA: I know. He asked me not to tell HR, which didn't make sense to me, but he said he was worried about our careers, especially mine. At the time, I thought he was sweet for looking out for me, but now I know he was gaslighting me.

MANDY: That bastard!

ANGELA: You're telling me. You want to know why he didn't want to tell HR?

MANDY: Why?

ANGELA: [unintelligible noise]

MANDY: Ah, tell us! We're dying!

ANGELA: *Because he was also in a relationship with the head of HR!*

MANDY: [gasp] NO!

ANGELA: YES!

MANDY: How did you find out?

ANGELA: I didn't feel great about keeping it from them, so I went to the HR department to get a relationship form just in case, with the plan to talk to him about it again that night, and when I walked in, there he was, sucking his other girlfriend's face!

MANDY: The balls on him!

ANGELA: I know! You'd think someone who graduated from Harvard would be a little smarter. I mean, the HR department is in another building—we work on a large campus—but still! Though I guess he'd gotten away with it until then, so maybe I'm the idiot.

MANDY: So what did you do?

ANGELA: What else? I got even. I learned from the best, after all.

[Mandy giggles]

ANGELA: I told the company about his other relationship, which I guessed correctly was also undisclosed. They fired both of them. I didn't name who he was in the relationship with, but I guess he'd been around HR enough that they traced it back to her. They'd been together much longer than we had, and apparently weren't as careful—which, I know I should feel bad, but c'mon. She was the *head of HR*. Shouldn't she have known better?

MANDY: And you got off scot-free?

ANGELA: Yeppity-doo-da!

MANDY: [whistles] So you got double the revenge!

ANGELA: Last I heard he's still looking for a job.

MANDY: That'll teach him to mess around!

ANGELA: So thanks, Mandy, for inspiring me. I wouldn't have even thought to do this without you or *Dish Served Hot*. And, Thornies, take it from me! Mandy's right! The dish is SO much better when it's served piping hot!

MANDY: There you have it, folks! Another happy, satisfied Thornie. Thanks for joining us and sharing your office revenge story today, Angela!

ANGELA: No, thank YOU, Mandy!

CHAPTER 26

"This has to be it," Olivia said once we finished the episode. "It matches his LinkedIn—worked with cancer drugs at a large medical research facility, went to Harvard, lost his job."

"And, as he said at the boba café, the podcast took everything from him, including his *relationships*, plural."

Olivia nodded. "Angela also stated that she wouldn't have gotten revenge if it hadn't been for *Dish Served Hot*—"

"Which could explain why Eugene was so angry at Mandy in particular," I finished for her. "It's all adding up."

So we had Eugene's LinkedIn page, the name of the company, and now we knew his exes' jobs. Putting all this together, Double-Oh-livia typed away until she tracked down Luz Lopez, a.k.a. Angela, who worked in vaccines, and Seraphina Greenberg, former head of HR.

"Wait!" I exclaimed, pointing at the screen. "Angela and Seraphina—*A-S*! What if Eugene was telling us to look at his two exes?"

"Then why wouldn't he have written *L-S* for Luz and Seraphina?"

"I don't know! Why can't you just throw me a bone?"

"Because I'm not Adrian," Olivia said with a salacious eyebrow waggle.

"Are you channeling Elle or do you really need to go on a date?"

Olivia sighed. "If you promise not to push me, maybe it's both?" Then she switched gears. "Why are you so obsessed with those two letters?"

"Because they have to mean something."

"Agreed, but don't get so obsessed you can't see the forest for the wrong tree you're barking up."

"That malaphor actually kind of makes sense," I said. "Except it's incorrect. That *A-S* tree isn't wrong. We just haven't figured it out yet."

"*A-S* if."

I chuckled. "Okay. We think we've found Eugene's exes. Now what?"

"I mean . . ." Olivia had that gleam in her eye.

"I promised Adrian—and myself—that we'd be careful."

If anything, Olivia's eyes twinkled *more* now.

"What?" I said cautiously. "We've done enough. Maybe we should stay behind the scenes for a bit."

"We will. At least, Kat and Olivia will," she said cryptically.

"What does that mean?"

Olivia's eyes darkened with mischief. "We're going in disguise."

Kathryn's Seventh Law of Life: Don't ask questions you don't want the answers to.

CHAPTER 27

"I am not wearing that."

Olivia replaced the fake beard with a frizzy blond wig.

"Or that."

"Stop being such a party pooper!" (Origin: debatable, possibly based on the word *pooped* or *pooh-pooh.*) "It's not like I'm asking you to wear a ball of flames."

"And just like a ball of flames is not a disguise, neither is this," I said, gesturing to the wig.

"What're you talking about? This is great; neither of us are blonde."

"It's a bad disguise because I'm not wearing it. It looks itchy."

"You are and it is. Just think of it this way—bad hair hygiene is part of your cover."

"Maybe we shouldn't do this." It had been several days since we formed the plan, and it was feeling dumber by the minute. Luz had agreed to meet us at Bubblicious at 2:00 p.m., and Seraphina, at 2:30, and we only had an hour left to get ready.

"We used fake names, remember?" Olivia said. "And if we use good enough disguises, we won't have to worry about our safety." And at least we hadn't spotted Luz or Seraphina at the Dish Gets Served meeting, meaning they hopefully weren't potential murderers, though they certainly had motive.

Olivia plopped the fake beard, blond wig, and several other items onto the table. "So suck it up and pick: old ladies, bearded bikers, or hot models who never take their sunglasses off?"

"Old ladies," I mumbled. It was sadly the only one I thought I could pull off.

• • • •

An hour later, drinks in hand, we were folding ourselves into a booth at the boba café where I'd first met Olivia what felt like a million years ago. Except this time, we were wearing baggy floral dresses, crocheted cardigans, gray wigs, and giant fake spectacles with beaded chains. And Olivia had done a movie-level makeup job on both of us. I wish it had aged me in the opposite direction, but here I was, with an unwanted glimpse into my future. At least my teeth held up; I'm a diligent flosser.

"We look ridiculous," I couldn't help saying as my beaded eyeglass chain caught on my crocheted cardigan.

"We look perfect. Not at all like ourselves."

"Speak for yourself." Though I guess my normal clothes were only old-lady adjacent—not *this*.

"You chose."

"Don't remind me."

"Have you talked to Adrian?" Olivia asked.

"Barely. He's been consumed by the case. Though he did tell me the preliminary cause of death came back as the knife wound."

"No surprise there," Olivia said.

The only other thing he'd said was to be careful, again, which only made me feel more squirrely that I was here, even if I was in disguise.

Olivia checked her watch. "I have something to tell you."

I leaned forward. "What is it?"

"I went on a date last night."

"*What?!* And you're telling me now, with only"—I checked my watch—"three minutes to spare? You waited on purpose!"

"Of course I did. Look, what you said to me the other day made me realize I've been in a standstill, frozen, and it felt like the only way out was to rip the Band-Aid off—which feels fitting to tell you that here, at Bubblicious, where we first ripped off the Band-Aids talking about Tucker—"

"There's no time! Tell me about your date! Did Ricky—"

"Not with Ricky."

"Why not? Then with who? How did it go? What's he like? Show me a picture!"

"Tanner McCluskey. Setup from a colleague. It was awful. *He* was awful. I should've known better than to trust another lawyer to set me up. Total bro douchebag. Here."

She pulled up a photo of an attractive guy with muscles bulging out of his suit. "Looks hot," I said. But with Olivia's glare, I quickly added, "And looks like a total douche."

"So I tried, but I'm done putting myself out there."

"No! The problem was Tanner, not you going out on a—"

"Velma? Nancy?"

That's right, I finally got to be Velma.

"Yes, hello," Olivia said, all too eager for the interruption. "Please join us."

"Um, hi." Luz was clearly thrown off by our outfits, but she didn't comment on them. Though she did say, "You two are law enforcement?"

We had told her that we were contacting her on behalf of the police—which was partly true, I was technically part of the precinct—and that we couldn't tell her why, but we needed to know more about Eugene.

"Yes, we got your contact information from Mandy Thorne," Olivia said. Then she barreled on before Luz could ask more questions. "We heard your podcast episode. Can you tell us what happened in more detail?"

Luz sighed. "I laid it all out on the show. What more do you need?"

"Did Eugene know that you got him and Seraphina fired?" Olivia asked. "Did Seraphina know?"

Luz shrugged. "Probably. Especially after the episode aired."

"Were they mad at you? At Mandy?"

"I mean, probably? But they got the last laugh. I got fired, too, for going on the podcast and bragging about what happened."

Olivia and I had noticed during our recon that she was at a different company now, but we hadn't realized she'd been forced to leave.

"Why did they fire you?" Olivia asked, and I could almost see her lawyer gears turning.

"Because they figured out from context that I was Angela on the podcast . . . I shouldn't have mentioned so many details, but I was nervous and they just came out . . . and by admitting to also having had a relationship with that fucker—I mean, Eugene—I was in breach of my contract since I didn't disclose it to HR, his *other* girlfriend." Luz laughed. "It's so fucking absurd, isn't it? Or does it serve me right for going and shooting my mouth off about how I got revenge?"

"So are you mad at him?" I asked, wondering if she could've had a hand in this.

"Of course I'm mad at him! He cheated and cost me my job."

"What about Seraphina?" Olivia asked. "Do you blame her?"

"Of course not. She was a victim, too."

I hesitated, then asked, "Do you blame Mandy? The podcast?"

"Why would I?"

"Because you said in your episode that Mandy inspired you,"

I answered. "And that you wouldn't have even thought to do this without the show."

Luz paused. Then said, "I don't regret the revenge. I regret going on *Dish Served Hot* and causing my own demise. But at least I handled my firing quietly. Eugene was yelling, threatening, screaming obscenities as security escorted him off the property. Then he snuck back in the next day, and the next, as if he was just going to go back to work and hope no one noticed—did you know Larry David did that on the set of *SNL*? It worked for Larry, but not for Eugene—he was found out pretty quickly, causing *another* ruckus when he was escorted out, by the police this time."

"So Eugene was upset about what happened, losing his job and both relationships," I said.

"No shit."

I had hoped she'd elaborate, but it wasn't like I'd asked her a question. I tried again. "Were you worried about his state afterward? About what he might do?"

"I haven't spoken to him since the day we broke up. What is this about?"

Olivia and I glanced at each other.

Luz asked, "Is he in trouble? Did he do something?" Her spine straightened. "Did he attack Mandy or something?"

"Do you think he would? Did he have a violent streak?" I asked.

"I mean . . . I heard things, after. I saw some of what he posted online before I blocked him. He seemed really pissed. At her, at me, at the world."

I nodded, then asked the question I needed to ask but didn't want to. "Did he ever talk about poisons? Was it a hobby? An expertise?"

"Well, he did research on cancer drugs, and most of those are literal poisons. And I mean, we use dangerous chemicals in our research all the time, and in the wrong context, many of them can be poisons."

I knew that better than most.

Suddenly, Luz's head jerked back. "Wait. Right after everything . . . blew up . . . a few bottles of chemicals went missing at work. Some drugs, solvents . . . all of which, in another context, could be, well, deadly." Luz's eyebrows drew together in concern. "You don't think Eugene could have . . . Am I in danger? Should I be worried?" Her hand clutched her purse tightly, and I couldn't bear the thought of her continually looking over her shoulder for her ex.

So even though we hadn't planned to, I told her, "Eugene is . . . gone. You don't have to worry about him."

Her eyes widened. "Wh-what? He's gone? What do you mean?"

I couldn't say it. So Olivia had to. "He's dead, Luz. I'm very sorry for your loss."

"What do you mean he's dead? How? What happened?"

"We don't know," I answered solemnly. "That's why we're here. So any information you can tell us would be helpful."

"Was it an accident? Was it . . ." She trailed off.

"We believe he was murdered."

Luz suddenly rose and ran off to the bathroom.

I hesitated, not sure if I should give her a moment or try to help.

"I'm surprised she got fired, too, as a result of all this," Olivia said to me. "A lot of firings because of the podcast."

I sighed. "Actions have consequences."

"I think she was truly surprised when she heard about his death."

"Agreed. So do you think the missing bottles are what Eugene was referencing when he told Yasmin that he could 'make it look natural'?" I asked with a shudder.

"You know, I've been thinking . . . Eugene talked to Yasmin about a knife *and* poison. Doesn't that seem like overkill? Oh, uh, bad use of that word. Though I guess we know where it comes from now."

For once, I did not want to know the origin.

"Maybe Eugene didn't know the best way to get to Mandy and he had multiple plans?" I suggested. "Though it sounds like he stole the chemicals a while ago. Why wait to use them?"

Olivia shrugged.

I glanced toward the restrooms where Luz had disappeared. "Should we go check on her?"

Olivia shook her head. "It's a lot to take in," she said, and I knew she was thinking about Tucker.

"I would've wanted someone to talk to," I pointed out.

"Maybe, but I don't think she wants Rose and Blanche."

"Dorothy and Sophia," I said. "We're missing our Blanche." And then I couldn't stop thinking about how I would love to be Golden Girls with Olivia and Elle, but we'd never have our Blanche if we didn't solve this case.

Olivia must have been thinking the same thing because she gave me a melancholy smile. She opened her mouth to respond but froze when the door to Bubblicious opened. Because in walked Seraphina Greenberg, fifteen minutes early.

I jumped into action, pulling Seraphina to another table in the corner while Olivia stayed behind to wait for Luz.

"Hi! I'm Velma. Thanks for meeting me here."

Seraphina gave me a doubtful once-over.

"Here's my badge," I said, waving my actual badge quickly and hoping she wouldn't look closely at the name or photo. "I just have a few quick questions for you. Have you seen or talked to Eugene recently?"

I would have assumed *no* given the situation, but Seraphina still managed to surprise me by saying, "Of course not; he broke my heart when he ended it."

"*He* ended it?" I repeated, stunned that she had wanted to continue their relationship after what had happened.

Seraphina nodded. "I mean, there was a lot of shit that went down, but he didn't do anything wrong. We weren't exclusive. It was that other girl who flew off the handle. Got us both fired for no reason."

"So . . . are you upset at her, then?" I asked.

"Wouldn't you be?"

"Were you upset at Eugene?" I followed up.

"I already said we weren't exclusive. So, no."

"What was Eugene like?" I asked.

"Oh, Eugene." A nostalgic smile filled Seraphina's face. "He was brilliant. Passionate. Emotional. A rare combination, don't you think? He wasn't just this cerebral robot churning out numbers and formulas. He was so . . ." Seraphina waved her hands in a vague circle. "He was Eugene."

All I could think about was how he was so Eugene and he was also now so gone. Unable to find any words, I grabbed my still unopened boba and pushed it toward her. "Would you like this?" I said even though it pained me to offer it to her.

Seraphina's lip curled in disgust. "How can you drink this stuff? It's like, pure sugar."

Now I was even more pained. Both from her words and from having to bite my tongue to keep from responding.

The only relief I felt was that at least the drink wouldn't be wasted on someone who wouldn't appreciate it.

But as I pulled the cup back, to my horror, Seraphina's hands sprung out and latched on.

"Eugene would love it, though," she said. "I would always say, 'would you like some coffee with your cream and sugar?'

And he'd laugh and laugh." She smiled at the memory. "Maybe I should give him a call."

"Actually, um . . ." As much as I didn't want to, I had to tell her.

But I didn't get a chance to.

"What the hell are you doing here?"

Luz had returned and spotted us despite our being in the corner and Olivia trying to distract her.

Seraphina stood. "What the hell are *you* doing here?"

So Luz had more beef with Seraphina than she'd let on. Though Seraphina hadn't been shy about her feelings. This was information we'd been after, and thus why we'd set up the timing of our meetings as such, in the hopes they would see each other. Though we hadn't meant for it to overlap quite this much.

Seraphina pointed a finger at Luz. "You caused all this. This is your fault."

"What are you talking about?"

"If you hadn't gone on that show, none of this would have happened! You ruined our lives!"

"It's not my fault he was murdered!" Luz yelled.

At that, the entire room went silent. This was not how I'd wanted Seraphina to find out.

"He was what?" she said in disbelief.

That calmed Luz down instantly. "Oh. I'm sorry. I thought you—"

"That's why we're here," I said gently to Seraphina. "We're trying to figure out what happened to Eugene."

Seraphina clutched her chest. "He was . . . murdered? My god . . ."

"Are you okay?" I asked.

Seraphina nodded, but she couldn't seem to catch her breath.

Should I call for help? Before I could decide, Luz ran over. And it was a good thing she did, because just as she reached Seraphina's side, Seraphina tried to sit back down but stumbled. Luz's arm shot out and grasped Seraphina's arm, steadying her. Then she helped her back into the chair.

"I'm sorry," Luz said, placing her hand on Seraphina's forearm. "About all of it. I'm sorry he's gone. I'm sorry how my actions affected you. I never meant for you to get hurt or fired. And if it makes you feel any better, I just found out what happened to him a second before you and I was throwing up in the bathroom, so . . ."

With those words, they fell into silence. Heavy, emotion-filled silence that said more than words could.

And I suddenly felt like I couldn't catch my breath. This conversation, happening here . . . I looked up and locked eyes with my unexpected sister. Olivia's eyes were as glassy as mine felt.

Regardless of everything else, at least we were able to get Luz and Seraphina to have a long-overdue conversation. And for them to be there for each other when they got the news about Eugene—well, I knew personally how much that could help.

• • • •

"Do you think she's hiding something?" Olivia asked on the way out the door after I filled her in on my conversation with Seraphina. "Do you think she's just pretending not to be mad at Eugene?"

"And why did Luz pretend not to be mad at Seraphina when she actually was?"

"And Seraphina wasn't even pretending not to be mad at Luz."

"Not everyone becomes friends with the other woman," I joked.

"*Best* friends," Olivia amended, and I couldn't help but smile.

"They should try that," I said. "Ten out of ten recommend."

Olivia pulled me into a hug.

Kathryn's Eighth Law of Life: Even the worst storms can lead to a rainbow.

CHAPTER 28

"Adrian, we have a lead!" I called out excitedly as I walked into the precinct.

And despite the room having been noisy a second before, it suddenly became dead-ass silent.

Not because I was working a case that maybe I wasn't supposed to be.

No, it was because Olivia and I were still dressed as old ladies.

A raucous roar of laughter pierced through the silence. Coming from Ricky, whose desk abutted Adrian's. And it was so loud it dragged the captain from her office.

"Um, can we get out of here?" I asked Adrian. Then, as I spotted Ricky and Olivia peering at each other—yes, even though she was dressed as an old lady—a light bulb went off (origin: cartoons). "Actually, let's all go grab some lunch. Together. The four of us. Right now."

Adrian glanced at the clock. "It's three in the afternoon."

"A snack. Coffee."

I grabbed his coat, then made my way toward the exit.

Luckily, the other three followed.

• • • •

At a nearby French café, I picked a cozy booth most likely meant for two people, shoved Adrian in, then scooched in beside him.

"Uh, is this table a bit small?" Adrian said, trying to cram his legs underneath.

"No!"

Adrian was good at his job, but he was terrible when it came to reading romantic cues. Not that we couldn't have found a slightly bigger table, but I figured, if the one-bed trope can work in movies and books, why not one side of a tiny booth?

"Ow!"

"You're okay. I mean, sorry." I hadn't been trying to step on Adrian's toes—literally or metaphorically (origin of idiom unknown)—but, yeah. This was a little cramped.

The server arrived and I quickly ordered. "A boba milk tea and whatever pastry you want to share," I said, directing the last bit at Adrian. After a few bad experiences of hard tapioca and tea that tasted like pure sugar, I usually avoided ordering boba at non-Asian cafés, but I knew from experience this one was decent.

"Almond croissant," Adrian supplied. "And a boba for me, too."

I bit my lip to suppress my grin. Seeing my burly man order a boba when he used to only drink black coffee will never get old. Yet another new thing I'd turned him on to.

Ricky didn't react, which made me wonder whether Adrian ordered boba often, not just when he was with me, or if Ricky was just a good guy who didn't judge. Regardless, both of those options made me happy.

After Olivia's matcha latte and Ricky's black coffee were ordered, I spoke up. "And we'll have a second almond croissant. For them."

Olivia gave me a wary look—I was laying it on too thick—but I shrugged. I was having too much fun. Not to mention, if the tables were reversed, she'd have been doing way more, making me sit in the guy's lap or share a milkshake with two straws.

When I looked back at the server, she was staring at us, her eyes darting from one face to another before finishing on Olivia's and my gray hair.

"What? You didn't expect these young men to want to share croissants with us?" I said, unable to help myself. Maybe Elle had rubbed off on me.

Olivia grinned and joined in. "Well, you're right. They're escorts."

"We are not escorts!" Adrian boomed.

"Don't worry, it's legal, you don't have to lie. Right, honey?" Olivia said, turning to Ricky.

To everyone's surprise—including Adrian's, given the bulge of his eyes—Ricky said, "Sure thing, honeybun. As legal as free speech and apple pie."

Olivia giggled—*giggled!*—and the server hurried away with flushed cheeks.

"What an ageist!" Ricky joked. "If we want to rob the grave, it's no one's business but ours, right, partner?"

Adrian was not amused. As was clear from the purse of his lips and the I-don't-want-any-part-of-this grunt that followed.

Olivia asked Ricky, "So have you learned to decode the grunts yet or do you need Kat to teach—"

Adrian grunted. We all laughed.

"I like your grunts," I said, but then all I could hear was the double entendre and Elle in my head. So I quickly switched gears, trying to get a different conversation going. "So what made you want to become a detective, Ricky?"

"Well, the honest answer is the *Teenage Mutant Ninja Turtles*. Loved them as a kid—I'm a Michelangelo, of course. But when I became old enough to realize I couldn't be reptile nor vigilante, I started looking into *actual* job options. This one seemed pretty good, though I wish it involved more travel, but no better way to get to know the beautiful city we live in, warts and all. Just hope I can do my part to make it a slightly better place."

And suddenly, my goal went from conversation-starter to matchmaker. Because Ricky and Olivia were a promising match. His boyish charm and enthusiasm for life were a good balance to her need for order. And Ricky's zest for life didn't border on reckless like Tucker's, so that was also a step in the right direction.

The irony was that what Olivia and I needed seemed to be pretty opposite, yet we had once fallen for the same man. But we had fallen for different parts of him, and, of course, he had been wrong for both of us.

My plan seemed to be working because Olivia followed up by asking, "And how did you two become partners?"

"Our meet-cute?" Ricky said.

I glanced at Adrian, who stared straight ahead and was *not* amused by the phrasing.

Like I said, opposites.

"I got lucky," Ricky said. "Transferred in, Adrian needed a partner, and somehow he didn't hate me as much as he hates the others." Then he turned to Adrian. "Maybe it helped that I sided with you against the captain about how you handled Elle's case, though it probably held less weight since I didn't get here until after everything happened."

Adrian just grunted, but I knew the low pitch of it meant he believed Ricky had his back (and mine, since I was the captain's main point of contention). I hoped Ricky hadn't done it just to suck up to Adrian, though. And I hoped it didn't mean Ricky had terrible judgment—that case had been quite the mess and probably wasn't handled exactly how it should have been.

My matchmaking skills were better than I thought because Ricky suddenly leaned close to Olivia as he said, "You have a . . ." He picked a tiny feather out of her wig.

Embarrassed, Olivia swiped a hand through the wig hair while saying, "Oh, it's this new couch I got . . ." She trailed off, and I knew she was at a loss for words, not wanting to talk about how she'd gotten rid of the old couch because she'd picked it out with Tucker and it was too painful to look at.

Ricky put the feather on the tip of his finger. "Make a wish."

Olivia's eyes widened. "Oh! Um, okay." She was hesitant at first, but once she closed her eyes, a smile spread across her face—a real one, wide and glowing. I grasped Adrian's arm to suppress my squeal, and finally getting it, he relaxed into his seat, draping an arm across the back of the booth and my shoulders.

Olivia's long lashes fluttered open and her glossed lips puckered to blow the feather into the void.

"What'd you wish for?" I asked.

"Don't tell her; then it won't come true," Ricky said.

"I think I know . . ." I started to say with a teasing tone, but then my brain registered Olivia's face.

She was beaming. At me. Her face was serene and peaceful. Happy.

Her wish had been about me, our friendship. Or *for* me.

Now my face filled with a wide glowing smile.

Of course she had been thinking about us and not a silly crush. Sisters before misters.

Olivia blew me a subtle kiss across the table and I returned it.

"So," she said, shifting her attention to Adrian and Ricky and reminding me why we were here in the first place. "We have some intel for you. My brilliant PhD friend here thinks you need to look into something that happened at Eugene's former workplace."

Part of me bloomed at the praise and the other part felt like a fraud, hearing Gerard's fancy-pants taunts in my head.

"Right," I said. "So we spoke to some of the people who

talked to Eugene during the meetup, and then we talked to his ex-girlfriends."

Adrian raised an eyebrow, then glanced at our wigs just as Ricky said, "Oh, so that's why you're dressed as Rose and Blanche."

Olivia's eyes sparkled. "Exactly."

"Though it doesn't totally explain it?" Ricky added. Olivia punched his arm jokingly and Ricky pretended to be hurt.

"We were safe," I said quickly to Adrian, then moved on. "A woman named Yasmin said Eugene was talking to her about making Mandy pay using a knife and poison, about how he's a scientist and could 'make it look natural.' And then Eugene's ex Luz told us he used to research cancer drugs and worked with dangerous chemicals, and that some of them went missing around the time he was fired. We need to get a list of what those chemicals were and figure out what he was doing with them."

Adrian pursed his lips to one side. "Just because one has access to dangerous chemicals, doesn't mean they used them for harm, as someone once told me."

Yes, I had said those very words to him when he'd suspected me of using the buffet of chemicals I had at my disposal to hurt Tucker.

"And," Adrian continued, "Eugene was the victim. Not the perpetrator."

"And the preliminary cause of death came back as stabbing," Ricky added.

"I know. But since Eugene talked about the knife to others and that ended up being the murder weapon, I think we need to follow up on the chemicals, too. We need to know what he was doing leading up to his death. It could help us see the bigger picture. I just don't want to miss the poisoned forest for the tree with the obvious knife sticking out."

Adrian's mouth curved up. "Noted."

Ricky was observing Adrian with a surprised curve to his own mouth, and Olivia gave him a knowing nod. I had to say, it did feel nice that I was the only one who apparently brought some softness to my gruff man.

"So you two have been keeping busy, huh?" Ricky said, nudging Olivia's elbow with his.

"Actually, um, there's one more thing . . ." I hesitated, wondering if I should be telling Adrian this. But then I told myself I was part of the forensic lab, even if Gerard didn't make me feel like it. "I have a fingerprint from a possible suspect—his name is Asher—and while we're pretty sure he's not the killer, I thought it would still be good to compare it to the fingerprints on the knife—"

"No," Adrian interrupted. "You didn't tell me that."

"But I'm part of the—"

"Did you obtain his permission?" Adrian asked.

"Not exactly—"

"Unless you had consent or a court order—"

"What if we have proof he committed a different crime?"

"Proof we can legally use?" Adrian asked, though his tone implied he already knew the answer.

"Never mind," I mumbled. I briefly wondered if I could access the knife fingerprints in the database to compare to Asher's fingerprint myself—but no, that was a line I couldn't cross.

Ricky glanced at Adrian a few times, and Adrian pointedly did not look his way.

"What is it?" I asked.

Neither of them responded.

Olivia leaned forward. "We can help you. As we've already proved."

Adrian was still sitting there brooding, so I said, "Remember what you said to me last time? Well, it applies here. Olivia and I are entrenched in this one. And we have access in a way you two don't. Not to mention, Mandy trusts us. The perfect moles, right?"

Adrian's mouth softened at the memory. But it quickly returned to a hard line. "And look what happened then. It's not worth the risk."

"That's why we work together."

Adrian shook his head. "But I can't always be there."

"I'll be there, too, partner," Ricky said.

I bet you will be, I thought to myself.

"And I still have this," I said, pulling out my Life Alert. Then I gestured to the rest of the safety items attached to my ginormous keychain courtesy of my mother.

Ricky's eyes widened. "Uh, what're all those—"

But Olivia gave him an it's-a-long-story shake of the head.

Looking at my keychain, Adrian chuckled, unable to keep it in. "Alright. I can't wait to meet this mom of yours. So I can thank her."

I coughed, my stomach twisting. Olivia glanced at me, but I refrained from meeting her eye. "So what're you not telling us?" I asked.

Ricky looked at Adrian, who nodded. Ricky then said, "We already identified the fingerprints on the knife."

I scooted forward in my seat. "And?"

"They're Mandy's."

My gaze met Olivia's. Mandy had claimed to use gloves and said she hadn't touched the knife when it showed up at her house—*I'm not a fucking idiot*, she'd said with the utmost class—so if she was telling the truth about that, this seemed to fit the narrative that later, after Eugene threatened her publicly, she grabbed the knife in the heat of the moment and did the horrible deed to defend herself, red-panda style.

"How did you get Mandy's fingerprints?" I asked, thinking

back to our conversation just a few minutes ago about consent or court ordered.

"She offered them to us, willingly," Ricky answered.

"That . . . doesn't make sense," I said. Either she was offering them up in the hopes of proving her innocence, or she was a genius, knowing we'd figure out they were her fingerprints eventually anyway, and was voluntarily handing them over to throw us off the track.

But, *genius*? The star of *Bikini Babe Rebels 4*?

"Who else's fingerprints were on there?" I asked.

"No one else's. Just hers," Ricky answered.

"That doesn't make sense, either."

"I know," Adrian said with a sigh. "But . . . with this new information, we have a plan of how to make it make sense."

"What kind of plan?" I asked.

"One that involves potential evidence that Mandy *won't* be giving up so willingly," Ricky said.

Olivia perked up. "You mean—"

"Yes," Adrian said.

Olivia's eyes gleamed. "Does that mean we can also maybe . . ."

Ricky nodded encouragingly at a reluctant Adrian.

Adrian sighed but relented. "How would you two like to join us in searching Mandy Thorne's home?"

• • • •

That café visit felt like a win in so many ways. I got to drink boba and eat 80 percent of an almond croissant, we were accompanying the upcoming search, and Olivia's and Ricky's fingers kept grazing while they were sharing their croissant.

"I know you were reluctant to get back in the dating pool, but did you have to wait until your sixties?" I joked with Olivia as we drove back to her place.

"That wasn't a date."

"Well, whatever it was, maybe it was a sign you shouldn't wait until you're really sixty."

Olivia was contemplative as she pulled her gray-haired wig off. But then she said, "You're right, because by sixty, I might still be making stupid decisions. Better make it seventy."

Kathryn's Sixth Law of Life, addendum: Some wounds need much more time to heal than others.

CHAPTER 29

"Who would've thought we'd get to search Mandy Thorne's place without needing a little help from our friends?" Olivia said, patting the side pocket of her jacket where she kept her lockpicks.

"We did need some help, but from our more-than-friends."

Olivia rolled her eyes. "Speak for yourself."

We were early, and likely the first ones here since there weren't any squad cars in the massive driveway. Just a very old Volvo that definitely did not belong to Mandy.

"Someone else from the team?" I suggested, gesturing to it.

But when we passed through the iron gate (yes, seriously) and started up the path to the house, we spotted someone kneeling by the front door, doing what we had just joked we wouldn't need to.

"Hey!" Olivia shouted.

The girl jumped up so fast she lost her balance and fell over, her tools clattering to the ground—bobby pins, I realized as we ran over.

It took a second to place her, but once I did, I realized how different someone could look wearing an old T-shirt and jeans versus a sexy firefighter costume.

"Jocelyn?"

"Why're you breaking in?" Olivia asked.

Jocelyn winced. "I, um, lost my set of keys and I don't want Mandy to know that I screwed up again—"

At that moment, the door swung open and Mandy's head popped out. "You lost your keys? Why didn't you just tell me instead of scratching up my lock? *And* you're late!"

Jocelyn dropped her head as she mumbled, "I just didn't want to mess up again, not after you've been so good to me."

Olivia raised an eyebrow at me. I returned the gesture but even more heightened—I knew Mandy was a nightmare to work for; she made Jocelyn message her OnlyFans clients.

Mandy turned her attention to Olivia and me. "What're you two doing here? Do you have news? You've figured a way out of this for me, right?"

She could not be further from the truth.

"Actually . . ." I started to say, but I didn't need to finish. Because Adrian and Ricky walked up to the front door. Ricky lifted his chin in our direction in a quick, informal greeting. Adrian, of course, was all business.

"Mandy Thorne, I need you to step outside at once. You may not touch anything or take anything with you. All other occupants must step outside as well." Adrian was using the authoritative voice that once made my knees buckle but now made them weak in a different way.

Jocelyn walked out slowly, her arms in the air, but Mandy stood her ground. "What the shit is this?"

Adrian held up a piece of paper. "Ms. Thorne, we are here to execute this search warrant."

"I object!" Mandy exclaimed, snatching the paper from Adrian. She scanned it, then held it out to Olivia. "Is this legit?"

"Afraid so," Olivia said without looking at it.

Officers streamed past us and into the house. When Gerard stepped up, I forced myself to meet his eye despite wanting to look away.

"You going to run into your boyfriend's arms again if we find anything today?" he said quietly, looking disgusted.

Needing comfort after finding a dead body is normal, I tried to tell myself, but I couldn't help wondering if Gerard was right, that I wasn't cut out for this.

I couldn't come up with a single thing to say.

He scoffed. "You shouldn't be here," he muttered. But given that Adrian was in charge and standing just a few feet away, he moved on without causing any more trouble.

Or maybe he was just trying to escape the shitstorm that was erupting around us.

"You can't do this!" Mandy was yelling as she took a step toward the house, but Adrian held a firm hand out and she stopped. Desperate, she turned to Olivia. "You have to do something!"

"Ms. Thorne, do you know how we were able to obtain this warrant?" Adrian asked.

"However you did, it was probably corrupt. And wrong. You're barking up the wrong fucking tree!" (Origin: hunting with dogs that are off the scent.) "I don't even have trees here, y'all! I made them cut 'em all down because there was too much shade and pollen and shit!"

"Ms. Thorne," Adrian said, unfazed. And his face remained neutral as he said his next sentence even though the information was anything but. "The fingerprint analysis from the knife came back. We got a match. To you."

Mandy's jaw dropped open. "That can't— It's just not— Well, didn't you also find the killer's prints on there?"

"Only yours were present, Ms. Thorne."

"That's not possible."

Adrian said nothing, just continued staring with those pH7, Switzerland, neutron eyes that saw everything. I couldn't help thinking about how not so long ago, I was on the other end of that stare thanks to Mandy.

When no one else said anything, Mandy clenched her fists so hard she crumpled the search warrant. "This is so fucked! I'm telling you, this is not possible. I didn't touch that fucking knife. It was left in *my* house to threaten *me*. And now it's incriminating me of a crime I didn't commit? Can't you see what's happening?" She paused, looking at each of us for a second longer than was comfortable. "*I'm being framed.*"

"She is," Jocelyn piped up. "She couldn't have done this. Not Mandy. I promise. You have to look elsewhere, I'm telling you."

A high-pitched shriek erupted from Mandy's mouth, and in a heartbeat, Jocelyn was rubbing her shoulders.

"I didn't do anything!" Mandy wailed.

"Ms. Thorne and Ms. Morningstar, you must leave the premises now while we search," Adrian said. Then he gestured to Ricky, Olivia, and me to head inside.

Mandy's head whipped toward Olivia and me. "Wait, you two are with them? What the fuck; I thought you were helping me!"

"We are," Olivia said. "If you have nothing to hide, this will help prove it."

"Not if I'm being framed! You traitors!"

"Mandy," I said gently as if she were a wild animal I was trying not to spook. "We'll be in there the whole time. We'll figure this out, okay?" *Including if you did it*, I couldn't help thinking, but she didn't need to know that.

Finally, Mandy's fist unclenched. "Fine," she said, her voice barely audible.

I wasn't sure how I felt that Mandy seemed to respond the most to me. It was like being the mean feral cat's favorite—a blessing, but not exactly something to write home about (military origin).

"Take her somewhere else," Ricky instructed Jocelyn.

"Buy her a coffee, on me," Olivia said, handing her cash. Then she grabbed my arm and led me inside, whispering, "Every time I start to give Mandy the benefit of the doubt, she does everything in her power to make that as hard as possible."

"Tell me about it," I mumbled back.

But once we stepped into the foyer, empathy surged through me.

They were tearing her house apart. Which, of course they were, but they were leaving cushions overturned and books littering the ground and carpets bunched to one side. Again, of course they were . . . I'd just never thought about the logistics of a search like this.

Even if Mandy were innocent, even if this helped her prove it, this sucked. And not just because of the mess, but the severe invasion of privacy, which was all I could think about as I watched a police officer pull a lacy thong from the crevices of the couch and inspect it closely. And he wasn't embarrassed at all—apparently that was part of the job. Maybe he was looking to see if it was worn, if it had DNA on it?

My attention swung to Olivia as she snapped powder blue gloves on. I almost wanted to laugh, thinking back to Elle snapping similar gloves on all those months ago.

"Here." Olivia handed me a fresh pair. "At least it doesn't smell like shit in here, right?"

I smiled. Of course she'd been thinking about the same thing.

But then the more I thought about it, the more my stomach turned. Elle had thought it through so brilliantly, making us not question her gloves while also ensuring her DNA was nowhere to be found, unlike ours. But she'd done that to frame us. To frame me. Just like Mandy was claiming someone was doing to her.

And suddenly I knew exactly why Mandy had come to me,

why I was the feral cat's favorite. Because I was the only one who'd understand, even if she was part of the reason for that understanding.

I turned my attention to the task at hand with renewed determination.

Olivia and I wandered from room to room, keeping out of the officers' way. We weren't supposed to be actively searching or touching things, but we could go through rooms they'd already cleared in case we noticed something they didn't. It was almost as if we were the calm after the storm, walking through the wreckage silently and passively.

I wished I were here as a CSI instead, but that wouldn't happen until after my certification. I only had a handful of training days left to log, but that didn't mean Gerard couldn't find a way to kick me out before that happened.

Ugh, Gerard. Who was here somewhere, basking in bossing his minions around and sending me hate from wherever he was. I would have to keep away from him to minimize drama and avoid embarrassing myself in front of Olivia, Adrian, Ricky, and the rest of the officers who were technically my colleagues now, too.

"I got something here!" someone yelled from the other end of the house.

Olivia and I paused to look at each other, then we both broke into a jog, rushing toward where the voice had originated while also trying not to bump into anything on the way.

Adrian and Ricky were already there, gloves on, when we arrived in the kitchen. I gasped when I saw it.

"Is that . . . a knife missing from the block on the counter?" Olivia asked, her hand flying to cover her open mouth.

"Not just any knife," Ricky said.

Adrian was sizing up the empty notch. "Make and size likely matches the murder weapon," he concluded.

"Although . . . that would explain why Mandy's fingerprints are on it," I said, not really sure whose side I was on. I guess the side of truth. "That technically still matches the story she told us. Though . . . she didn't recognize her own knife?"

"Maybe she's never used it," Ricky said.

Olivia shook her head. "Nope. She has." She retrieved her phone and scrolled until she found what she was looking for. "Here it is. This video she posted went viral. She's trying to cut celery, emphasis on the word *trying.* It's like she's never held a knife—or had hands—before."

Olivia turned her phone around so we could all watch as Mandy held the knife in an upturned fist, then used her entire arm to try to cut the celery.

"This has to be a joke, right?" I said. "Like, done on purpose for views?" Though Mandy didn't look like she was acting.

Adrian sighed. "We never seem to know with that one, do we?"

"That's one of the main problems here," Ricky said.

"Boss, check this out," an officer called from the pantry.

We all filed in. The pantry was large enough that we could fit easily.

"What is it?" Adrian asked, looking at the clear bottle the officer was holding up.

"Something that doesn't belong in the pantry," the officer answered.

Adrian and I both stepped closer to examine the bottle.

The liquid inside was clear but syrupy. And the label—I sucked in a breath. "Ethylene glycol," I said, lifting my eyes to meet Adrian's. "Poison, if used in the wrong context. It's also a common solvent in medical research—meaning easy access for someone in the field like Eugene." Or Luz, or maybe even Seraphina. "And I mean, many people do have it—it's used as antifreeze and to de-ice—but, in its pure form and the kitchen?"

Adrian was looking at me the way he did when he was admiring my brain, but there was something else there. Confusion. Disbelief. And his wheels were churning (no known origin).

"You looked into the missing chemicals from Eugene's work like I asked, didn't you?" I said. "And he stole ethylene glycol."

"Ethylene glycol, chloroform, and hydrogen cyanide," Adrian answered.

I couldn't help a shudder. Yes, I'd been around and even used those chemicals before in the lab, but hearing them in this context? It was a reminder why Adrian had previously suspected me and my access to a buffet of chemicals.

What was the bottle doing here, though?

A second later, I concluded, "We need to run a tox screen on Eugene Maxwell."

Adrian tilted his head at me. "Because . . ."

"Eugene talked about hurting Mandy with a knife and poison, and then the knife—covered in Mandy's fingerprints—ended up in his back. And now the poison he stole is resurfacing, and if it parallels the knife, then it might have been used on Eugene, too."

And if Eugene had been poisoned, either Mandy did it and is the dumbest killer on earth, or she really is being framed. And if he wasn't poisoned, then there was another reason why the bottle was in the pantry, and we had to figure out what that was.

Adrian grunted. He was on the same page as me.

"Tell the medical examiner to check for ethylene glycol in Eugene's blood," I said. "And to check his kidney for calcium oxalate crystals. And if he was poisoned, we want to know whether this was the cause of death or if it was the knife. And we need to dust the bottle for prints."

Adrian signaled to his team. "You heard her. Bag all this." Then he grabbed his phone and called the medical examiner.

I couldn't help feeling a *little* fancy-pants as everyone around me jumped into action on (sort of) my orders.

Olivia and I left the pantry to continue our hands-inside-the-boat tour of the mansion, stopping first in the already-searched non-master bathroom. It was filled with normal toiletries, but I couldn't help asking Olivia, "Is there a part of you that wants to stick any of those items down your pants?"

She laughed. "Please don't remind me of that." She had stuck Tucker's toothbrush, floss, and loofah down her pants in revenge, but that felt like a different lifetime now.

So did Elle farting on his pillow, which I was reminded of as we entered Mandy's bedroom, which was devoid of officers, and for a reason.

"The tornado's already been through here," I said as I looked around at the destruction.

"Yeah, no kidding. They couldn't have been a little more sympathetic about that?" Olivia pointed to Mandy's nightstand, which was now covered in sex toys.

"Well, I'm not putting them back for her." I looked away, trying to find anything else to focus on.

But Olivia didn't seem bothered. "She's got good taste. Think she gets these for free from sponsors? Lucky."

"Should we start looking around?"

"I am." Olivia paused, then caught my eye. "Are these making you uncomfortable? Wait . . . don't tell me you've never—"

I busied myself looking through Mandy's closet but stopped as soon as I realized how personal that was. In fact, all of this was too personal. Why had I agreed to come?

"Well, don't knock it till you try it," Olivia said. (Possibly referring to doors; don't knock until you've tried the handle.) "And if I can give you a tip—double entendre intended—they aren't just for solo use, either."

A laugh bubbled out of my mouth unbidden.

"What's so funny about that?" Olivia asked. "Again, don't knock it till you've—"

"As if we're even at that stage!" I burst out.

A police officer walked by the open door and peeked over at us.

"What—" Olivia started to ask, but I grabbed her hand and dragged her down the stairs and into the recording studio, thankful that it was soundproof.

As soon as the door closed, I blurted out so many of the things I'd been bottling up. "Adrian and I haven't been intimate yet. I don't know how to."

"You mean—"

"No, not like that!"

"Oh, so, small penis?" Olivia said sympathetically with a knowing nod.

"No!"

"Huge penis?"

"No!"

"*Oh*, that bad, huh? Is it splotchy? Stinky?"

"*I meant*, I haven't been able to after Tucker . . . I just don't know if . . . I just can't . . ."

Olivia put her hand on my shoulder. "I get it. Completely. As you already know. I don't want to let anyone in. On *any* level, let alone that level." She hesitated. "I'm scared."

I hadn't ever expected Olivia Valentina McCarthy, Double-Oh-livia, badass boss bitch, to admit that out loud.

I sighed. "I keep thinking that I'm over it, everything's fine, but the effects are so deep I can't see how far it goes."

"You're doing well, though. Better than me. You just have to keep taking steps forward."

"But the idea of being that vulnerable, of being that intimate..."

I ran a hand over my weary face. "And I lied to Elle about it. She wanted to hear all the spicy details, and she guilted me so much I made some up."

Olivia laughed. "That sounds about right. But don't worry about her."

I did, though. All the time. "If she were here, she'd make a joke about how we shouldn't give Tucker's penis that much power."

"She'd also say something about how Adrian's penis probably has the power to heal you from the inside, end this night and cycle and dry spell with a—"

Bang! Bang! Bang!

Someone was pounding on the door to the recording studio, which they hadn't searched yet and were probably trying to.

Olivia opened the door to reveal Ricky. "Need this room?"

"Uh, yeah." His cheeks were slightly red. More so than usual, even when he was talking to Olivia.

Then I noticed Adrian behind him. Adrian, who wasn't meeting my eye.

"Everything okay?" I asked, not sure who I was directing the question to.

"Why don't you see if anything jumps out at you from Mandy's mail, which is on the dining room table." Ricky gestured down the hallway to the left.

"Sure, okay," Olivia said, but she'd noticed the weirdness, too, her eyes ping-ponging between Ricky and Adrian.

I glanced back toward Adrian. He nodded at me slightly, then disappeared into the room across the hall. I looked at Olivia, who shrugged.

Ricky accompanied us, and after we turned left out of the recording studio, we passed a door that had been closed the last time I was here. Inside was a smaller room containing technical equipment. A giant window on one wall offered a view of the recording studio.

"That, uh, is the producer's room," Ricky said. "Gives access so they can hear what's going on."

I stopped in my tracks.

Oh no.

"Hear what's going on? In the recording studio?" My brain simultaneously refused to wrap around what had happened and was also already screaming into the void.

Olivia had also stopped. "Is it . . . always on?"

"Not sure. But it definitely is right now. And not only that, but it's projecting the sound to other parts of the house."

Just as he said this, an officer walking by me ducked his head and scurried past.

Fuck me.

"No." Olivia was shaking her head. "No. That can't—no. Why didn't you come in sooner?"

"I was at the other end of the house! I ran here as fast as I could!"

"Did he hear?" It was me asking, but the words had come out before I realized I was saying them.

"Yes."

"Did everyone hear?"

"Yes."

Well, I understood even more now why Adrian liked Ricky. He didn't sugarcoat things, just like Adrian. Adrian, who had heard me talking about how I was scared to get intimate with him, who had heard Olivia calling his penis small and stinky and splotchy . . .

I didn't need Gerard to embarrass me, apparently. I was great at doing that all by my lonesome (or with a little help from Olivia).

Kathryn's Ninth Law of Life (and Death): Maybe one *could* die from embarrassment.

CHAPTER 30

I was debating whether I should make a run for it or hide for the rest of time in one of Mandy's closets (she had so many she probably wouldn't even notice) when a dreaded voice called out.

"Everybody needs to congregate in the master bathroom! We have an active threat!"

Gerard was yelling at us from downstairs, basking in the one rare time he got to boss not just his minions around, but everyone.

"What could the threat be?" I asked Ricky, who shrugged. I was so distracted I barely noticed him placing a hand on the small of Olivia's back and directing her upstairs. "This isn't protocol," I continued. "If it's a chemical threat, we should go outside. If it's biological, again, we should evacuate."

"Unless the threat is outside," Ricky stated, still moving at a brisk pace and forcing me to keep up.

"Is a bathroom even big enough? How many people do we have—" But I shut up the second we walked in. Because everyone was there. Everyone. And yes, it was big enough, but just barely. Bodies were crammed between the opposing vanities, around the Jacuzzi, and even inside the walk-in steam shower.

And standing at the front of the crowd, with a crack in his pH7 neutral veneer, was my strong, confident, handsome man who didn't deserve what had just happened to him in front of his colleagues.

Should I apologize? Pretend it hadn't happened? Wait until later to address it?

Yes, yes, all of those.

But also, I'd never seen a fissure in Adrian's facade before. Not even when he was flirting with me when I was a murder suspect, not when his captain was pissed at him for how he was handling my case. So I had to fix this, any way I could.

"Adrian's penis is just fine!" Oh my god. The plan had been to talk about our *relationship*, but I apparently had penises on the brain. Now that it was out, I couldn't take it back. "There's nothing unusual about it, it's completely average . . . I mean, not average at all, it's really excellent . . ." I should just try to take it all back. "I mean, none of this is any of your business. Though I guess I sort of made it your business. Adrian's the best, okay? I'm not. I'm the worst."

Every single eyeball in that bathroom was staring at me like I'd, well, just talked about their boss's penis. Ricky was trying not to laugh. Olivia was begging me with her eyes to shut up. Listening to her, I clamped my mouth as tight as possible, then averted my eyes like a wounded animal.

I heard a throat clearing next to me and dreaded what words would be coming next—*my penis isn't the problem, it's her, clearly* . . . or, worse, *Ms. Hu, we're through*—but of course my consummate professional did neither. "Why are we in here? What threat did Gerard cite? There is no threat I can think of that would require us to take shelter here."

"I assumed it was a threat outside," Ricky said.

"What kind? Explosive? Chemical? Biological? None of them dictate we should be in here—there are windows, and we're on the second floor." Adrian grabbed his walkie-talkie and pressed the button. "Gerard. Details on the threat. Now."

Two seconds later, static, then Gerard's gravelly voice. "All clear."

Adrian's jaw flexed. Then he said into the walkie to Gerard, "Meet me here. Now."

Everyone filed out like their asses were on fire. And they were—on fire from the explosive situation I'd accidentally created.

I couldn't meet Adrian's eyes as I sheepishly (cow-ishly?) shuffled out with the herd.

But as I walked through the door, Gerard was on the other side.

"I told you, you don't belong here," he hissed at me under his breath.

My head snapped up.

I guess I should be worried about being my own worst enemy *and* Gerard's. I had suspected it, of course, but I hadn't thought he'd be this blatant about it.

I glanced backward. Adrian was watching us with those silent, ever-knowing eyes. Even though they were emotionless, I knew from the minuscule downward angle of his mouth that he had heard and was now wondering why I hadn't told him about Gerard—and a million other things. I'd had an excuse for each one: I didn't want to involve him with Gerard since it was complicated with Adrian also working at the station, and how do you tell someone you're scared of being intimate with them because your last boyfriend really fucked it and you had no idea how to move past it? But now, looking at that tiny tilt of his lips, I knew I was the one who'd fucked it.

And still, in this moment, all I could think about was how I didn't want him to ream Gerard out. Because that would only make it worse for me. It would only confirm all of Gerard's complaints about me—that I was the fancy-pants Harvard asshole who wasn't good enough and needed my boyfriend to come in and save me.

I gave Adrian an almost imperceptible head shake. I couldn't tell if he saw or understood.

So I walked away from the bathroom at the slowest pace possible in order to eavesdrop.

"And the threat was . . . ?"

No response from Gerard.

"You must have had a reason to put us all in here."

Still no response. Gerard clearly did this just to embarrass me.

Adrian cleared his throat. "I expect a report on my desk detailing all your reasons for this alert and how you followed protocol for it. And if you didn't follow protocol, I'm sure the captain will want to know and send you back to training to refamiliarize yourself."

At least he hadn't mentioned me. But Gerard was going to put two and two together and have my ass for this.

As I picked up my pace and speed-walked out of there so I wouldn't have to see either Gerard or Adrian, all I could think about was how I was truly fucked now. In my relationship, in my job . . . and it was completely my fault.

Kathryn's Second Law of Life, amended: The universe isn't out to get you; turns out, life is just hard, especially when you keep digging holes for yourself.

CHAPTER 31

Days later, in the precinct viewing room that was unfortunately reminiscent of the producer's room in Mandy's mansion, Olivia said, "It wasn't that bad, I promise."

"Well, we're still talking about it."

"Reminder, you said his penis *wasn't* small or stinky or splotchy."

"I also said it wasn't huge. And that it's average."

Olivia laughed. "Yeah, but after you doubled down, you also said it was *really excellent*."

"Aren't you supposed to be making me feel better?"

"Aren't I?"

"Does Mandy Thorne have any good qualities?"

Olivia chuckled. But once it died down, her face turned serious. "Um, Kat? Is everything okay with your boss? Because the way that he—"

"It's okay," I said much too quickly. "I mean, it will be okay. I've just finished my training hours"—*finally*; it had felt like an eternity—"and since I already passed the test, my certification should be here any day. And then I can apply for other jobs." I'd miss being in the same precinct as Adrian, but I needed a better work environment.

"Okay, but if you need me to step in—"

"I know. Thanks, Liv."

Just then, Ricky entered the interrogation room through our viewing window, draping himself casually in the chair across from Mandy. Adrian joined and took the opposite approach, towering over her.

Olivia sat up straighter and nudged my shoulder with hers. "Here we go. Wish we had some popcorn."

I pulled out the "survival kit" my mother sent me that I was pretty sure was meant for a child, with a plastic compass, fire starter, and snacks. "Fruit Roll-Up?"

"Thank your mom for me," Olivia said.

"Ms. Thorne," Adrian said from the other side of the glass, his tone clipped. "Do you recognize this knife?" He slid a photo of the murder weapon across the table.

"No duh. Of course I recognize the knife left inside my front door to scare the ever-living shit out of me. And it's apparently also the knife that stabbed that guy, but I don't know how it got there, I swear to gods!"

"When that knife showed up at your door, did you recognize it from any other context?" Adrian asked.

"I fucking recognized it as the threat it was intended to be! What is going on here? I'm the victim! Do your jobs and figure this out!"

Adrian slid another photo across the table, this one of Mandy's kitchen counter. "Are you aware that a knife is missing from your set?"

"I don't even—" She paused, finally spotting the missing slot in the knife block from the photo that was definitely of her kitchen—which was unmistakable with the Do Me, I'm Dirty sign above the sink. "That can't be."

Adrian raised an eyebrow. "You didn't recognize your own knife?"

"It's a knife, not a Birkin. And like I said, I don't cook! I didn't even know I owned knives!"

"Are you saying you haven't used that knife before?" Adrian asked.

"Of course I haven't! You think someone like me needs to use knives?"

Adrian pulled a video up on his phone and slid it across to her. "So then who's this using that very knife to cut celery?"

From beside me, Olivia mumbled, "If what she's doing can even be called cutting," and I couldn't help a snicker.

"I—" Mandy went silent.

"That is you in the video, is it not?"

"It is, but . . . It was just the one time . . ."

"Clearly," I muttered to Olivia.

"Wait, holy gods, that's exactly it!" Mandy suddenly exclaimed.

"What is?" Adrian asked. "That *is* you using the knife."

"And everyone knows it!"

Adrian sat patiently, waiting.

Mandy rolled her eyes. "Do I have to solve this whole case myself? *Everyone knows it.* Making it incredibly easy to frame me with it. Holy hells, wait. This is all adding up. The fingerprints! The fucking fingerprints! That's why they're on there! Because it's my knife and I used it the one time! Ha!" she concluded in triumph.

Adrian didn't flinch. Didn't bat an eye. Ricky continued leaning back, simply observing, just like Olivia and I were doing on the other side of the glass.

"What's wrong with you two?" Mandy asked. "Bang-up job y'all are doing here. I just gave you frickin' gold on a platter, and you just sit there staring? Yoo-hoo! Are you in there? Are you listening?"

Adrian ignored her and simply slid another photograph forward, this time of the ethylene glycol bottle. "Ms. Thorne, does this look familiar to you?"

"No, what is that?"

"It was in your pantry," Adrian answered, face neutral.

"I have shit in there from years ago. And you saw the size of it. It's probably bigger than your kitchen and dining room combined. What, am I supposed to have an itemized list? It's probably vinegar or sauce or something."

"This looks like vinegar or sauce to you," Adrian stated, his voice and face still Switzerland.

"I don't know—I don't cook. Or clean. Maybe it's cleaning supplies? I don't know where my peeps keep things, okay? I have staff for all that stuff. Ask Jocelyn to get you the contact info for my maid and cook."

"Ms. Thorne, we ran a toxicology screen on the victim, and the preliminary report has come in."

I held my breath. Adrian hadn't told me this yet. And I couldn't help wondering, was it because he'd just gotten the results? Or was he avoiding me because of Penis-gate?

"Are you familiar with ethylene glycol?" Adrian asked.

"Do I look like a frickin' nerd? Where's Kat?"

"Real nice," I mumbled.

Olivia nudged me. "Hey. You *are* a nerd. And you should be proud of it."

"Okay, I'll be *positive*."

"There's my little proton."

"*Kat*-ion," I corrected with a smile.

Meanwhile, Mandy was doing anything but smiling. "Whatever all this is," she said, gesturing to the photos, "it wasn't me, okay? I don't even know what that ethel-lini thing is."

"Ethylene glycol is the chemical in antifreeze. And when ingested, is lethal."

Mandy froze. "Wait. You're not saying . . . I don't even know what that is!"

Adrian pointed to the photo. "Yet here it is in your kitchen."

"Didn't y'all just say it was antifreeze? Why the hells would it be in the kitchen?"

"That is exactly what we would like to know."

Mandy had nothing. She sputtered for a few seconds, then shut her mouth.

Adrian moved on. "Tell me, Ms. Thorne, this is you, is it not?" He played the clip from *Dish Served Hot* episode 36.

"If I ever murdered someone, it would be with poison—the hardest to trace back! And so easy to do if you think about it. And not messy at all."

Mandy opened and closed her mouth a few times before saying, "Yes, it's me—you fucking know it's me—but that's just chitchat. Idle talk. What you say on a podcast about revenge and murder. It doesn't mean I'd actually do it."

"Not even when you want to red-panda someone?" Adrian said.

Mandy's eyes flicked over to the glass, and I swear she was looking right at me even though she'd missed her mark by a few feet. "Pillow-talking, now, are we? I didn't fucking do this. Why would I? Poison takes a ton of planning and shit! I just figured out who Eugene was at the café! You think I just carry around poison with me to take down my enemies?"

"You certainly have a lot of them," Adrian pointed out.

"I didn't do that!"

"So, then, are you saying you stabbed him with the knife?" Adrian asked calmly.

"No! Stop putting words in my mouth! And, wait! The knife! I thought he died by stabbing! So which is it? You can't have it both ways."

"Either way, Ms. Thorne, both methods point to you."

"Yeah, how convenient," she said sarcastically.

Ricky clasped his hands in front of him and leaned forward, speaking for the first time. "Mandy, give us something here. We're trying to help. Everything is stacked against you right now."

"Because. I'm. Being. FRAMED! How many times do I have to tell you that? My gods! It's fucking *Sesame Street* in here!"

"There isn't any explanation you can give us for all this evidence incriminating you?" Ricky asked.

"*F* is for fucking framed. Do I need to spell it out for y'all?"

Adrian stood. "I think it'd be best if you got your affairs in order."

"What affairs? I'm not dating anyone so I'm not cheating—and OnlyFans is just that, fans; they're not relationships!"

Adrian collected the photographs, returned them to the folder, then stood.

"I want Kat! And Olivia! I know y'all are behind there," Mandy yelled at the two-way glass even though she couldn't see us. "You must see what's going on here. It's exactly what happened to you! I'm being framed! Open your fucking eyes! And you seem to be mad at me, but I wasn't the one who framed you. That was Elle. You hate me yet you don't seem to hate *her.* She was the one who did it—framed you, hurt you, not to mention, *the murder.*"

Olivia and I both glanced away—her at the ceiling, me at the wall.

Mandy was right, but I didn't want to hear those words. Even with the progress we'd made, the emotions were still too complicated. And it was easier to just hate Mandy.

Besides, I wasn't sure who could help her now. She had threatened to kill the victim in public, her fingerprints were on the first possible murder weapon that came from her kitchen, and the second possible murder weapon had been found in her pantry.

Kathryn's Fifth Law of Life (and Death), now proven: Karma's a bitch.

CHAPTER 32

"Are you sure about this?" Ricky asked.

"I'm not sure, and that's exactly why we're letting Mandy go—for now. Innocent until proven guilty," Adrian said.

Ricky nodded. "I agree. Was just checking with ya."

We were at Adrian's and Ricky's back-to-back desks, with Olivia and me in chairs pulled up to the side.

"What's not adding up for you?" I asked Adrian. I felt the same way, but I thought it might help to discuss it out loud.

"For starters, she's turning over all her texts and emails as we speak. *Without* us asking. It feels like she's trying to prove her innocence."

"Unless she's just trying to get ahead of what you would figure out anyway," I said, again wondering if Mandy could somehow be a genius underneath the fake accent and ridiculousness.

Ricky frowned. "That's not the usual way a guilty person would act."

Adrian nodded. "Instinct is to hide what you can, even recklessly—not turn over evidence."

"There's also the matter of the empty pockets," Ricky said.

"Empty pockets?" I asked.

Adrian clarified, "The victim had nothing on him. No phone, no wallet, no keys. We're not sure what motivation

Mandy would have had for taking those, and we didn't find them anywhere on her person or in her house."

"And if Mandy's guilty," Olivia said, "why the two modes? Why the poison *and* the knife?"

Adrian rubbed his chin stubble. "Poison wasn't working fast enough? Wanted to make sure he'd end up dead?"

"Or maybe it was to confuse us," I mumbled, only half joking. "Okay, wait." I closed my eyes briefly, trying to rearrange the pieces in my mind. "We know for a fact that Eugene stole ethylene glycol—"

"And other dangerous chemicals," Olivia interjected.

"—from work. And according to what he said to Yasmin, he was planning on using it on Mandy. But then *he* was poisoned with it, as confirmed by the tox screen, and then the poison showed up in Mandy's home." My eyes flew open. "But here's the kicker." (Possible origin: poker, with the kicker being the card that determines the winner between two players with hands of the same rank.) "Eugene was poisoned *before* he yelled at Mandy, before we figured out he was the one threatening her."

"How do you know that?" Ricky asked.

"At the boba café, Eugene was unhinged when he was yelling at Mandy. I thought he was just irrationally angry"—I remembered the glass on the verge of shattering—"but ethylene glycol toxicity can cause disorientation and erratic behavior. And at the time, I also wondered if he was drunk, because he was slurring his speech, struggling with balance, and breathing rapidly, but all of those are also toxicity symptoms. And there was vomit." All over the floor and that poor guy in the bathroom I embarrassed myself with. "If Eugene was the one who vomited, that's also due to the poisoning. So unless Mandy knew before we did that he was the one threatening her—which, if she did, why would she ask for our help and set up the whole Dish Gets Served meeting to draw Eugene out?—she likely wasn't the person who poisoned him. And whoever did poison him didn't have to work very hard. As we learned from Seraphina, Eugene loved his drinks extra sweet." *Would you like some coffee with your cream and sugar?* she'd said. "Ethylene glycol in its pure form—as it was in the bottle we found—tastes sweet. Eugene would drink it without realizing something was off."

Adrian was looking at me as if my brain was the most beautiful thing in the world; Ricky was leaning back, impressed; and last but not least, Olivia was beaming at me. "This is a Kathryn Hu–specific epiphany that may not have come to anyone else."

I blushed, still not sure how to take a compliment. "Do you have footage from the café? Maybe we can see someone handing Eugene his drink. Or making it." *The very same glass I'd had in my hand*, I thought with a lump in my throat. Too bad I'd lost it in the scuffle.

Adrian pulled up the security footage. "Unfortunately, there was only one camera, pointed at the door. Very minimal coverage."

We watched in silence, and I couldn't help noticing that Olivia and Ricky had scooched closer together, their heads almost touching. They needed to crowd in to see Adrian's screen, but not *that* much.

Adrian was right—the footage didn't capture most of what was happening.

"Oh, people are fleeing now," Olivia said.

"We can't see if it's Eugene vomiting. Or where he goes after." I sighed.

We continued watching.

"Wait!" I exclaimed, pointing. "Go back! Right there!"

Adrian, Ricky, and Olivia leaned closer to the screen (and the latter two even closer to each other).

"Holy shit . . ." Olivia said.

"That's Seraphina," I said. "Seraphina Greenberg. Former head of HR and Eugene Maxwell's ex-girlfriend. And she lied about having seen Eugene recently."

Adrian picked up his phone. "Guess it's time to have a little chat with Seraphina."

CHAPTER 33

"We could've gone undercover, you know," Olivia said from beside me. We were back in the interrogation viewing room together.

"And surprisingly, Ricky seems just as attracted to you when you look like an old woman," I teased. "Is that something we should worry about?"

As predicted, that shut Olivia up.

"Oh, come on," I prodded. "Just admit you have a crush."

"Shh! It's starting."

Adrian had requested Seraphina come down to the station, and even though Olivia claimed she had the wigs and clothes from our old-lady disguises in her car, I knew she didn't have the makeup, and Seraphina would've been suspicious when our skin suddenly appeared thirty years younger.

"Ms. Greenberg," Adrian greeted her. "Thank you for coming."

Seraphina clicked her long nails on the table. "Happy to help. Anything for Eugene."

Adrian glanced at her nails and they abruptly stopped.

"Do you know what happened to him?" Seraphina asked.

"That's what we were hoping you could help us with," Adrian said, lifting his eyes from her fingers to her face.

"Like I said, happy to help." The fingernails started again.

"What's making you nervous, Ms. Greenberg?"

"I'm not nervous," she answered quickly. Too quickly.

"Do you have something you want to tell us?"

Seraphina shook her head.

Adrian moved on. "When was the last time you saw Eugene?"

"Is this a conversation or an interrogation?"

Ricky jumped in. "We brought you into this room for privacy, and it's just a conversation. We all want the same thing—to figure out what happened to Eugene. And to do that, it would help us to know how often you were in contact leading up to his death."

Ricky's good-cop act worked, and Seraphina rested her palms on the table, more relaxed now. "I haven't talked to him in a long time. Not since the breakup."

"Have you seen him?" Ricky asked.

"Didn't I just answer that?"

Adrian leaned forward, his time to shine. "Did you?"

Seraphina stuck a fingernail in her mouth. "What're you getting at?"

Adrian pulled out a photograph and slid it toward her. "Is this not you at Live in Our Bubble during the Dish Gets Served meeting?"

"Yeah, I got invited via social media. I just wanted to see what it was about."

"And is that meeting not the exact location where Eugene Maxwell made a scene . . . and then was subsequently murdered?"

Seraphina's jaw dropped, her fingernail plunking onto the table noisily. "What? He died *there*?"

Adrian waited, patient. I knew not to play that game with him; no amount of silence made him uncomfortable.

Seraphina only lasted thirty seconds. "How did he die? Who

did it? Was it Mandy? Was it one of her stupid little minions from Always Hot? Was it an accident in all that shit that went down?"

Adrian ignored her questions and said, "You claimed you hadn't seen Eugene since the breakup."

Seraphina rolled her eyes. "I mean, I saw him there, from afar, but I didn't get a chance to talk to him before things went to shit. Once the yelling began—and yes, I know he initiated it—I ran out of there before it could escalate. He clearly should've, too."

"Do you know anyone who would want to hurt him?" Ricky asked.

"I mean, Luz was obviously mad at him, but if it happened during that godforsaken meeting, it was probably some freak thing."

"How many people knew that Eugene liked his drinks sweet?" Ricky asked.

"What does that have to do with anything? I'm guessing the people he worked with—or had coffee with, or slept with—knew. Why?"

"You knew," Adrian said ominously.

"How did he die?" Seraphina asked.

"Are you familiar with the chemicals he was using for research?" Adrian asked.

Seraphina paused, putting two and two together. "You should talk to Luz. And I think we're done here."

Guess Seraphina and Luz hadn't become best friends, because neither Olivia nor I would throw the other under the bus like that. Unless Seraphina truly believed Luz did it? Though, even facing that same situation, Olivia and I hadn't thrown Elle under the bus.

Kathryn's Eighth Law of Life, variation: Not all storms lead to a rainbow.

CHAPTER 34

Luz was much more hostile than Seraphina, which wasn't surprising based on our previous interaction.

"Where are the two grannies with terrible fashion sense?"

See? Hostile. At least we were behind the glass again.

But Olivia saw it differently. "She's complimenting my makeup skills."

"Maybe you can use them to age me the other way next time?" I suggested.

"You want to look like a baby?"

I laughed.

In the interrogation room, Adrian said to Luz, "You do medical research."

"You obviously already know that. That's not a question."

"Do you work with dangerous chemicals?"

Luz sighed. "Again, you already know the answer. Yes."

"So a person—an expert—who knew how to use these chemicals could use them for dangerous purposes as well, correct? Including, say, murder?"

This brought me back to when Adrian asked me the same question after discovering that Tucker had died from hydrogen sulfide poisoning. I gripped the table to ground myself and remember that we were past that. I was safe. When Olivia took my hand in hers, my shoulders relaxed again.

Luz crossed her arms defensively over her chest. "Obviously, yes; stop asking these inane non-questions. But anything can be a weapon. Construction equipment, cleaning supplies, that pen you're holding. So yes, most things can be used for murder. So?"

Adrian's potential future-weapon went to work scratching across his notebook. "You seem quite knowledgeable about murder."

Luz didn't answer, seeming to play Adrian's game right back at him.

Adrian spoke first, but only because he was going on the offensive again. "It's true most things can be considered a weapon. But it's quite the coincidence when the murder weapon used on your ex turns out to be the very thing you're an expert at."

Well, one of the weapons, but yes.

Luz's arms slacked briefly before regaining their confidence. "I haven't even seen him since we broke up."

"Have you heard of Dish Gets Served?" Adrian asked.

Luz didn't answer.

"They had their first meeting recently. Were you invited?"

"So what if I was?" Luz countered. "I didn't go."

"Can you tell us where you were that day?"

"With my girlfriends at brunch. You can check my credit card transactions."

Adrian nodded. "How did Eugene like his drinks?"

"What?"

Adrian waited.

Luz's eyes slowly widened as she put it all together. "Sweet. Very sweet. And with your earlier questioning . . . Wait. Eugene coming back to the lab, the chemicals that went missing . . ." Her arms dropped along with all her defenses. Now she just looked like a scared child. "But if Eugene took them, how did he end up . . . ? Why was he the one . . . ? Was he that unhappy? Did he do this to himself?"

I grabbed Olivia's arm. "How far do you think Eugene would go to get revenge on Mandy Thorne?"

Olivia shook her head at me. "No. Do you think? He couldn't have."

"It's not that different from what Elle had been thinking," I pointed out. "Frame the one you want to get back at. And now we're suspecting Luz and Seraphina. Two—I mean, three birds, one stone?"

We both turned back to Luz, who was now being comforted by Ricky.

"Or is Luz doing this just to get us off her tail?" I said. "Seraphina pointed a finger at Luz, Luz is pointing hers at Eugene . . ."

"And round and round we go," Olivia said. "We have jack squat."

"Did you know that's a malaphor, combining *jack shit* and *diddly-squat*? One of the few popularized ones."

"No shit."

"Jack shit."

We shared a smile, but they both quickly fell into frowns.

Just as it was with the last case, it felt like the more we dug, the more questions and suspects we found.

At least this time, we weren't in danger.

CHAPTER 35

I should've known better than to tempt life with thoughts like *at least we weren't in danger.*

When Olivia and I arrived at her townhome later that evening, on her front stoop, there was a thick, sturdy, expensive-looking cream envelope. No address, no stamp—meaning whoever delivered it had been physically here, at the door. Inside was a handwritten note.

Stop investigating or else

Somehow the lack of punctuation made it even more threatening, as if it were leaving the possibilities open and endless.

"Shit." The word seeped out between Olivia's teeth, and as my head darted to and fro—trying to see if the person threatening us was still here, watching—Olivia grabbed my arm and pulled me inside.

Frantically and wordlessly, Olivia locked the door and shoved a chair beneath the handle as I locked the windows and shut the curtains.

Then Olivia and I started talking in a breathless rant, our words overlapping but still making complete sense to one another.

"They know about us—"

"Which, how? We've been undercover or just watching and definitely in the background—"

"And why now?"

Olivia turned the envelope over in her now-gloved hands. "Agreed. What's changed?"

"The biggest shift was today—"

"The two new suspects—"

"So this could be from Seraphina or Luz."

"Or both."

"Luz was more confrontational—"

"But Seraphina seems to be hiding more secrets—"

"Yeah, she showed up at the Dish Gets Served meeting—"

"And tried to keep it from everyone."

Finally, out of words and breath, we both paused.

Then, a second later, Olivia exhaled loudly. "Fuck. This changes everything."

"Should I—" I started, and Olivia was already nodding.

"Make the call."

• • • •

Like sending out the bat signal, my man showed up with his Robin in tow.

I had to admit it was very hot, though there wasn't any time for that right now.

He gave me a once-over to confirm I was in one healthy piece, making me wonder if maybe we had a *little* time?

"Show me," he said gruffly.

Olivia handed the envelope over.

"No prints; I dusted," I said.

He nodded, and I couldn't help feeling like an integral part of the team, much more so than I'd ever felt at the forensics lab.

"We have to keep you two safe," he said.

"Agreed," Ricky chimed in immediately.

Olivia glanced at Ricky and hesitated, but then said, "I have a state-of-the-art security system. I'm fine."

"Are you sure—" I started to ask, but Olivia cut me off.

"I'm sure."

I briefly considered staying here with her, but there was a very important reason I couldn't.

"Cinny," I said, and both Olivia and Adrian understood.

"I'll take you home," Adrian said.

Olivia gave me a long hug. "Stay safe."

"You too."

I couldn't say what I was really thinking—that I was so sorry I'd gotten us into a mess like this again.

CHAPTER 36

I should have realized what I was getting into before I buckled myself into the front seat of Adrian's car, but the note had really shaken me. So it wasn't until the silence descended that it hit me.

This was the first time we'd been alone since . . . the incident. The accidentally broadcasted discussion that changed the words *splotchy*, *stinky*, and *average* for me forever.

I wanted to ignore it, brush it under the rug like I always did. But what if that was part of the problem? Under the rug, things would only fester, grow splotchy and stinky.

I had to try to take down this invisible wall I was feeling, the one created by Tucker and all the baggage he'd come with. And there was no better time than the present, with this huge—oh no, another word with an altered meaning now—with this *large* elephant in the car to address.

"So, um . . . I'm sorry about what happened, during the search at Mandy's place."

I should leave it there. It was succinct, from the heart, and true. That was all that was needed. Anything else would just undermine the apology.

But it was like the pink cupcakes, only instead of turning red or sweating, this time I couldn't stop blabbing. "I'm sorry about what I said, especially when I don't know what it . . . your penis . . . actually looks like—not that it matters, not at all—but I'm also sorry that everyone heard, including you, because that was worse than—"

"Kat. I know it was an accident. And I know you were trying to help when we were all in Mandy's bathroom. I know you."

Even though he was staring at the road ahead, his hands perfectly at ten and two on the steering wheel, his words proved he was looking right at me, always.

He saw me. So why was it so hard to let him in?

"If it makes you feel better," I said, "you can tell the precinct I have an average fishy vagina—I'll understand."

Not only did Adrian's hands slip to nine and three—scandalous!—but he *laughed*. One quick short *ha*, originating from deep within his belly.

Then, his mouth still curved up on one side, he said, "I'm telling you, Kat, you don't need to worry about it so much. All those guys on the squad have heard worse. Or are dealing with worse. Santos has hemorrhoids he won't stop talking about, Johnson's wife has slept with half the force, and have you heard about Ike, who can't keep his hands off his butt? When people work together, that close, dirty laundry comes out—both true and untrue. Who has time to sweat the untrue?"

I never would've imagined Adrian sharing precinct gossip, especially not to make me feel better about publicly declaring his penis average. But maybe this was a good reminder that he was so much more than he appeared. And if he could always give me the benefit of the doubt, I needed to be able to do that for him, too.

"So then it's untrue?" I joked.

His hands returned to ten and two, but the other side of his mouth also curved up. Which meant, there may be a murderer after me *again*, but at least Adrian and I had put the huge, not average, great penis discussion of the twenty-first century behind us.

CHAPTER 37

When Adrian and I arrived at my apartment, there was a giant package as tall as a human leaning against my front door.

Adrian held a hand out, stopping me in my tracks. He quickly checked the hallway, then peeked at the label. "Know who it's from?"

The return address was a company I hadn't heard of.

"No, but it could just be something from my mom," I said, panicked—if that was the case, the package was definitely not safe to open, though for a very different reason.

Retrieving my phone, I shot off a text to my mom.

Did you send me a package?

Immediately, my phone began ringing.

Of course. I knew my mom wasn't a texter—*the buttons so small, so hard to see!*—but now was not the time.

Can you just answer me by text? It's an emergency.

Before she could respond, Adrian hurried me inside and locked the door.

"Backup's on its way. They're sending a team to check the package." Before I could protest, he barreled on. "Stay here.

Use this if you need to." He grabbed a plastic poster tube from where it was leaning against the wall and handed it to me. As if that would do much damage. I grabbed the Kubotan defense tool on my keychain instead, the one from my mom, and I couldn't help feeling both grateful and annoyed at her.

Adrian left me to scour the rest of the apartment. By the time he'd checked every closet, corner, and curtain, the team must have arrived because I heard sirens outside, then noises in the hallway.

"Wait, Adrian—"

"Stay inside, okay?"

"No, Adrian—"

But he was already leaving and closing the door behind him.

Shit.

Since my mom still hadn't responded, I called her back.

"Yushan! Yes, I send package. And you better use!"

I muted it briefly so I could yell through the closed door, "It's just a package from my mom! It's fine!"

Unmuting, I quickly asked her, "What did you send?"

"What you mean? Is not obvious?"

I resisted the urge to let out a strangled groan and instead said, as patiently as I could, "Can you please just tell me what it is?"

"For protection. Put in window."

"Um, Kat?" I heard through the door.

What in god's name could it be?

Someone from the hallway opened the door just as my mom said, "Can also use for carpool lane."

Adrian was standing there holding . . . a life-size cardboard cutout of Glen Powell.

My god. There were no words.

The rest of the officers were a few paces back, but I could tell a couple of them were trying not to laugh.

Could the earth open up a wormhole for me to fall through this instant, please?

"It's from my mom!" I exclaimed.

"Um, why?"

"I told you, she's just weird. She told me to use it for the carpool lane." Half true.

"As a police officer, I have to advise you against doing that."

In the background, low and muffled, came: "Aiyah!!! Yushan! I not weird! And why police there?"

Shit, I'd forgotten to hang up. I yanked the phone back to my ear.

"Ma, it's fine. It was just a really big box and they were worried what was in it, okay? Next time, warn me before you send me these things."

"My Yushan is good girl! Is just dangerous for single—" my mom yelled loudly just as I hung up the phone.

I couldn't meet Adrian's eyes. I didn't want to know if he'd heard her or not.

"Thank you," I said to the officers. "Everything is A-OK here."

Except for maybe my relationship and sanity.

My cheeks flushed, I grabbed the Glen Powell cutout in one hand and the cardboard box in the other and dragged them into the apartment behind me, a walk of shame. But as I pulled the latter across the threshold, a cream envelope appeared that had been previously underneath it.

His eyes dark, Adrian turned to his colleagues. "I want someone patrolling by here every hour."

After we disappeared inside and locked the door, Adrian opened the envelope.

Stop investigating or else

Same note.

Without saying a word, he took my hand in his and led me outside to his car. Twenty minutes later, we were back in my apartment, him drifting here and there to put up the security system he'd procured. Then he installed two extra bolts on my door.

When he was finished, he plopped onto the couch beside me.

"Thank you," I said, feeling like those two words weren't enough.

He turned to look at me, and my gaze landed on the scar above his eyebrow. For the first time, I reached out and caressed it.

"That's a gift from the partner who betrayed me," Adrian said. Though his words were serious, his tone wasn't as sharp as I would have expected. Instead of recounting with anger, he was showing me another piece of him—an important, usually shielded piece—and he seemed to want to. "Even after he skipped town, I couldn't give it up. On and on, I chased him, devoting more time than I should have, needing to find him so I could charge him." He tapped the scar. "This was my wake-up call. I asked the wrong person about him, and this was his answer. So I let it go—I had to, for my sanity and for my job. I haven't forgotten about him, but sometimes you have to put yourself first."

I tilted my face up and brushed my lips against the scar. He grunted, low and soft. As I started to lower my head back down, he caught my lips with his.

I felt our kiss deep within, like our physical connection extended to my soul.

When we came apart, I said, "I'm sorry I got us into this."

He touched my cheek with his hand. "You never have to be sorry for being yourself. That's my favorite part of you—your big heart, your desire to figure everything out." He paused, and his face pulled down, forlorn. "I just hate that you're in this world with me now."

I sighed, knowing exactly what he meant. I hated that part of it myself.

Reaching my arms out to encircle his shoulders, I climbed onto his lap, my legs on either side of his. But instead of it feeling sexy, I just felt cocooned as I leaned forward and buried my face in his chest. His arms wrapped around me.

My chest rose and sank with his, our heartbeats feeling like one. And for this brief moment in time, I felt safe. Home. And thank god, because my actual home was feeling less and less so.

CHAPTER 38

I was worried about Olivia going to work, but I at least felt safe in the forensic lab.

Unfortunately, though I wasn't worried about my safety, I was worried about plenty else.

"Focus, Hu," Gerard chastised when I almost let my chromatography column go dry.

"Who?" asked Diane.

This was getting old.

"Sorry, I'm here," I said instead of saying what I actually wanted to say, which was, *I can normally do this in my sleep and* you're *the one distracting me.*

"What's one of the most important characteristics for a forensic chemist?" Gerard asked the entire room.

"Integrity," answered his minions.

That was getting old, too.

"Exactly," Gerard said smugly. "The ability to remain unemotional and uninvested in the case is crucial. Once emotions become involved, you can no longer be an effective scientist."

Why did it feel like everyone and everything in my life was telling me to stop having emotions? It was why Olivia and I were in danger, why we'd been in danger in the past, why I'd been emotionally shattered by Tucker . . . and apparently I still hadn't learned. If I could just find a way to stop caring, maybe we'd all be better off.

Gerard lowered his voice so he was only addressing me now. "Stop sticking your nose where it doesn't belong. I've told you, our job is to be in the background, to use science and stick to the facts. We should be more computer than human, but also better than computers. We use every tool at our disposal *except* emotion."

Honestly, that was how I used to think of myself during my PhD and postdoc. Or at least, it was what I strived for. But now, getting there was impossible; I was the heart of the Ex-Girlfriend Murder Club.

Gerard continued, "I heard from your paramour that you've gotten yourself into some trouble, and he's using his position to make sure I keep an eye on you—which is *not* part of my job. So, speaking of integrity . . . nepotism is something I look down upon."

Just great. While I didn't bemoan Adrian worrying about my safety, he was not helping my work situation.

Where was that damn certification? I should have gotten it by now. But until then, I was under Gerard's thumb.

As if to prove just how under his thumb I was, he took a step closer and said, "You don't belong in my lab, Hu. We do *serious* work here, instead of whatever you were kicked out of doing at Harvard. If you get in the way of any cases, I'll make you regret everything you've ever done."

After Gerard left to go annoy someone else, I mumbled, "Trust me, I'm already regretting my actions enough for the both of us."

• • • •

Later that night, even though I wanted to, I couldn't bring up Gerard to Adrian. What would I say? *Hey, so, my boss thinks I'm fancy-pants when I'm actually old pajama pants, but I can't change that no matter what I do, and every time you talk to him, you seem to make it worse.* Was it even worth getting into when I was going to get my certification and be out the door any day now?

Luckily, there wasn't even a good opportunity to talk about it.

"And we're here because . . . ?" Adrian asked, looking around at the rows of easels, aprons, and long-stemmed glasses.

Part of the reason was because Olivia and I had agreed we'd only go out if the boys were in tow, but as for why we were in this particular spot . . .

I nudged his side as I said in a low voice, "Play it cool."

Adrian's brow furrowed. "You tell me to play it cool, but are you doing the same? Kat, this place is called Paint Night, as in, a play on *Date Night*."

I ticked my head subtly toward the corner where Ricky was laughing way too hard at something Olivia had said. I mean, sure, she was funny, but not *that* funny. "Hey, whatever I'm doing, it's working."

Adrian shook his head, but he also chuckled slightly. "Or maybe there's no need to meddle and we can let nature take its course."

I couldn't help thinking his words reminded me of what Gerard had said earlier today. Deflecting, I went to grab us paint supplies and wine, emphasis on the latter.

Thirty minutes later, the wine was working, but only some of our paintbrushes were.

"You're not even going to try?" I asked my grumpy man.

"Actually, I'm finished," he said.

I peered over at his canvas, and as soon as I saw what was there, I burst into laughter. "A gray rock?"

That was what he had painted. While the rest of us were following instructions to create a simpler version of Vincent van Gogh's *Starry Night*, Adrian had marched to the beat of his own drum (origin: Thoreau's *Walden*) and painted the most boring object in the entire world.

Adrian nodded as if to say, *What else would I have painted?* "I like rocks. They're simple, dependable, and always interpreted the same—no fuss, no frills. Unlike a starry night."

With those words, I saw the gray rock in a new light, and it only made me like my dependable, no-fuss man more.

Across our shared table, Olivia asked Ricky, "How is yours so good?"

I leaned over to get a glimpse, and his swirling sky somehow deviated from the example painting in all the best ways, with new paths and better colors.

Ricky shrugged. "This makes sense to me. Doesn't help me very much with my job, but I guess it's fun."

He raised his paintbrush and added a Ninja Turtle in the sky.

"You ruined it!" Olivia exclaimed.

"Or did I make it awesome, gnarly, and radical?"

Olivia laughed.

Ricky raised a pleased eyebrow. "So you've seen the show?"

She scoffed. "Who hasn't?"

He looked at her like the sun shone out of her eyes.

My own painting was a bit of a soupy mess, but I didn't care since my goal had been reached.

"So, any progress in the case?" I asked Adrian since he was done with his Paint Night masterpiece.

"Mandy's phone and email are still being sifted through. Not surprisingly, there's quite a bit of data, and there were a slew of potential suspects she'd been communicating with anonymously. We did manage to speak to a few people of interest today, though."

"Oh?" Olivia said, her and Ricky joining the conversation. "Who'd you talk to?"

"Luz and Seraphina again, and also Eugene's sister, Katrina," Adrian answered.

"Anything of note?" I asked.

"Some trends we noticed, but nothing damning."

Ricky nodded. "They all seemed to be in disbelief that Eugene was the one threatening Mandy—said it was out of character for him."

"Well, don't they always say that?" I mused.

"Yeah," Olivia said. "They never interview the friends and neighbors and they're like, 'Of course he did it! I knew it!'"

Olivia and I glanced at each other, and I knew we were both thinking about how we hadn't known with Tucker. Or with Elle, at least not at first.

"Or it could be true what they said, that it was out of character for Eugene," Ricky said. "Doesn't mean he wasn't behaving out of character, though."

"Or could they all be in cahoots?" Olivia suggested.

Ricky shrugged. "Maybe."

"But why would the sister be?" I asked.

"We can share the transcripts with you," Adrian said, and I knew he didn't want to make any conjectures without evidence.

"None of that tells us if either Luz or Seraphina had anything to do with his death," I pointed out.

"Unfortunately not," Adrian agreed. "Though their prints were not found on the knife, ethylene glycol, or any of his belongings."

"That could be on purpose," I said, thinking out loud. "They had reason to be mad at Eugene *and* Mandy. They could have framed her for this." Again, two birds with one stone, and that made more sense than Eugene doing this to himself.

I knew what Adrian was going to say before he said it. "Good hypothesis—we just need the evidence to back it up."

Easier said than done.

"Any leads on the threatening note?" I asked.

"You tell me. Isn't the forensic lab working on it?"

My gaze fell to the floor. "Oh, uh, Gerard doesn't want me working on this case. Which is fine. But I don't know if they have any results back yet—you'd know before me."

Adrian arched a scarred eyebrow.

"Do you think my sky is spooky enough?" Olivia asked suddenly, most likely to help me deflect from a conversation I didn't want to have.

Ricky glanced over and beamed. "I don't know. I think you should check it out, Kat."

I stood and walked to the other side of the table. When I saw Olivia's canvas, I smiled so wide my cheeks hurt. "It's perfect."

Under the sky, Olivia had painted Velma and Nancy in their classic outfits plus a beanie for Velma and a cloche hat for Nancy. And the two of them were looking through binoculars, but not at the sky. They were looking right out from the canvas, right at the viewer.

Even though that very trait had gotten us into heaps of trouble, at least it had also brought Velma and Nancy together. So as much as I regretted putting us in danger again, at least some good came out of my need to meddle.

Interrogation Room Transcript

DETECTIVE BIRCH: Thank you so much for coming down here, Ms. Maxwell.

KATRINA MAXWELL: Katrina, please.

DETECTIVE BIRCH: Thank you also for identifying the body. I'm so sorry for your loss. Eugene was your older brother?

KATRINA MAXWELL: Yes.

DETECTIVE BIRCH: Can you tell me about your relationship with him?

KATRINA MAXWELL: We weren't all that close anymore, unfortunately. Our parents died when I was thirteen and he was fifteen, and my aunt took me in while my grandma took Eugene in. When my grandmother passed, Eugene was about to turn eighteen, so he applied to college early. He was always smart—got into Harvard on a full ride—and then he made something of himself, getting a job at a top medical research facility. He was always invited to my aunt's place for holidays, but he never came. Too busy working.

DETECTIVE BIRCH: Are you aware that your brother was out of work for the past year?

KATRINA MAXWELL: Out of work? That can't be. Wait. Was this because of his health issues?

DETECTIVE BIRCH: What health issues in particular are you referring to?

KATRINA MAXWELL: He called me once, drunk, really upset, telling me about how he'd been diagnosed with kidney disease. I couldn't make out all the details, but the gist of it seemed to be that he was having a hard time and had been self-medicating, but it wreaked havoc on his body. Is that what got him?

DETECTIVE BIRCH: Unfortunately, no. We're still trying to get to the bottom of what happened. We're investigating foul play.

KATRINA MAXWELL: As in . . . murder?

DETECTIVE BIRCH: Were you aware of any relationships he had?

KATRINA MAXWELL: I don't think he was that interested in having romantic relationships. As for friends, I'm not sure. He was always a bit shy.

DETECTIVE BIRCH: Did your brother talk to you about someone named Mandy Thorne?

KATRINA MAXWELL: That name sounds vaguely familiar. Maybe he was upset at her at one point? Is she a colleague?

DETECTIVE BIRCH: She's the host of a podcast called *Dish Served Hot*.

KATRINA MAXWELL: I'm not familiar with it.

DETECTIVE BIRCH: We have reason to believe that Eugene was threatening her.

KATRINA MAXWELL: Eugene? My brother, Eugene? That can't be. I mean, it's just not like him. He was bullied all the time growing up and never once defended himself or even talked back. It got so bad he wouldn't even walk to school without me. And his default was to run away—from bullies, even teachers and babysitters and other kids. I think you've got the wrong guy.

DETECTIVE BIRCH: Can you think of anything else that might be relevant for this case?

KATRINA MAXWELL: His work was everything to him. It was his identity, his pride, his joy. Losing his job might've been why he was having a hard time and self-medicating. So maybe see if you can find out what happened there, and also see if you can get his medical records.

DETECTIVE BIRCH: Thank you for that information and for your time, Katrina. Again, my condolences on your loss. We'll keep you informed.

KATRINA MAXWELL: Thank you.

Interrogation Room Transcript

DETECTIVE BIRCH: Ms. Greenberg, thank you for coming down again.

LAWYER: And we'd like to note that she did this voluntarily. My client has nothing to hide.

DETECTIVE BIRCH: Ms. Greenberg, were you aware that Eugene Maxwell had been threatening Mandy Thorne?

SERAPHINA GREENBERG: Look, I was very surprised at how he was acting at the Dish Gets Served meeting. But something was clearly wrong with him that day. He wasn't himself. And while the yelling was out of character, that's also all it was—yelling.

DETECTIVE BIRCH: He also sent her death threats and a bloody knife.

SERAPHINA GREENBERG: Eugene? No way. He doesn't have the guts.

DETECTIVE BIRCH: Why do you say that?

SERAPHINA GREENBERG: Because he was Eugene. He was passionate and emotional, but about science and saving people's lives. He worked well with others, always happy to contribute and collaborate. Does that sound like the same person who would send death threats?

DETECTIVE BIRCH: Are you aware of any health issues Eugene Maxwell may have had?

SERAPHINA GREENBERG: He was virile when we were together.

Why, was there something wrong? Is that why he was acting differently? Is that why he *died*?

DETECTIVE BIRCH: Are you upset at Mandy Thorne?

[Seraphina Greenberg looks to her lawyer, who then confers with her]

SERAPHINA GREENBERG: I mean, I'm upset in the expected way. Her podcast led to my firing, but also, it's not like Mandy forced Luz to go on the show. So I'm more upset at Luz—

[Lawyer clears her throat]

SERAPHINA GREENBERG: I mean, I *was* upset with Luz, right after everything imploded. But we've since made up. She didn't know all that would happen. She was hurt and just wanted to get back at Eugene. I get that.

DETECTIVE BIRCH: Because *you* wanted to get back at Eugene?

SERAPHINA GREENBERG: No! Don't put words in my mouth!

DETECTIVE BIRCH: Have you wanted to get back at any of the players?

SERAPHINA GREENBERG: Of course not! I've moved on. I'm doing well. I'd like nothing more than to put all this behind me.

[beat]

DETECTIVE BIRCH: Thank you for your time today, Ms. Greenberg.

SERAPHINA GREENBERG: Again, I'd like to put this all behind me. Yes? I've told you everything I know.

LAWYER: Please do only reach out if there's a new development in the case. Otherwise, my client has been generous enough with her time.

DETECTIVE BIRCH: [noncommittal grunt]

Interrogation Room Transcript

DETECTIVE BIRCH: Thank you, Ms. Lopez, for coming down today.

LUZ LOPEZ: Sure.

DETECTIVE BIRCH: Did you have any additional contact with Mandy Thorne after the podcast recording?

LUZ LOPEZ: No. Why?

DETECTIVE BIRCH: Are you upset that her show convinced you to take action that resulted in your firing?

LUZ LOPEZ: I mean, if you think about it like that, sure, but it's not such a direct causal relationship, is it? I could just as much blame the company for hiring me, which resulted in me meeting Eugene in the first place.

DETECTIVE BIRCH: Except that's not the same thing at all.

LUZ LOPEZ: Fine, bad example. I could just as well blame the company for not taking my side, or the HR person—who was probably a friend of Seraphina's, by the way—who told the company about the episode and processed my firing.

DETECTIVE BIRCH: Are you? Upset at Seraphina? Or that HR person?

LUZ LOPEZ: Can we move on from this useless questioning?

[long beat]

LUZ LOPEZ: I didn't do anything wrong.

[beat]

LUZ LOPEZ: I might've been upset about everything that went down—like any normal person would be—but I've had enough distance from it now. I don't blame Seraphina or the HR person or the company any more than I blame myself.

DETECTIVE BIRCH: What about Eugene? Do you blame him?

LUZ LOPEZ: Does it matter? He's gone.

DETECTIVE BIRCH: It matters.

LUZ LOPEZ: I was of course upset at him, like any normal person would be after being cheated on and fired.

DETECTIVE BIRCH: How long were you upset at him?

LUZ LOPEZ: For a normal amount of time!

DETECTIVE BIRCH: Which is?

LUZ LOPEZ: Seriously, Detective, I'm kind of at my wit's end. Do I love the guy? No. Do I wish I hadn't dated him? Yes. Did I wish he'd have a cold that didn't go away or bad acne for the rest of his life? Sure. But did I want him dead? No.

DETECTIVE BIRCH: Are you aware of any health issues Eugene Maxwell had?

LUZ LOPEZ: I think he had asthma? Was that somehow related to what happened?

DETECTIVE BIRCH: Are you aware Eugene was sending Mandy Thorne death threats?

LUZ LOPEZ: Eugene? Shit, I didn't think he had that in him. I'd heard he was super pissed after everything, but he was also the guy who needed me to talk to his landlord for him or order at a restaurant. He was so nonconfrontational he was practically dependent on me. If he threatened Mandy, it was just talk; he rarely followed through on anything. Or I don't know. Maybe I didn't know him after all.

DETECTIVE BIRCH: Yet, you seemed confident in saying that it was just talk, and he didn't have it in him.

LUZ LOPEZ: Are you always this annoying? I think we're good here. I didn't have anything to do with this, and I don't have any other information, so please stop contacting me. I don't even want to know what happened; he's been dead to me for a long time now.

[chair scrape]

[door slam]

CHAPTER 39

Ricky and Adrian drove Olivia and me home from Paint Night, respectively—both meanings, ha.

After spending the first part of the ride skimming the transcripts, I blurted to Adrian, "Eugene had kidney disease."

"Yes, and?"

"And I think whoever poisoned him knew about it."

"How come?"

"Because ethylene glycol poisoning is sped up by kidney disease." I should have put all this together sooner, seeing as I'd noticed Eugene's swollen eyes, scaly patches of skin, and thinning hair—all signs of kidney disease.

"Whoever poisoned him didn't necessarily know that," Adrian stated.

"True, but I think we should still figure out if anyone else knew about the disease."

"If they did know about it, then why the knife? And speaking of, the ME confirmed that the knife was the cause of death, though the victim was, of course, also poisoned."

I liked that Adrian was always skeptical, asking questions, playing devil's advocate—really, I did—but also, could we not just consider a hypothesis for a little longer than twenty seconds?

"What if the knife and the poison were committed by two

different people?" I suggested. "That possibility means we shouldn't ignore potential leads if it only fits one of the two methods."

Adrian nodded slowly. "Good thinking."

"Or," I said, my mind churning quickly now. "It could still be one person. Maybe the killer chose poison because they thought it would work quicker with the kidney disease, but then it wasn't working fast enough—I mean, these things aren't predictable—and so they resorted to the knife?"

Adrian nodded again. "I'll see who knew about the diagnosis."

• • • •

I spotted it first.

A cream-colored envelope leaning against the door.

Adrian immediately shielded my body with his while his eyes checked the perimeter. We continued like this as he searched the apartment, then locked the door.

My phone rang.

"Did you get one, too?" Olivia asked instead of saying hello.

"Yeah."

"Meet us at my place," Adrian called out toward the phone.

As I texted Olivia the address, Adrian donned gloves and opened the envelope.

This is your last warning
Stop investigating

Again, no punctuation. And behind the cardstock with the handwritten threat was something even worse: a photo of me and Olivia looking at her canvas at Paint Night, with red *X*'s drawn in Sharpie over our faces.

"They were just here?" I whispered. The fact that we might

have just missed each other made the danger feel ever more present.

Adrian's gaze was locked on the photo as he said, "Pack your bags. You're not staying here. And we're hunkering down for the foreseeable future."

I couldn't find any words. I couldn't even nod my head. I just packed as fast as I could, all the while thinking about how this time, the murderer after me was not my Ex-Girlfriend Murder Club sister who regretted her actions and would never hurt me.

CHAPTER 40

"This will be home base," Adrian said to welcome Olivia in. His delivery could have been warmer, but this was his way of saying *my home is your home.*

Like a gentleman, he took Olivia's bag from her and started to lead her down the sparse hallway. His three-bedroom house was the clean version of a bachelor pad, with blank white walls and minimal furniture, but it was functional and sturdy, just like him.

"I'll leave you to it," Ricky said with a two-finger salute. But just before he could head to the front door, Adrian paused and turned around.

"You're not staying?"

Ricky surprised me by saying, "Oh. No. I don't want to intrude—"

"You wouldn't be; we need you."

"No, really—"

But Adrian just grabbed a blanket and threw it at him.

Was Ricky being shy because of Olivia? You'd think he'd want to spend more time with her.

"Where's the bathroom?" Olivia asked.

"Right there," Adrian said just as Ricky also pointed. But Ricky seemed to catch himself and his finger quickly dropped. Adrian glanced over but his face remained as neutral as ever.

"The couch folds out" was all Adrian said to Ricky. Then he disappeared into the guest room to drop off Olivia's bag.

Unsure what to say to Ricky, I busied myself setting up Cinny's cage. But no matter how hard I tried, I couldn't get the weird feeling out of my stomach.

• • • •

I couldn't sleep, even with Adrian's arm resting gently on my hip—then my stomach, then my waist as I tossed and turned—and despite knowing that Olivia was safe in the next room.

Around two in the morning, I gave up, slipping away from Adrian's warm body and padding into the kitchen without turning any lights on.

"You couldn't sleep either?" I heard from my right.

I would've jumped if I didn't know that voice so well.

"Why're you sitting in the dark?" I asked Olivia as my index finger flipped the switch for the under-cabinet lighting—the dimmest option.

Still, Olivia shielded her squinted eyes from the brightness. "I don't know. It felt . . . safer. Also, um, why the hell does Adrian have a life-size cutout of Glen Powell?"

With anyone else, I would have flushed red, but with Olivia, I laughed. "Because my wacky mom sent me that to put in the window *Home Alone* style to scare people off—"

"And Adrian thought it could protect us here?"

I shook my head. "He brought it as a joke. I didn't even see him pack it in the car earlier, and he set it up here without a word."

"Who knew he had such a sense of humor?"

I patted Glen's arm as I passed by him to plop next to Olivia at the dining room table. Before my butt even made contact with the chair, my hands were reaching for the open Pocky box in her hands. "You found the good stuff."

"Wouldn't have pegged Adrian for a Pocky man. So many surprises."

"I've rubbed off on him." And maybe he also kept those here for me.

I bit into the long, thin chocolate-covered biscuit and, as usual, my chest filled with nostalgia.

"My parents used to buy these for me at the Asian grocery stores. They were so strict about sweets, but not when it came to Pocky. Not when it came to things they knew and loved." Which was exactly why biting into one of these felt like a hug from them.

"I could use some comfort food from my childhood right now."

I took her hand in mine and squeezed. "I'm sorry."

"You didn't do anything."

"Didn't I? I was the one who couldn't let it go, even after both you and Adrian warned me." I put the Pocky down. "Why did I do this to us?"

"Because you're you. Your heart is just that big."

"Well, it sucks."

"Hearts don't suck. Mouths—"

I threw a Pocky stick at her.

She picked it up and bit into it. "Seriously, though? Stop blaming yourself. I was just as in, remember? We did it for Elle. And . . ." She smiled sadly. "What's done is done."

Even though Elle wasn't physically here, she was still with us, everywhere. And just like before, when we were trying to figure out who had killed Tucker, those same words focused me, draining the panic and replacing it with resolve.

"So let's not make all of that in vain," I said. "We solve this while also staying safe."

"How're we supposed to figure anything out while holing up here?"

"With our best assets."

"My tits?" Olivia said.

"You think those are your best assets?"

Olivia shrugged. "They certainly get the most attention."

"Well, those people are wrong." I placed a hand over my heart and gestured to her head with the other.

Olivia smiled. Then, wistfully, she said, "Guess we don't need the guts if we're staying in."

"At least we won't need the old-lady clothes, either."

"Hey! They worked!"

"Can we dress up as Velma and Nancy next time?"

Olivia beamed. "Deal."

Dish Served Hot Podcast Transcript–Episode 106: *New Release*

[Podcast theme song plays, sung by creator, host, and star Mandy Thorne]

MANDY THORNE: Hello, Thornies. It is with a heavy heart that I greet y'all today. [pause] I am, through no fault of my own, in some trouble. Someone—a deranged, deluded, and probably jealous psychopath—is out to get me. I am declaring it here first: I am innocent. I have committed no crimes. I am as innocent and pure and clean as a virgin's hoo-ha. Cross my heart and, well, I'm not going to say the rest. Because given that a psychopath is after me, death might actually be coming for me for reals. But not if I have anything to say or do about it.

I am Mandy Thorne—award-winning podcast creator, host, and star; mega influencer; OnlyFans superstar; best contestant ever on reality dating show *Love Hut*; masterful actor; and last but not least, survivor.

I am going to fight this. Because that's what I do best. I'm a fighter. And y'all know what I'm capable of.

So I'm going to use all the resources at my disposal to fight back, including this show and all of your wonderful, lovely, fantastical selves. Please, *please*, if you know anything, contact me. And if you're a lawyer or cop or CSI or PI, please also reach out. I need all the help I can get.

So here's the scoop. Ever since the fucking dumpster lava fire that was Lassy McBush, I've been a victim. Of hateful messages, death threats, and much more. So, yes, the scuttlebutts you've been hearing are true: the person who died at the Dish Gets Served and Always Hot meetup was someone who had been threatening me. But I swear to gods, I did not have anything to do with his death. *He* was threatening *me*—as you all saw!—and, unfortunately, that was just another Monday for me. I did *not* decide to do something about it. Y'all know me. I'm only about the kind of revenge that elicits frustration *and* a laugh. Replacing their website with photos of them cheating. Using up their rewards points. Taking all the buttons off their clothes. *Not* murder.

So here as my guest today to tell you more about this case—and also about yours truly, who could never have done this—is my assistant and right-hand woman, Jocelyn. Thanks for being here, Jocelyn.

JOCELYN: Of course, Mandy. Whatever will help you. And, Thornies, believe me when I tell ya, Mandy has been stressing over this. So much so that I've even seen her eat . . . a *carb*. That's right, I saw her put butter on her steamed broccoli.

MANDY: Jocelyn, what's the carb there? I would never eat a carb.

JOCELYN: The butter.

MANDY: Butter's not a carb.

JOCELYN: But I thought . . . in *Mean Girls* . . .

MANDY: No, Regina *asks* if butter is a carb. She's not stating it. And even if she did—

JOCELYN: Okay, okay. Can we just cut this out? [clears throat] Thornies, please do what you can to help Mandy. Your shero needs you.

MANDY: Thank you, Jocelyn. I don't know what I'd do without you. Seriously, y'all, without Jocelyn, I'd forget my head! [whispering] And for my other *special* fans, I sometimes forget my clothes, too.

JOCELYN: [also whispering] And for those special fans, there's a discount on Mandy's OnlyFans page for the next three days. [speaking at normal volume] So, Mandy, tell everyone why the police wrongly suspect you.

MANDY: Well, they claim they found my fingerprints on the murder weapon, but get this—they're not even sure what the murder weapon is! Apparently, so many people wanted this guy dead that someone tried to poison him *and* someone stabbed him. So, c'mon, how am I the prime suspect here?

JOCELYN: And you probably weren't the only person he was threatening. Just the most famous one.

MANDY: Exactly, Jocelyn. Clearly, there is a lot of shit going on here, and *I* am the victim. Also, this guy had a ton of health problems! So how do they know he didn't just drop dead from that? The bottom line is: I will not go down for a crime I did not commit.

JOCELYN: And you have help.

MANDY: I do. Remember our Queens from the previous unprecedented award-winning True Crime season? Well, they're on my case! Because they know as well as I do that I'm innocent. So they're helping me, and they're going to nail the true murderer, just like they did last time. Thanks to them, Lassy McBush is rotting away where she belongs, so this murderer better watch out. We're right on your tail!

And, of course, that leads me to my epic, out-of-this-world, truly awesome announcement.

JOCELYN: So exciting, Mandy!

MANDY: Drumroll, please.

[drumroll]

MANDY: This is going to be the *second* True Crime season of *Dish Served Hot*. Where the Queens and I prove my innocence and sentence another vile murderer to life in prison.

Stay tuned! Detective Mandy and Detectives Kat and Olivia are on the case!

JOCELYN: And Detective Joce—

[end episode]

CHAPTER 41

"That little ratings-hungry piece of shit!"

"You didn't say *lying* this time," I pointed out to Olivia. We were still at Adrian's, though the boys were in the office with the weekend shift.

"Well, sadly, I'm not sure if she lied. She actually told way too much of the truth. What was she thinking, giving away all those case details and using our real names?"

"Exactly what you said. Ratings."

We hadn't given Mandy many updates since the threatening notes showed up at our doors, and in our brief absence, she'd gone and done this?

"We cannot talk to her again until this is solved," I said.

"Agreed. She's a liability."

"A nightmare."

"The giant thorn in our asses we cannot pull out no matter how big our tweezers."

I chuckled at the malaphor combining *thorn in your side* with *pain in the ass*. Then I said, "You know, there *is* a silver lining here."

"Mandy has proven to us she's the absolute worst and we were right about her?"

"That and something else. She proved she knew about Eugene's health issues, which none of us told her about. I think that's damning."

"So what do you propose?"

"We dig into Mandy."

Olivia frowned. "Gross. Do we have to?"

"We know for a fact she's tied up in all this—she's a definitive source Elle would tell us to look into."

"But it's *Mandy Thorne*."

"We'll wash our eyeballs after. You can even use the eyewash station at the lab."

"That thing that has two prongs sticking out of it? No thank you; that looks like a torture device."

I shook Olivia's arm. "Come on, Brains, what would Guts say?"

"I'm not looking at Mandy's OnlyFans."

"Well, I can't afford to subscribe to it, so, not it." My index finger flew up to touch the tip of my nose.

Olivia followed suit (origin: cards), but that was the downside of having just two players. "Ricky can look into that part."

"Do you actually want him to?" I teased.

Olivia ignored me. "I'll take social media if you look into press coverage."

"Deal."

"Too bad we don't have our—" I started to say, but Olivia reached into her backpack and pulled out the beanie and cloche hat. "You brought them?"

"Of course. How can we do any sleuthing without our sleuthing hats?"

For the first time since the threatening notes arrived, I felt some much-needed hope as I tugged the knit beanie onto my head.

• • • •

"This girl has dated reality stars, influencers, a boy band—and I mean that how I said it; she dated every member of an up-and-coming boy band," Olivia said an hour later.

"And don't forget DJs," I added. DJ Quiktrix had been the original revenge seeker, serving a cheating Mandy her hot dish by asking her to get matching tattoos. She went first, then he dumped her before getting his. According to our favorite columnist, Lassy McBush, this incident was where the idea for *Dish Served Hot* came from, though Mandy would never admit that, having denied the origin of the tattoo as staunchly as she denied shitting in the hut.

"What happened with the boy band?" I asked.

Olivia read off her screen. "The Boystown Boys were 'a promising boy band from Boystown, Illinois, that combined pop, R&B, jazz, and folk.' Yikes. Their tagline was 'Boys! Boys! Boys!' And they rose to fame after their appearance on *America's Got Talent* went viral, mostly because the audience couldn't get over how terrible yet good-looking they were. And, oh, shit, they were all brothers."

"Of course. Somehow they plus Mandy equals a lot of sense."

"Ooh, was that a 2gether reference?" Olivia asked.

"Yes!" I was over the moon she got it. (Over the moon origin: the "Hey Diddle Diddle" nursery rhyme.)

"Somehow that makes sense, too, that the boy band you liked was the one *making fun* of boy bands," Olivia said.

"It almost feels like the Boystown Boys should also be a parody, but they're clearly not. So how did they meet Mandy?"

"On the reality show *Traitors*. That's where Mandy hooked up with all of them."

"During one season of a TV show?" I had to hand it to her, that took commitment.

"She claims she was 'using her best resource to determine who the traitor was.'"

"And?" I asked.

"She accused every brother except for the one who *was* a Traitor."

I . . . sort of knew what that felt like, having chosen the lying asshole cheater, and not in a reality show but in this game called life.

"Oh, shit," Olivia said as she scrolled further. "When the season aired and the brothers found out that she slept with all of them, they disbanded—all went their separate ways to try to make it solo."

"Shit," I repeated. Then I wrote all five Boystown Boys onto our growing list of people who have beef with Mandy (possible origin: Cockney slang, where one would yell "hot beef" to cry for help because it vaguely sounds like "stop thief!").

Olivia sighed. "I feel like I know Mandy and nothing surprises me all that much, but at the same time, she's still such an enigma. Almost like she's a . . . caricature. A part she's playing for the public."

"Except she's like that in private, too," I said, thinking about all my interactions with her at her mansion, in the police station. "And Jocelyn claims she's like that with her, too."

"What about her weird-ass background? The fake Southern accent?"

"Right?" I pulled up Lassy McBush's articles. "And she's from Idaho, though she tried hard to hide that."

"Maybe there's a reason. It's also suspicious that we don't know much about her past or her family."

I nodded. "Let's switch gears."

Olivia tilted her head at me, and I smiled.

"Related to changing gears in a manual transmission."

"Ah, of course. Shall we shift to Drive and set our course for Idaho?"

"Already on it."

CHAPTER 42

A few days later, we switched course again. Because all we'd managed to dig up was that Mandy's parents had passed away—her mother ten years ago and her father when she was a baby. Which could explain why there wasn't much information to find, but it was a bit peculiar that Mandy *never* talked about her family when she was so open about everything else.

So even though we were supposed to be lying low, we convinced Adrian to take a field trip with us. And while we *were* looking for information, this visit was about more than that.

"Kitty Kat! Double-Oh! And . . . well, well. What do we have here?" Elle said as we filed into the visitation room. "Is it thanks to you that we have some space to spread out, Detective?"

It indeed was; Adrian had pulled some strings so we could talk in person without the glass between us, which was such a lovely change, though we were prohibited from any physical contact with Elle. So no hugs.

Adrian cleared his throat. "Hello, Lauren. How are you?"

"Oh, just peachy keen." She beamed at us—a full, genuine smile—and my heart sank that this was such a highlight of her day, to be in a sterile guarded room with us. "How are you, Detective?"

Her eyes swept over him, landing on his hands, and there they stayed.

"Stop it," I whispered.

"What, I can't enjoy myself for a second?"

"How are you, Elle, truly?" Olivia asked.

"Don't you worry about me. I want to hear all the updates. Let me at least live vicariously through you."

Olivia and I glanced at each other, not sure if we should oblige, but how could we not? We weren't going to force her to tell us how prison life was going. And if I were her, I probably wouldn't want to talk about it, either.

So we filled her in. And she gasped and whistled in all the right places. When we finished, she steepled her fingers.

"I don't want to defend her, but . . . if this was truly the work of Mandy Thorne, doesn't it seem a bit too complicated?"

"You were the one who warned me not to trust her." *And that you weren't all that different*, I didn't add.

"I'm not saying to trust her. I just don't know if she's capable of all this. Though poison does tend to be a woman's weapon of choice."

"Do you think it's possibly Luz or Seraphina?" I asked.

"I think we don't know enough yet. Which I'm guessing is why you're here. What can I do to help?"

"We were hoping you—or Lassy McBush—might know more about Mandy's background. We hit a dead end looking into her past, which made us even more suspicious that there might be something there."

Elle laced her fingers together and put them behind her head. "I don't know how much this has to do with everything else, but I do have a juicy nugget for you. I've been conducting further research on Mandy for my book with the help of a PI and some pen pals I've made, and . . . here's what I know. Mandy grew up in a tough situation. Had a single mom with limited resources and was an outcast at school who dropped out junior year. She worked at the local ice-cream shop and gas station until she saved up enough money to leave home, hoping to make something of herself. But before she became, well, whatever she is now—infamous?—her mother passed away. From liver failure, though her sister—Mandy's aunt—thinks it was from heartbreak."

"That's your pen pal?" I interrupted. "Mandy's aunt?"

Elle's eyes sparkled as she said, "I never reveal my sources. Anyway, a little birdie told me that when Mandy was young—around five or six—her mother gave a child up for adoption. The man didn't want anything to do with her or the baby, and since she was a single mom already struggling with one kid, she did what she thought was best. But she never forgave herself for it. And she also never told Mandy."

Wow. That was . . . a lot. "How do you think this is connected?"

"I don't. I think you're looking in the wrong direction, looking at Mandy. But you asked what I knew about her, and that's it."

"Do you have the aunt's contact info?" Olivia asked.

Elle shook her head. "Sorry, can't share that. But if there's something specific you want to know, I'm happy to help. Though . . ." Her eyes narrowed. "I'm happy to help *you*, my girls, but if Mandy wants my help, she'll have to come down here and ask me herself on her hands and knees. That should be a position she's familiar with."

Olivia and I shared a look. That . . . was never happening. And not to mention, we weren't doing this for Mandy. We were doing this to try to help Elle, though we didn't want to tell her that piece of it, not yet. We couldn't get her hopes up prematurely.

Elle's tone lightened as she said, "I'll keep my ears peeled for you. I have access to information in a very different way than *y'all*, including Mandy. Might as well use it for good, yeah?

And I'll also put some feelers out about the other two girls." She glanced at Adrian as she added, "Especially if there's a way to offer that information up in exchange for some other favors. You know, good behavior and all." She winked.

Adrian shifted in his seat. There wasn't much that rattled him, but apparently Elle's flirting did. He stood, and Elle reached a hand out toward us, suddenly desperate.

"Hey. You all should be living—and not just Liv because it's in her name. Take it from someone in my position. Everything looks different from in here. So remember that our time is short. And that it's all the little joys in life that make it worth living."

My vision was blurry as Olivia asked, "Elle . . . are you okay?"

"I love you girls," she said instead of answering the question.

As Olivia and I walked out, our eyes met. We had to do this. For Elle. Even if the chance was slim.

That night, I couldn't get Elle's words out of my head. So when we got into bed, I pulled Adrian close and didn't let go. And I kissed him like there was no tomorrow. And for the first time in our entire relationship, as his mouth pressed into mine and his fingers trailed over my back and into my hair, everything else disappeared from my head. There was no past, no baggage, no worries or embarrassments or self-consciousness. It was just him and me, today's Adrian and Kat, and the perfect little moment we could share, even amid everything going on.

Elle's First and Only Law of Life: It's the little joys in life that make it worth living—don't waste it.

CHAPTER 43

Olivia, Adrian, Ricky, and I were really embodying Elle's Law of Life, trying to spray Febreze all over our shit-covered situation. Just because our lives were in danger and we had to hole up together outside of work didn't mean we couldn't enjoy each other's company or our meals, especially on the weekend. (And it was also freeing that I was ignoring my mother's calls and only sending brief texts—I rationalized it was my only course of action since I couldn't explain that I was in danger and staying with my boyfriend whom she didn't know about.)

"Ta-da!" Olivia announced as I did the Vanna White hand gestures to present our reverse-seared steak.

"Oh, wow," Ricky murmured, closing his eyes and inhaling.

Adrian smiled and silently clapped in our direction. I curtsied playfully.

It was chaotic in the best way as we set the table, cut the steak, and poured drinks. Everyone was in each other's way and trying to help, which only led to even more laughs and maybe some brushing of hands between Olivia and Ricky.

"This is nice," Ricky said when we all sat down. "Growing up, my dinners were mostly box mac and cheese or instant noodles, so this is quite the treat. Thanks, girls."

He raised his glass of red and the rest of us followed.

"To finding the rainbow after the storm," I said, glancing at Olivia.

She met my eye and added, "And to catching a murderer."

My insides warmed even though I hadn't sipped the wine yet. Olivia, Elle, and I had made that same toast when we reverse-seared our first steak, and even though it didn't play out as any of us expected, we did accomplish our goal.

Ricky glanced at Adrian and said, "And insert inside joke for us as well."

Adrian just grunted.

I couldn't help laughing as our glasses clinked.

Ricky took the first bite and groaned. "Un-fucking-believable."

Adrian was next, taking a bite and then smiling so wide his dimple appeared. "Delicious. Thank you."

It was funny how different the two of them were, with Adrian being reserved and Ricky wearing his heart on his sleeve (origin: medieval jousting where knights would wear a token from their lady on their armor's sleeve).

Adrian swallowed, then cleared his throat. "Speaking of the case, Elle reached out today. She found something. We should go visit."

"I knew our girl would come through," Olivia said, vocalizing exactly what I was thinking.

Like I said, we were doing our best to Febreze this shit.

After dinner, I couldn't help noticing that Adrian was the first to grab other people's plates. And when I picked up a few of the wineglasses and started to stand, he pulled my chair out for me.

Ever the gentleman—to everyone, but especially to me.

I looked up at him, my mouth curving into an enormous smile, unable to be contained, just like my emotions. Elle was right. It was all the little things. The way his eyes softened just for me, the way he was always aware of exactly where I was and what I was doing.

Suddenly, time slowed.

Shattering glass. Screeching tires. A scream.

My first thought was that the glasses in my hand had somehow broken, but the shattering sound was so loud, my brain quickly deduced it must have been something much bigger. The scream had come from Olivia, who was staring at the living room. But before I could discern what was happening, I felt arms wrap around me, knocking me to the ground.

This time, the shattering *was* the wineglasses.

Adrian had taken me to the floor and covered me with his body.

As I said, he was always aware of where I was.

"What's going—"

From the gap below Adrian's arm, I just managed to see Ricky leap over the couch into the living room.

Large plumes of smoke billowed into the air as an acrid smell assaulted my nose. I tensed, burying my head in Adrian's chest.

A second later, Ricky's movements stopped. His voice hollow, he declared, "It's out."

Adrian lifted himself off me, then inspected me from head to toe before joining Ricky to assess the aftermath.

The living room was filled with smoke, and standing above a broken beer bottle surrounded by charred cloth and leftover liquid was Ricky. The floor around him was also covered in shattered glass from the bay window.

"You're bleeding," Adrian said to Ricky, running over to help.

Ricky must have put the Molotov cocktail out by stomping on it, but he wasn't wearing shoes.

"Shit," Olivia mumbled as she ran over. I followed.

We bandaged Ricky's foot in silence, with Adrian periodically glancing out the broken window.

As soon as we finished, Adrian stated, "We have to move. We can't stay here anymore."

Olivia and I nodded, hurrying to pack up the belongings we'd flung around Adrian's place in the time we'd been here.

Somehow all of my stuff had fit into my bag earlier, but now, in my haste, I couldn't get it all back in. Maybe my shaking hands were also a problem.

As I tried to pack everything in tighter, I pushed too hard and the bag fell off the chair, spilling its contents onto the floor.

The threatening notes that I'd saved as evidence landed on top, as if telling me my time was running out.

Stop investigating or else

This is your last warning
Stop investigating

As I hastily picked everything up, I saw it.

"My gods," I said for the first time ever.

"Kat, what is it?" Adrian asked from across the room, aware of me from any distance.

I waved him over. He had to see it for himself.

Adrian, Olivia, and Ricky all hurried over.

"Look," I whispered.

I first showed them the threatening notes on the cream cardstock.

Then, I pointed to a third note six inches away that had also fallen out.

Please, Kat. I'm innocent. I know you know that in your gut. Please help me.

It was the note that Mandy had slipped into my purse at the Magic Lounge. And the handwriting was an exact match.

Olivia's eyes were as wide as mine. "That little ratings-hungry lying piece of shit."

Kathryn's Tenth Law of Life, a.k.a. Occam and Hu's Razor: Sometimes the simplest answers in life are correct.

CHAPTER 44

"We have to end this," Ricky said, waving away some of the residual smoke in the air. The rest of us had gathered our things and made our way to the front door.

"Agreed," Adrian said, his eyes smoldering with resolve. "We need to get you two somewhere safe," he said to Olivia and me before turning back to Ricky. "Then we take Mandy in."

We were right to be wary and ignore Mandy until we solved this (we'd rejected and ignored countless calls and texts). And Elle was right that Mandy was dangerous and couldn't be trusted.

"You have to be careful," I said, the worry clogging my throat. "Mandy's a wild card. We don't know what she's capable of—"

"Clearly," Olivia interjected, and then we went on to finish each other's sentences.

"She's irrational."

"Unpredictable."

"Frightening."

"A human piece of shit."

Adrian opened the front door.

"Well, this human piece of shit has a bone to pick with y'all," Mandy Thorne said from Adrian's front stoop with one hand on her hip and the other poised to knock. (Bone to pick origin: dog picking at a bone to get every last bit of meat.)

We were fucked, weren't we?

Even though I didn't believe in luck anymore, sometimes my previous hypotheses were still apt. And when it rains, it pours shit and beta-mercaptoethanol straight into the fan.

CHAPTER 45

Mandy peered past us into the living room, sniffing. "Some sort of ritual happening in here? Burning ole Tucker's things to cleanse the juju for the next relationship? You're gonna need a bigger fire than that."

"Are you joking?" Olivia said, incredulous.

Ricky grabbed his handcuffs. "Mandy Thorne, you have the right to remain silent."

"What the shit?" Mandy threw her arms in the air but took a step back.

"Did you do this?" I asked, pointing first to the remnants of the Molotov cocktail, then to the broken window it had come through. "Because we know you did *this.*" I thrust the threatening notes at her.

"What—Why is Jocelyn telling you to stop investigating?"

"Jocelyn?" I repeated, and then it all clicked. It *was* the same handwriting, but it wasn't Mandy's—it was *Jocelyn's.*

"Yeah," Mandy said. "She does everything for me."

She had implied as such in her latest podcast episode—*Seriously, y'all, without Jocelyn, I'd forget my head!*—but I wasn't going to just take her word for it.

"Prove it," I said, handing her a pen while trying not to be offended that she couldn't even be bothered to write her own note asking me for help.

Mandy quickly scribbled the same words out, and while the handwriting on the threats was small and neat, Mandy's was large and swirly.

"Look," she said, pulling out her driver's license and pointing to her signature. While a signature was obviously different than normal handwriting, it did have the same long loopy curls. "I couldn't write that neat if my life depended on it. That's why Jocelyn does it for me. That, and, well, what's the point of paying for an assistant if you don't give her stuff to do? And I pay her handsomely, let me tell you—better than she deserves. And still she claimed she had something more important to do tonight than to come here with me."

"Why *are* you here?" Olivia asked just as I said, "*How* are you here?" I wasn't sure how she'd found Adrian's address.

Mandy's hand flew to her hip. "That's all you can say after not speaking to me for gods know how long? You're the ones who made me *need* to find you."

"What does that mean—" I started to say.

Olivia's hand flew to her mouth. "Oh my god, you didn't."

And with her reaction, I put it together too. "How have you been tracking us, Mandy?"

Her eyes darted outside to where Olivia's Lexus was ensconced under a car cover.

"You should be thanking me for doing that!" Mandy argued. "Well, technically Jocelyn did it, but—"

"Goddamnit, Mandy!" I exclaimed as Olivia ran out to search her car.

As Olivia ripped the tracking device off the bottom of the vehicle and crushed it to pieces, Mandy kept running her mouth. "You're the ones who haven't been calling me back, and I have a new idea! If y'all come on my podcast, I think we can flush out the killer—"

"No flushing needed—*you're* the reason the killer has been able to find us!" I yelled at Mandy.

"What are you talking about?"

Adrian jumped in, taking control. "Where's Jocelyn right now?"

"At her place, why? She was the one who told me to come find you now to tell you about the podcast idea."

Olivia and I shared a look while Ricky and Adrian did the same.

"We need to pay her a visit," Adrian said, gesturing for Mandy and the rest of us to follow him to his car.

"Why? What does Jocelyn have to do with all this? Wait. You don't think she . . ." Her eyes traveled over each of our faces in succession. "She didn't. She couldn't. Trust me. I know her." She paused. "Oh my gods, what if she did it, and she did it *for* me? No. No. I mean, just, no."

That's what I would've said about Elle once upon a time. And Mandy didn't seem completely sure of her own words since she suddenly started sprinting toward the car.

Once we all crammed in, Adrian turned on the hidden siren he rarely used and floored it. Off we sped to chase down yet another potential murderer.

Kathryn's Eleventh Law of Life: Anyone could be a killer.

CHAPTER 46

The car was silent on the ride over to Jocelyn's, which showed just how nervous we all were.

I did briefly wonder whether Mandy and Jocelyn were working together to set a trap for us, but I took comfort in the fact that Mandy hadn't tried to contact Jocelyn since she joined us. Also, Adrian had alerted the department, and backup was on the way.

Plus, I always had my Life Alert.

Once we arrived at Jocelyn's, Adrian and Ricky did a quick perimeter check while Mandy knocked on the front door. When no one answered, she stuck her key in.

"Joce?" Mandy called out as she entered. Since the living room/kitchen was empty, she turned and went straight to the bedroom.

Adrian followed behind her, after which Olivia and I tiptoed inside. Ricky stayed outside in case Jocelyn tried to run for it.

The place was disorderly. Reminiscent of the state of Tucker and Lauren's place when Olivia and I had broken in. Cabinets and drawers were open and clothes strewn about, the latter of which especially stood out because the living room was sparsely furnished, with just a worn-down camel-colored couch sitting at an odd angle and an old cardboard box doubling as a coffee table.

I made my way over to the askew couch. A crumpled sweatshirt was sticking out from behind it, and I pushed the curtain aside to find that the sweatshirt was spilling out of an open, half-full, haphazardly packed suitcase.

"I think she already made a run for it," I said to Olivia.

She must have been packing, then realized she'd run out of time and left without her things. How had she known we were coming?

Was Mandy in on it? Had she found a way to warn Jocelyn?

"Maybe there's a clue in here," Olivia said, grabbing one side of the suitcase and trying to pull it out. But the other half was wedged tightly behind the old, hulking couch, and it wasn't budging.

Olivia grabbed an armrest and tried to move the couch out of the way first, but she only managed to slide it a millimeter.

Immediately I heard my mom in my head saying, *You cannot move couch because you not have man to do for you. I send furniture sliders.*

Determined to prove her wrong, I joined Olivia, and together, we heaved.

And then I screamed.

CHAPTER 47

"Jocelyn's not here—" Mandy said as she came out of the bedroom, but she stopped because of the screaming.

The bloodcurdling, hair-raising screams coming out of my mouth, then Olivia's.

And a second later, Mandy's.

Adrian's weapon was already out as he checked the rest of the living room, and a second later, Ricky joined him. After confirming that no one was hiding behind any other furniture or in any closets, Adrian called his team. Then he and Ricky joined us.

Face up, her eyes perpetually open, was Jocelyn. Her time indeed had run out, but not in the way I'd initially thought.

While Mandy continued screaming and Olivia and I stood shocked and frozen, Adrian swept forward and placed two gloved fingers on Jocelyn's neck. I was ashamed I hadn't gotten myself together to do it first, but that was also the least of my worries now.

Looking up, Adrian shook his head subtly at Ricky. With this confirmation, Mandy jolted forward.

I knew that instinct. I knew that pain.

I also knew there could be an ulterior motive to get your fingerprints on the body.

Mandy had sprung forward with such intensity that no one

could catch her. But instead of performing CPR—which had been my instinct—she just flopped onto the body, almost as if she was trying to keep Jocelyn alive by merging their cells together.

Adrian and Ricky hastily grabbed an arm each. Mandy flailed, shaking them off. When they regained their grip and got her to her feet, she went limp, her legs buckling.

Sirens wailed outside. Mandy wailed with them in disharmony, discordant nails on the chalkboard.

I wanted to comfort her or shove my hands over my ears or run away, but I couldn't seem to make any of my muscles fire.

As the boys managed to pull Mandy away from the body, her screams turned into sobs.

"Joce—Jocelyn—please—no—"

I couldn't tell if Mandy was begging Adrian and Ricky not to pull her away or imploring the universe to give Jocelyn back. Either way, my hands finally found their way to my ears, paradoxically to protect my heart.

Wordlessly, Adrian and Ricky guided us outside and into the back seat of Adrian's car, with me in the middle. Moments later, a squad car arrived. Then another. And another. Ricky stayed with us, standing guard, while Adrian went back in with other officers to process the scene.

Mandy's wails returned and split my heart in two. But instead of covering my ears this time, I grasped her hand in mine.

Olivia leaned on my shoulder, and I rested my head against the top of hers—supporting each other, as always.

How had this happened *again*?

And if Jocelyn wasn't the murderer, who was?

CHAPTER 48

"None of this makes sense," Mandy said between moans. The boys had joined us in the car and we were now on the road. "She can't be gone. She can't. I never got to tell her . . . I just didn't know how . . ."

"What is it?" I asked. "What didn't you tell Jocelyn?"

"Why did she tell you to stop investigating?" Mandy asked, ignoring my question. "Why would she keep something like that from me?"

Maybe because you were also keeping things from her, I didn't say.

Mandy began moaning again. "This can't be happening. This is all wrong."

She was right—something was wrong, but I couldn't quite put my finger on what. Even though this felt like a fairly standard reaction to finding out your assistant had just died, it felt out of character for Mandy, especially given how she'd treated Jocelyn in our presence, either yelling about her incompetence or acting like she wasn't even there. And given how Mandy treated her, Jocelyn's previous words to me also didn't make sense. *I owe everything to Mandy,* she had said.

And then I remembered the rest of what she'd said—she was from Mandy's hometown. She was quite a bit younger.

Combining that with what Elle had told us about Mandy's background . . .

"She's your sister. Jocelyn's your sister," I blurted out. Adrian kept his eyes on the road but Ricky's and Olivia's heads whipped toward us.

Mandy looked at me, dejected. "Technically half sister. And now she's never going to know."

In some ways, this made even less sense—that Mandy would keep that information from Jocelyn, and that she would treat her *sister* the way she had. I mean, we were taken aback by the treatment when we thought Jocelyn was just Mandy's employee.

"Why didn't you tell Jocelyn you're related?" I asked.

She didn't respond. She couldn't, her hands grasping her skull as her jaw clenched shut.

"Mandy?" I said as gently as I could.

"Don't call me that!" she burst out, shocking both Olivia and me.

"Um . . ." I looked to Olivia for help, but she was as lost as I was.

"That's not even my name!" Mandy exclaimed. "Everything about me is made up!"

I mean, I wasn't totally surprised—Lassy McBush had unveiled lie after lie about Mandy, and Mandy herself had copped to shitting in the hut when we started this whole adventure. But her *name*?

"I'm Mandra Horn. All the kids called me Horny growing up. Worst last name in the whole fucking world. And Mandra sounds like a fucking plant. So once I left home, I told myself I'd never be bullied again. I was going to grow fucking thorns in place of the horns and never look back. I—*Mandy Thorne*—was going to become famous, a star, and I'd do whatever it took to get there. Hollywood calls me a bitch? Adopt a Southern accent to be sweet as peach pie. Can't make it as the sweet small-town girl? Become the villain and say what no one else is willing to. And look at me! I fucking did it! A frickin' plus

plus. I made it on my own, became independent, *survived*. But at what cost?"

She dropped her head into her hands. "I wasn't even myself with my own sister! I was too scared to tell her. To show her who I was. Because how could I when I didn't even know who I had become? What if Jocelyn hated me? Of course she would hate me. And then what if she left? Family isn't supposed to leave, but they still do. My father, and then, in a different way, my mother. She was never there, not fully. So when Jocelyn showed up at my doorstep, not knowing we were related but telling me she was from the same place and was trying to follow in my footsteps, I gave her a job to keep her close. I thought if we got to know each other, it would help. And it would make it less likely for her to leave after I told her she was my sister. Then . . . too much time had passed, and I didn't know how to tell her. She hardly ever talked about her adoptive parents or her past, so I got scared that it was bad, and that she resented her birth mother and anyone related to her." She sighed. "I didn't tell her. I couldn't. And now it's too late."

As delicately as I could, I asked, "Are you sure Jocelyn didn't know the truth?"

"Of course not! She would have said something!"

I pressed my lips together to keep from saying, *You didn't.* Instead I asked, "Did you have documents or proof of your relation lying around?"

"Just a letter from my aunt, but I kept that in my safe. So essentially, no."

But it was possible that Jocelyn had seen it at some point and learned the truth. Though was it too much of a coincidence that she happened to show up at her half sister's door? No, it made more sense that she sought Mandy out already knowing about their connection. And if she knew, maybe she resented Mandy for much more than what Mandy had been worried about. Maybe she resented her for making her an assistant and treating her like crap—and then she lied to us, saying she owed everything to Mandy to throw us off the trail.

"Why?" Mandy exclaimed suddenly, so loud that everyone in the car jumped. "Why her? I should've been there. Oh gods. What if the killer went after her *because* of me? What if she was trying to solve the case and the killer realized? Holy shit. What if she solved it and that's why she had to be taken out?"

That certainly was a possibility.

Mandy let out a deep guttural moan, and I glanced at Olivia.

Olivia sighed—an exhausted-to-her-bones sigh that I felt myself. But if Olivia wasn't going to do it, I had to.

"Mandy . . . we know how you feel. The conflicting emotions, the grief, the guilt—we're here, okay?" I couldn't quite bring myself to say *whatever you need* in case she asked us to respond to her OnlyFans messages, but I did reach out and pat her hand.

"I . . ." Mandy wiped her eyes. "I need to know who did this. Why. What happened. Everything."

I nodded. I knew that feeling, too. I wasn't driven to solve Tucker's murder just because I was under suspicion for it. Which, I realized in the moment, wasn't all that different from Mandy's current situation.

I leaned forward through the gap in the front seats toward Adrian. "I have an idea for our next step."

We had to figure out what happened to Jocelyn.

CHAPTER 49

"No! Absolutely not."

We were still in the car and I had just told Mandy about a possible lifeline, but she was, of course, making this as difficult as possible.

"What's the problem?" Olivia said. "You have nothing to lose."

"Uh, my dignity? My self-worth?"

Olivia sighed. "Those are the same things. And let's be real, how much dignity and self-worth do you have to begin with?"

Mandy glared daggers at Olivia. "The answer is no."

Olivia turned to me. "She doesn't have to come, you know."

"Actually, it'd be better if she doesn't," I said, realizing Olivia was right.

"No!" Mandy yelled, suddenly desperate. "I . . . I want to be there."

As Adrian made a U-turn, Olivia sighed. "Fine. But when we get there, you're going to have to get on your hands and knees and beg."

"What?!"

• • • •

"Well, well, well, what have we here?" Elle said with a wicked grin on her face. It was the happiest I'd seen her in a while.

I'd remembered in the car that Elle had reached out to Adrian about new information before everything had gone to shit with the Molotov cocktail and finding Jocelyn's body.

"Hi, Kitty Kat. Double-Oh. Tall Tree." Elle raised an eyebrow at Ricky across the visitation room. "New Candy." Then she turned her gleaming eyes on Mandy. "Steaming pile of horse shit."

I had been thinking *mortal enemy*, but Elle's description was certainly more . . . colorful.

"We all—w'all? What do you think, Mandy? New term for you? W'all have a lot to discuss, don't we?"

"Yes," Mandy said. "You said you had something that would help—"

"Ah-ah-ah," Elle interrupted. "First things first. That's a funny phrase, isn't it?" She glanced at me. "Thoughts, Kitty Kat?"

I couldn't help a grin. "Agreed, pretty redundant phrase. Might have origins in AA."

Ricky looked confused, Mandy looked annoyed, Adrian looked at me as if he thought this particular trait was adorable, and Olivia was beaming as she always did when the Ex-Girlfriend Murder Club talked idioms.

Elle's grin briefly shifted to wistful before curving back into wicked. "So. First things first. Come on, I don't have all day here."

Everyone turned toward Mandy. She swallowed, then said, "Uh, hi, Lassy—Lauren. Or Elle? Um, hi—"

"That's not what I meant," Elle interrupted, waving her hand toward Mandy's body.

"Are you serious?"

"As serious as a prison stabbing." Elle's eyes were as dark as her tone. "Do it."

Mandy stood and dropped to one knee. As soon as her knee

contacted the floor, Elle laughed. "I can't believe you did it! Do you know how dirty that floor is? I was just kidding. Get up."

"You—why—"

But Elle interrupted again. "To even start this conversation, I'm going to need something from you."

"Actually, I can help you! I have connections—" Mandy started.

I glanced at Olivia, wondering if Mandy was going to mention the governor, but before she could get into details, Elle said, "That's not what I want."

"Then what—"

"Tell me a secret." Elle leaned forward. "I want to know something so juicy, so worthy of Mandy Thorne and her Thornies, that I have no choice but to trust you after."

Mandy opened her mouth. Then stalled.

I waited, wondering if Mandy was going to admit to shitting in the hut again. We had already told Elle about that (and she had eaten that, uh, *information* right up).

But that wasn't what Mandy had in mind. She was thinking about a secret more befitting this audience.

"I . . . may not have hated Lassy McBush as much as I let on. I hate *you*," Mandy clarified, spitting the word at her. "And I hate the things you said and how you said them, but Lassy McBush's existence? Brought me a helluva lot of listeners. And at the end of the day—or season, in this case—that's all that matters."

"No press is bad press, right?" Elle said, repeating the words she'd said to Olivia and me right before she told us about her book deal. "Now, that's the girl from Idaho I know. The one who would do anything for more publicity. *Anything* . . . yes?"

"I didn't kill him."

"Just saying. This certainly has gotten you a massive amount of publicity, especially after your special little episode there—

I'm sure you didn't check with McTree about that one beforehand, now did you?"

"Making sure to stay up to date on your favorite podcast, even in the slammer, Lassy?"

"Nothing's more important to me than my girls, and the fact that I am staying up to date despite my *limitations*? Should be a reminder not to underestimate me. *Again*." Elle held Mandy's gaze until she looked away. Threat accomplished, Elle said, "Okay, I'm ready. Go ahead."

Through gritted teeth, Mandy forced out, "Can. You. Please. Help. Us?"

"Of course! You didn't even need to ask! What can I do for you?"

Mandy looked to me, exasperated, but I was already jumping in. "You said you found something related to the case?"

"I did. But we might want some privacy for this part," Elle said, glancing at Mandy.

"No fucking way! I already got on my hands and knees! Just tell us! Now!"

Elle's eyes met mine, then Olivia's.

"It's up to you," I said, unable to make this decision for her since I didn't know what her information was.

Elle decided to tell us while pretending Mandy wasn't in the room. "I managed to find out the name of the child Mandy's mother gave up. It's Jocelyn Morningstar."

"Are you fucking kidding me?" Mandy burst out.

Elle rolled her eyes. "I told you, we should have done this in private—"

"We already knew that!" Mandy screeched. "What else do you have?"

Elle hesitated. "That was it. I thought that would be helpful."

"You're useless!" Mandy wailed. "I can't believe all that was for absolutely nothing!"

To my surprise, Elle looked crestfallen. Her voice was small as she said, "It wasn't easy to find that out."

"We didn't know that until recently, so that would've been really helpful, Elle," I said, leaving out that Mandy had actually known for a while and failed to loop us in. "Do you know anything else about Jocelyn or who might've wanted to hurt her?"

Elle's eyes flicked to Mandy, then back to me, a question in them. I nodded subtly. That seemed to soften her because she turned to Mandy and said, "No, but I'll keep digging. I'm sure something will turn up."

We were still the Mortal Enemy Murder Club, but everything was grayer. And now we had to save not only Elle, but also our own asses. This time, it was lasses *and* asses. And I wasn't sure how we were going to pull it off.

CHAPTER 50

"You said she would help," Mandy whined once we were back in the car.

"And I believe she will," I said, thinking about how Elle had managed to uncover Jocelyn's identity, even if it had been too late.

"In the meantime, Ms. Thorne," Adrian said from the driver's seat, "we need to put you in police custody. For safety."

I couldn't help wondering, *And maybe to get her out of our hair—both because she's as pleasant as a tornado and also because she could still potentially be involved?*

"No!" Mandy yelled, startling us from the sheer outburst. Also, shouldn't she have been happy to have guaranteed protection?

"Ms. Thorne," Adrian said cautiously. "You're in danger. Whoever came after Jocelyn is likely coming after you next. In fact, everyone in this car is in danger."

"Oh, shit," Olivia said.

I'd caught on to Adrian's meaning as well. "The Molotov cocktail was from the killer."

We had originally thought it was Jocelyn escalating, but she must have already been dead then. I might've connected those two dots sooner if I hadn't been so shaken up by Jocelyn's murder. (Obvious origin of connect-the-dots puzzles.)

Olivia turned and glowered at Mandy. "So you still probably led the killer to us." Thank god Olivia had smashed that tracker to pieces.

Mandy shook her head vehemently. "There's no way anyone else knew about that, I promise! There must be another way you were being tracked!"

The car fell silent, no one wanting to entertain that idea.

"Ms. Thorne," Adrian said, cutting into the tense silence, "you will be safest in protective custody. I will pick the officers myself."

"I don't trust anyone but y'all," Mandy said, shocking me even further. "No one but the people in this car."

Adrian glanced in the rearview mirror and met my eye.

This was going to be bad.

CHAPTER 51

"I can't believe what a dump this is," Mandy moaned for the two thousand and seventeenth time. "If my number one Only-Fans client knew how y'all were treating me—he's a Saudi *prince*, thank you very much—he'd have you on your asses, and that's not just related to his kink . . ."

It wasn't bad.

It was soul-suckingly awful.

Adrian and Ricky had taken Olivia, Mandy, and me to a sparsely decorated department safe house that, I had to admit, reminded me slightly of Adrian's place with its minimalist interior design. Our phones were off, replaced by temporary burners. Two officers were stationed outside. Adrian and Ricky had gone to the precinct, leaving Olivia and me to deal with Mandy, who switched between complaining about our lodgings to complaining about not being able to bring any of her belongings to complaining about how uncomfortable and unflattering my and Olivia's clothes were on her.

And as soon as the three of us started looking into the people who'd been at the Dish Gets Served meeting, Mandy began complaining about that, too.

"If a tree falls in the woods and no one hears it because they've fallen asleep from boredom, does anyone in this room give a flying fuck?"

"Do you want to solve this or not?" Olivia snapped.

Instead of pointing out that she should be grateful we were here trying to help her grouchy ass, I said, "Somebody in that café killed Eugene. And if we can identify some of these people and figure out their podcast episodes and backgrounds, maybe we can figure out why."

"Like, here," Olivia said, pointing to the notes in front of her. "I just found this online. That girl Penelope is apparently starting her own rival podcast all about vengeance."

"Vengeance? That's bullshit! She's so blatantly copying me!" Mandy exclaimed.

"I don't know," Olivia taunted. "Vengeance is a step up from revenge, don't you think? That sounds like a *better* podcast."

Mandy was about to pop, but all I could think about was how Purple Ombré Penelope seemed to get over finding Eugene's body real quick. And her new podcast was extra interesting in light of what we knew.

"Penelope's goal at the meeting had been to get *Dish Served Hot* canceled," I said. "But maybe she was pushing for that because she wanted to be the new *Dish Served Hot*, which makes so much more sense than her being that angry at Mandy just for making her miss the finale of *Murder in Copenhagen*—"

"She missed the finale of *Murder in Copenhagen*?" Mandy interrupted, appalled. "The poor thing! No wonder she's so pissed at me!"

"Anyway," I said. "Maybe after she was unsuccessful in the cancellation, she took it up a notch—from revenge to vengeance," I couldn't help adding. "Though it still doesn't seem to be a big enough motive for murder."

"Of course it is!" Mandy disagreed. "We're talking about podcasts and listeners and ratings. We have to take that bitch down! I swear to gods, if she actually makes that podcast, I'm gonna show *her* vengeance."

"Can we focus?" Olivia said.

Mandy seemed to pair with us as well as bleach and vinegar—that makes a gas, and not the funny kind. But at least we were finally getting her to take the research seriously.

"Let me see those," Mandy said, grabbing Olivia's and my notes. "Okay, I don't recognize a lot of these names"—no surprise there, not just because it was anonymous but because it was Mandy—"but some are jumping out."

"Who do you recognize?" I asked.

"Gia and Russ, mostly because they're faking their rivalry for followers," Mandy said as if we should all know this.

"The WOAT?" I asked, surprised. "The ghost pepper and Tabasco on the sex toys people?"

"How do you know they're faking?" Olivia asked.

"C'mon, Sherlock, it's so frickin' obvious!"

When Olivia and I didn't respond, waiting for Mandy to clarify, she said, "Oh, great. Why am I trusting you two to solve this? Look at the clues, duh." She pulled up Gia's and Russ's social media accounts. "Isn't the timing of everything just a little too perfect? And they're the only ones to have ever both come on my show. And why did he have a photo of the Fleshlight with Tabasco before he stuck his ding-dong in if he didn't know it was already on there? And also, I might've accused them of this in person and their reactions gave them away."

"Was Jocelyn there when this happened?" I asked.

"Yeah, in the background."

Potential motive for Gia and Russ there, wanting to keep the secret to their success and livelihood under wraps (origin: keeping a racehorse's speed hidden until the race).

"Why didn't you expose that on your podcast?" I asked.

"Because," Mandy said, still using her *duh* tone. "That's not a good story—*it was all fake*. It's much better if the fight appears real. People tune in for that shit."

Of course, it was always about the ratings.

"Honestly, I love Gia and Russ," Mandy said. "Peeps after my own heart. Taking shit and turning it into gold Rumpelstiltskin-style."

"And they're actually good actors unlike some people," Olivia mumbled.

If Mandy were a cartoon, steam would be coming out of her ears. "You know what else they're good at unlike *some* people? They know how to take shit without losing their shit! They had just as much reason to be pissed at me as you!"

"What does that mean?" Olivia asked. "Wait . . ."

My stomach sank. "Goddamnit, Mandy. You didn't."

"Of course she did! How did I not realize this sooner?" Olivia turned to Mandy. "You spliced their episode together, just like you did to us, didn't you? Because you're as shitty as the present you left for the other contestants in the Love Hut! And all so you could create a better story."

I should have realized just how far Mandy would go for ratings, but somehow I'd still given her more benefit of the doubt than she deserved. I had naively thought when our episode aired that she'd never edited an interview that way before, but of course she had. Of course we weren't the first.

"All I did in their episode was make their revenge a little *spicier*, and look what it did! I launched their influencer careers. They should be nothing but grateful." Mandy stuck her nose in the air. "I did what any other producer and host would do to create award-winning entertainment."

"No respectful producer and host," Olivia said. "Mandy, how many other people did you do this to?"

She shrugged. "I didn't keep a list."

I couldn't get over just how despicable she was. "How could you do that to people who came on your show, who trusted you with their stories, who had just gone through terrible things—"

"I didn't think about it, okay? I was doing whatever I could to make it! I told myself I was leaving Mandra Horn behind and Mandy Thorne would never live in her car again. Stop making me think about them as human!"

So *Dish Served Hot* and Mandy Thorne were somehow even worse than we'd realized.

Olivia shook her head in disbelief. "That means the Dish Gets Served people had *even more* reason to be pissed at you."

"And it wasn't just victims of revenge, but guests, too," I added, thinking about how we didn't have enough paper to list all the potential suspects.

"Did Jocelyn know about all this?" Olivia asked.

"Of course—she was the one doing the splicing. You think I edit my own podcasts?"

That made me angry until I remembered Jocelyn's fate.

"Is that public knowledge?" I asked. Meaning, could a guest have known this and gone after Jocelyn for revenge?

"I mean . . . not many people knew about Jocelyn. She contacted podcast peeps using my name and accounts, and she was in the background otherwise."

"You need to tell us all of it," Olivia demanded. "Every last detail."

"No more secrets, Mandy—not if you want us to solve this."

"Um, I get it, y'all, I really do, but . . ."

There was always something with her. "But what, Mandy?"

"Jocelyn kept track of everything, okay? I only remember Gia and Russ, and one other one."

"Tell us. Now," Olivia ordered.

"There was this gal who worked in cybersecurity, and her revenge involved doing some shit or other to the guy's phone. So, I mean, the story practically wrote itself. I just had to . . . you know . . . *embellish*."

"Did you say she used work resources to break into his phone when you don't know if she did?" I asked.

"For the record, I didn't want to do that—I was scared of retribution, and I have a lot of . . . personal things to keep personal." I did not want to know how many nude OnlyFans photos Mandy had on her devices. "That's why I remember it so vividly. But Jocelyn convinced me it'd be fine. But the gal might've gotten in trouble after. Though she didn't get retribution on me."

"Not that you know of," I pointed out. Maybe all of this was her retribution—served cold, as it was meant to be.

"What else do you remember about the episode?" Olivia asked.

"I don't know, something about sexting the wrong people and being mad about him asking for an open relationship? Which, I mean, just between us—don't tell any Thornies—I sort of get his side. Like, doesn't he get any credit for trying to communicate?"

There was no time to address Mandy's ridiculousness or hypocrisy. Because with the comment about the open relationship, Olivia's face had snapped to mine.

"We know exactly who they are," I said. "And they were at the café."

Dish Served Hot Podcast Transcript–Episode 73

[Podcast theme song plays, sung by creator, host, and star Mandy Thorne]

MANDY THORNE: Hiya, my lovely Thornies! Welcome to another extra juicy revenge episode of *Dish Served Hot*! And *whoo* you are going to be so happy you tuned in for this one! What happens when you wrong a cybersecurity specialist? You'll wish you'd been dating a technophobe instead—yeah, I actually said that.

Please join me in welcoming Ms. Robot. Thank you for being here with me today.

MS. ROBOT: Hi, Mandy! Hi, everyone! I'm so excited to be here! And Ms. Robot—love the reference, but I'm not a hacker.

MANDY: Po-tay-toh, po-tah-toe. So, Ms. Robot, tell my darling listeners what you already told me in your initial email.

MS. ROBOT: So, my genius of an ex decided to learn about relationships through a reality dating show. A fantastic one, sure, but *Love Island* is not known for creating healthy, long-lasting relationships. I mean, we watch it for the drama!

MANDY: Duh.

MS. ROBOT: Just like *Dish Served Hot*! I mean, if every guest came on here and was like, "I had a great relationship with this person and we ended it amicably and I returned all their stuff like a calm, reasonable person," who would listen?

MANDY: Exactly. And we're doing gods' work here—seeking justice, making the world a better place.

[beat]

MANDY: Do you not agree? Why else would you have wanted to come on the show?

MS. ROBOT: I mean, you're right; I wanted to stick it to my ex. But I go back and forth. Is it justice? Is it petty?

MANDY: Why not both? Now, tell us what your relationship with him was like, and what went so terribly wrong.

MS. ROBOT: It started out good. I mean, if it hadn't been, it wouldn't have progressed, right? We met at a coffee shop—we both reached for the last free outlet. I thought it was a real meet-cute, you know? The perfect way for me, Ms. Robot, to meet someone. Anyway, we had fun times together; he asked good questions and took me on interesting dates, like to a pottery class.

MANDY: Pottery? Like that scene from *Ghost*?

MS. ROBOT: [laugh] No, there were a ton of people there. But still, points for creativity, right?

MANDY: Rare these days, indeed.

MS. ROBOT: Especially in a tech-focused world. So things were going well and after a few months, we had the I'm-not-seeing-other-people-are-you talk, and we were on the same page. Or so I thought.

MANDY: Uh-oh . . .

MS. ROBOT: Just a few weeks later, he asks me for an open relationship. The funny part is, if he had just told me he wasn't ready to be exclusive when we had the talk, I would've been fine! But not only is the timing weird, he then launches into this whole spiel about how on *Love Island*, the girls say that the guys just have to be upfront. *If he had just told me he wanted to see other people, I would have been on board. It was the lying that was the problem.* Which, that was exactly *my* point! We'd just had this conversation, and he *hadn't* been upfront! But he presented the *Love Island* example as if it were proof that he was a stand-up, top-notch guy, and I should be so thankful that he told me he suddenly wants to sleep with other people.

Then, he opens his bedroom door. And there's another woman waiting in there. For *us*. "Surprise!" that motherfucker says. The open relationship really is for us, for *me*, a gift, because he quote, unquote, "picked up on my hints" and "could tell I wanted a threesome," and, shocker, he was happy to oblige.

MANDY: What a stand-up, top-notch guy.

MS. ROBOT: When I told him I wasn't interested, he was actually confused. Completely, stupidly shocked, emphasis on stupid. To this day, I don't know what signs he was talking about and whether or not we were having completely different conversations without knowing it.

MANDY: Did you try to ask?

MS. ROBOT: It was just easier to break up with him. Which I don't regret. I'm pretty sure he slept with that woman as soon as I was out of there. But once I left, breaking up with him just didn't feel like enough.

MANDY: Oh-ho-ho, here we go.

MS. ROBOT: I swapped the contacts in his phone.

MANDY: I'm sure he was weird about his phone. Did you use your cybersecurity skills and resources for this? To hack into the phone?

MS. ROBOT: Of course! What's the point of being an expert in something if you don't use it?

MANDY: That's my gal! What a badass. See? The Ms. Robot nickname *is* perfect. So what happened after that?

MS. ROBOT: All the new girls he was sexting? I chose two of them and swapped their numbers with his mom and stepmom.

MANDY: [gasp] No! You didn't!

MS. ROBOT: Of course I did. I just wish I could've seen his face after he sent dick pics to his mom and stepmom. Which he definitely did because I got like two a week from him.

MANDY: Okay, your ex gets the Dumbass Award, and you get the Genius Award. Way to scandalize those poor old ladies! How did you even think of that?

MS. ROBOT: He's always had such a weird relationship with his family, so it seemed fitting, you know? I didn't even know he had a stepmom until I looked through his phone.

MANDY: What if that wasn't his stepmom but another girl he was hiding from you?

MS. ROBOT: Mandy! Don't take away my satisfaction!

MANDY: Well, it's a good thing you swapped a girl with Mom, too. So you got him, no worries. Have you ever thought about looking him up now to find out how it all played out?

MS. ROBOT: Yes and no. I did briefly try right after it happened, but you know what they say about curiosity and the cat. When I couldn't find anything right away, I told myself to give it up. That asshole doesn't deserve another second of my time, you know?

MANDY: You said it! [pause] Would you like me to look into him further?

MS. ROBOT: No, no. I came on this show to share my story because you were such a vital part of it, Mandy, but I want to be done.

MANDY: Well, you finished it epically! What a great use of your expertise—and work resources—to stick it to him. Me and all the Thornies are proud of you! Good job, and fuck that guy! We hope he got a talking-to from his mom.

You learned it here first, Thornies! Being an asshole doesn't pay . . . [ominously] except in how we make you pay.

Byeeee!

CHAPTER 52

"Wyatt and Isla seemed so chill at the boba café, though," Olivia said after we listened to their podcast episode.

"Maybe she was chill because she already had a plan in motion," I suggested. "And cybersecurity specialist—that could explain how she knew where we were at each step."

Double-Oh-livia typed away for a few seconds at her laptop. "You know, Isla did say something that day at the café that didn't make sense at the time, but after knowing what Mandy did—"

"Technically Jocelyn," Mandy mumbled.

"It makes sense now. Isla said her firing was a misunderstanding, with the company not believing her when she claimed she didn't do what they accused her of—which we now know is using work resources to access Wyatt's phone and get revenge on him." Olivia pointed to her screen. "And according to her LinkedIn, she's been out of work since."

"So going on the show led to Eugene's exes *and* Isla losing their jobs," I said. There were a lot of parallels here. Coincidence? Certainly a strong motive at the very least.

"But why go after Eugene and frame Mandy for murder instead of going straight for Mandy?" Olivia asked.

"You'd prefer that, wouldn't you—me being murdered?" Mandy said.

"We're just trying to be objective," I said. Then I turned to Olivia. "You bring up a good point. It feels like we're running in circles." I thought for a moment, then suggested, "Why don't we go back to the threatening notes?"

"They were from Jocelyn, even if the Molotov cocktail wasn't," Olivia said. "Why would she want us to stop investigating?"

Mandy opened her mouth to say something, but I spoke over her, not wanting to be derailed from my train of thought. "When did the first note show up?"

"Right after Luz and Seraphina were brought down to the precinct," Olivia answered. "Which was why we first suspected it was one of them. Not sure how that connects back to Jocelyn."

I tried to think back chronologically through everything that had transpired leading up to the notes.

"You know what else happened around that time?" I turned to Mandy. "You turned over your texts and emails. Did that include—"

"Jocelyn! She's on my phone plan. So hers would've been turned over, too. I just told the phone company to give the police whatever they wanted."

Olivia and I looked at each other. And I immediately picked up my burner phone.

• • • •

"I was wondering when you'd call," Adrian said in lieu of hello.

"What do you mean?"

"We just finished going through Jocelyn's texts."

I beamed. He knew me better than I thought. "And?"

"And she was talking to Eugene. And to an unknown number, which we assume belongs to the killer, but we haven't been able to trace it yet. She and Eugene did set up a meeting at a nearby Starbucks, and we just got the footage from that day and time. And before you say it, yes, I'll bring the footage and copies of the messages back with me."

"This is lovely, not having to say a word," I joked. "I see why that's your usual preference."

He chuckled. "Ricky and I will be there soon. And we'll pick up food on the way." Thank god, because Mandy had also been complaining about how unjust it was that her stomach was empty even though Olivia's and mine were growling just as loudly. He finished with, "I'd tell you to get some sleep, but I know better than that. So I'll just say, be safe."

A smile filled my face as I hung up, but it promptly fell when a loud *thump* sounded outside our window. All the curtains were drawn so we couldn't see out, but I was grateful no one could see in either.

"Are the boys back?" Olivia asked.

"You know, I dated the Boystown Boys, also known as the *original* 'the boys,' so I get confused when you use that wording."

I didn't even have time to respond to Mandy's ridiculous comment because I was grabbing my Kubotan defense tool in one hand while passing the pepper spray to Olivia with the other.

"It's not Adrian and Ricky," I whispered.

"Is it the team that's outside?" Olivia asked.

"They have our burner numbers. And why would they go to the window?"

"Well, how did whoever this is get past them?"

I didn't have to say my answer out loud.

After firing off a Get back here NOW! text to Adrian, I crept toward the door, Kubotan raised.

"Oh gods oh gods oh gods," Mandy chanted until Olivia silenced her with a glare.

"We do not open the door under any circumstances," Olivia whispered, mostly to Mandy.

"Go for the eyes, nose, chest, or groin," I instructed, repeating Adrian's words from our first and subsequent self-defense lessons.

"What? I can't go for all of those," Mandy said in a panic. "Which one if I have to choose?"

"Groin," Olivia and I said at the same time. Our eyes met and I knew she was thinking of the time she kicked Ray in the balls thanks to our secret code. Balls in. The one time Tucker's favorite underwear brand helped anyone.

Time slowed. All I could hear were our shallow, panicked breaths. And all I could think was how the Molotov cocktail had been the killer's step *one.* And how they'd already found us once and would likely find us again.

A loud and frantic knock sounded at the door.

Olivia and I raised our weapons. Mandy swung her foot out in a practice kick to the groin.

The knocking stopped suddenly. Then . . .

"Eigh, Yushan! You inside? The app say you here! But why you not answer? Why the curtains shut? And why your phone off?"

"Oh crap," I muttered as I lowered the Kubotan.

It had been so freeing ignoring her calls, but that was coming back to bite me in the ass now. Hard. Who knew she would take this drastic step of *showing up*?

I reached out and opened the door as Mandy hissed, "I thought we weren't opening the door under any circumstance!"

The petite woman barely reaching five feet now standing in front of me had the ability to make me feel even smaller than she was.

"Mom! What are you doing here?"

"What am *I* doing here? Why you not answer my many calls? I worried sick!"

"I texted!"

"You know I not know how to text! I did not see!"

Olivia moved aside so I could hurry my mother indoors. But her stubborn ass was not budging.

"What is this place? Why you here? You kidnapped? I call police!"

"Mom, come in. This is a police safe house. We're under police protection."

Finally, she came in and we shut the door. "Those two men who ask me for ID are *police*? Why they dress like farmers?"

"You think farmers wear polo shirts and jeans?" I knew that wasn't the most important thing at the moment, but I couldn't help it.

"They faded and ripped!"

"They're undercover," Olivia explained kindly as I lost all patience and exclaimed, "Mom! Why are you here?"

She huffed. "That the thanks I get? For dropping everything to come here and save you? What trouble you in?"

Honestly, it never occurred to me that my mom would go to these lengths to help me. Find me a husband or get me a career in dermatology, sure—but not this.

I pulled her into a hug, shocking her.

Her body remained stiff and unyielding as she exclaimed, "I knew it! You in trouble!"

"I love you, too, Mom."

She stiffened further. "Yushan, you tell me now. What you do?"

"Nothing, Mom. Why do you always assume it's me that's the problem?"

"Where Glen Power? He protect you. Why he not here?"

Yes, the cutout of Glen Powell, which would have just ignited with the Molotov cocktail instead of shielding me like my real-life boyfriend had—but of course she didn't know about Adrian.

"Uh, hellooo?" Mandy broke in. "Are we all ignoring the obvious here?"

I wasn't sure what she was talking about until Olivia asked, "Mrs. Hu, how did you find us?"

"Ah, who are you?" my mother said, her face glowing as she gently touched a strand of Olivia's silky hair. "So pretty. Too pretty. You need Life Alert like my Yushan. Or better, Helicopter Mom. Not only is flashlight and alarm, but have GPS tracking. Even better than Life Alert because Life Alert, have to press button to activate GPS."

Shit. That was why she had taken the packaging off before sending me the Helicopter Mom—so I wouldn't know she'd been tracking me all this time. And even though this was royally messed up, my first thought now was, *Does she know I've been staying at Adrian's?* I tried to remind myself I wasn't in high school, but I already knew my fears weren't unfounded. If she knew I'd stayed overnight at my boyfriend's, that would be an even bigger deal than the fact that there was a killer after us.

"Mom, you have to turn the GPS off."

"No! Your baba using it to track right now, make sure you okay."

Suddenly, the front door banged open. Adrian entered first, gun drawn, followed by Ricky. Behind them, the undercover cops slash farmers raced toward us.

"It's fine! She's cleared!" they called from a distance.

Of course the first time my mother meets my secret boyfriend is him pulling a gun on her. Because this was my life now.

Adrian looked at my mom, then at me. Probably clocking how I have her eyes, nose, and ears. He stowed his gun quickly.

"Mrs. Hu, so lovely to meet you. Sorry about that." Without missing a beat, he said, "I'm Adrian, the police officer protecting your daughter and her friends. This is my partner, Ricky."

Every single head in the room turned to stare at him—mine included, just as my heart dropped to my stomach. All this time, he knew that I was keeping our relationship a secret from her? Was it the Glen Powell cutout? How I reacted when he asked me to meet his parents? Or had he heard when my mom called me "single" through the phone that one time? Whatever it was, I felt like the awful person I'd proven myself to be.

But there was no time for that right now.

"Mom, everything's fine, I promise. I'm sorry to have worried you. You didn't have to come all the way here."

Adrian's wheels were churning—I could tell by the furrow of his brow. His gaze traveled from my mom to the massive number of items dangling from the keychain attached to the Kubotan still in my hand. When his gaze finally landed on me, I gave a subtle nod to signal his hunch was right—something my mom gave me had been the reason she found us.

My mother, who had been watching us, looked Adrian up and down as she said, "You a police officer? What your SAT score? Your parents together or divorce?"

No, no, no. She'd put it together. At least Adrian would maybe understand now why I hadn't told her.

"Um . . ."

"Answer the questions," Mandy said with glee.

But my mom didn't care what the answers were because she turned to me and said, "You can't be with police officer! Too dangerous a job! That why you here, in safety house? Because of him? He also why you change to worse job? I take you home right now!"

"Mom, no. I changed jobs on my own, because it was the right decision." Though a part of me couldn't help asking, *Was it?* "He's saved me, multiple times. If anything, I'd be in so much trouble without him."

Her eyebrows rose. "Oh, because you making trouble? That

why you with him, to save your behind? That not how I raise you!"

I really wished there weren't so many people here witnessing this, especially Mandy, who had disappeared and reappeared with Twizzlers—which, also, WTF, she'd had those this whole time and hadn't shared?

"Yushan, you tell me what going on. Everything. *Right. Now.*"

Adrian cleared his throat. "Actually, our current priority is to turn off all GPS tracking, then move to a new location." Even though his words were authoritative, his tone was less so than usual—guess my tiny mom had the ability to make him feel smaller, too.

"It was this," I said, holding up the Helicopter Mom. And now, as I was looking at it in this new light, I noticed a toggle on the side. I switched it off to my mother's protests.

"Yushan, you leave that on!" Then she turned to Adrian. "And the priority is me—your mama not teach you anything?"

The jig was up, and in the worst way possible. My mother was never going to like Adrian now.

CHAPTER 53

I thought nothing could be worse than being stuck in a safe house with Mandy Thorne, but haha, you win, Life. Kathryn's Twelfth Law of Life: It can always be worse.

Since the safe house wasn't safe anymore, we were now crammed into two connected motel rooms that Adrian had paid for in cash. And this was worse than a sardine can because at least sardines have oil to wriggle around in and plenty of other sardines to choose from for company. But here, I was stuck with a whole bunch of ticking time bombs: Adrian, my mom, Olivia, Ricky, and *Mandy Thorne.*

"Ow!" I yelled as Mandy bumped my chair and sent my rib cage into the table. She was hurrying past me to perch on the bed near my mom.

"Okay, so," she said between handfuls of M&M's—that she was *not* sharing, by the way. "Mama Hu, you are just my new favorite person. Do you want to be on my podcast? Actually, no. I'll come up with a whole new one just for you, a complete rebrand. *Fierce Mama Bear.* No, *Mama Hu Knows Best.* No, *Mama Hu Finds Your Soulmate.*"

"Mandy," Olivia said. "Can you give us a little space, please?"

"Hey, I'm part of this, too!" she exclaimed, though she was on the bed and the rest of us were seated around a tiny table, having brought chairs in from the second room. "*I'm* the one that was framed."

"And you the one who pull my daughter into this. Put her in danger." My mother's voice was ominously low, and while it wasn't enough to shoo the pest away, it at least shut Mandy's giant annoying mouth.

Then my mother turned back to Adrian and me. "So how this happen?" she asked, gesturing broadly in our direction. "The *when* I know."

As usual, my plan had been to divert-divert-divert, but with her latter comment, I had to follow up. "What do you mean you know the when? How?"

"When you learn, Yushan? You really think I not know? You begin act strange to my packages."

"Um . . ." To be fair, wouldn't anyone react weirdly to packages of Glen Powell cutouts and self-Heimlich machines?

"Why you think I send more and more package this year? I push you, try to make you tell me."

"You've always sent that many," I said, but even as the words came out, I started realizing that my mother's gifts had grown more frequent and more ridiculous lately. But I'd just assumed it was my mom being my mom.

"So?" she pushed. "Tell me."

I was not letting her derail this. "Mom, we're trying to talk to you about something serious. We're in danger. You really need to go back home. We're actually on a case here, look." I pulled out our folder of notes.

The page with my summary of Isla's podcast episode was sticking out, and my mother grabbed it before I could swerve out of the way.

"What is . . . dick pic?"

"A picture of a guy named Dick," I said as Mandy said, "A picture of a guy's junk."

"A guy named Dick's junk?" my mother said. "Like food wrappers? Empty bottles? Candy?"

"Sure, Mom."

"Aiyah, what a mean thing to do, to send to his mama. I sure she so angry to see he not clean up his trash."

A shocked Mandy turned to my mother to clear up the misunderstanding, but Olivia spoke first. "What's this?"

She picked up the piece of paper on top of the folder, which was the printout of messages Adrian had promised.

Seeing the names on top, Mandy wrenched it from her. "Yes, what the fuck is this?"

"Texts from Jocelyn to Eugene and, we presume, the killer," Adrian said in that even tone of his.

"How you be so—what the word? No heart," my mom said.

"Heartless," Olivia supplied at the same time I said, "Callous?"

Adrian turned and lifted a scarred eyebrow at me. *Sorry*, I mouthed. I didn't actually think he was callous; I was just trying to fill in the blank for my mom. It was second nature.

"He's a detective, Mom. He can't do his job if he's . . ." But I trailed off. I refused to agree with Gerard here. "There are just times you have to be separated from it, okay?" *But not always.*

I took the sheet from Mandy to read the text messages.

First, between Jocelyn and Eugene:

<Eugene>

Thanks for responding

What'd you have in mind?

<Jocelyn>

Something she won't forget

Something she'll have to respect

I think we can manage that

We need to meet in person

Next Monday, 5pm, at the Starbucks at the pin below

Then, the messages between Jocelyn and presumably the killer:

<Unknown>
I know you have it.

<Jocelyn>
And I know what you've done

Hand it over before I make you.

Over my dead body

Jocelyn's last text sent a shiver down my spine.

"What do you think Jocelyn had that the killer wanted?" Olivia asked.

"We're still trying to figure that out," Ricky answered.

The texts between Jocelyn and Eugene made it sound like they were planning some kind of revenge on Mandy, but I couldn't say that out loud without sending Mandy into a spiral.

"You said you had the footage from Jocelyn and Eugene's meeting?" I asked instead.

Adrian nodded, then pulled it up on his department laptop.

The meeting itself began calm and amicable, but pretty quickly, Jocelyn grew uncomfortable, shifting in her seat. Then she began leaning away from Eugene just like all the Dish Gets Served people had in the boba café. Unfortunately, we didn't have audio, but it was clear that Jocelyn was scared and Eugene was growing increasingly irate, the anger radiating off his jerky movements.

And then—I gasped. Adrian paused the video.

"What? What is it?" Mandy was frantic.

"Go back," I said. "Right there."

Jocelyn had said something that caused Eugene to bang his fist on the table so hard that Jocelyn's drink toppled into her lap. And as soon as Jocelyn was distracted cleaning herself up, Eugene reached down and slipped his hand into her purse.

"The missing keys!" Olivia exclaimed.

I nodded. "Exactly."

"Why did Eugene want them?" Olivia asked.

"That's probably how he got the knife," I said. "And how he got that same knife back into her house, newly covered in blood, to threaten her. And I guess he could've been the one who planted the ethylene glycol, too"—*if* it was planted—"since that had been in his possession at some point."

And this implied that Jocelyn wasn't in on whatever revenge Eugene had planned, so they must have been talking about something else in their meeting and text messages.

"Why was Jocelyn meeting with someone who hated me?" Mandy lamented.

But she was drowned out by my mother saying, "See, Yushan? This is why I say the new job is no good. Knife, ethylenie glycoo, *killer*—you not need to invite these into your life. Have I not done enough? Provide enough? I sleep in your room at foot of bed until you thirteen because study say it help."

That . . . was a memory I'd chosen to block. "Mom, I heard you, okay? I'll think about the risks of the new job. But we're already in this, and like you said, it's dangerous, so, you can't stay here. Time to go."

"Aiyah, you need me! Who will protect you? Only I care enough to sleep at your feet and warm your lotion when you a baby. And yes, is dangerous, but I not worry. Because you will figure out. You always do. Ever since you little, you make lists of this and that, put everything together in your head—I so proud! Thought, she can do anything she want! Will be dermatologist, for sure!"

How could she be both so encouraging and demeaning at the same time? That was her superpower, and no one could match her doing it.

My mom tapped on the next page in the folder, her index finger landing on my notes about the *A-S* and the crime scene. "See? You already making lists! And you always able to see things different, not like the other kids. Recess time? They see time to play games, you *make* games. Remember Kangaroo Tag, where you tell other kids to jump around? So creative! And a leader! Maybe president, I thought then, but now I know better."

I flushed, hoping Adrian and Olivia wouldn't ask me for more details later. (Teams of two would hop around in a potato sack and, of course, nobody wanted to be in my sack.)

"They show you those inky blots—psychology or whatnot—other kids see butterfly, dog, two faces; you see beakers, chemical spill, two frogs. Same when you learn Chinese. I show you character for fire—everyone else see dancing flame, you see person making fire with two stick."

"Oh my god," I suddenly blurted.

"Yes, see, I write for everyone," my mother said, grabbing a pen and writing 火 in the margin of my notes so they could decide what the Mandarin character for *fire* looked like to them.

"No, no," I said, frantic, as I snatched my notes back from her.

"Now, is clever that the middle part of the *fire* character is actually Mandarin word for *person*, so even more genius she think the character show person holding two stick. And my Yushan think of that at age seven! Can you believe?"

"Mom! Just . . . one second."

I expected her to say something like, *I brag about you and you tell me to stop? So ungrateful!* But she must have realized what was going on, because she stopped talking and leaned forward, anticipating.

And she was right to. Because hearing her words and seeing her point to my notes, something clicked.

"The *A-S*," I said slowly, still fitting the final pieces together. "What if they aren't letters?"

Adrian grabbed the folder of evidence and pulled out the crime scene photo of what Eugene had written on the floor.

It had been written painstakingly, with the last of Eugene's energy. "Yes, it looks like *A-S*," I said, "but it could also be—"

"Forty-five," Olivia finished breathlessly.

"And . . ." I flipped through my notes, then pointed to where my research on *Dish Served Hot* was neatly organized. "The easiest way for us to keep track of the podcast episodes was by episode number."

Olivia's eyes widened. "We need to look at episode forty-five."

I nodded. "Maybe Eugene wasn't writing a name because he didn't know it. Just like how we haven't been able to track that many people down. But maybe he knew enough about the person to have tracked down their episode." Just like we'd done with several suspects.

I looked over at Adrian and saw he was smiling at me like he was simultaneously proud and not surprised. In some ways, it was similar to how Tucker used to tell me my brain was hot, but also completely different. Because this wasn't about attraction or lust, but about respect and admiration.

"See? I tell you," my mother said, unimpressed. "Yushan

solve just like I say. What a waste of PhD—instead of Harvard professor, she here looking at scribbles of dead man."

Again, the queen of pumping me up just to pull me back down.

I glanced at Olivia, who was beaming at me.

"You were right about the letters—well, numbers—being vital." She gave me a small fist bump. "My partner in crime, forever."

I wanted to respond with *Ex-Girlfriend Murder Club forever*, but I couldn't, not with my mother here. She would hear *murder club* and jump down my throat. And not to mention, I'd like to keep the whole dating-the-same-man-at-the-same-time thing under wraps.

"I still confuse, though," my mother said. "What this forty-five business?"

Mandy stood. "Please allow me."

I had thought the Ex-Girlfriend Murder Club had been an unlikely trio, but this was the ultimate ragtag team. Somehow, though, it was working.

Kathryn's Third Law of Life, now proven: Well, shit, life does sometimes have a sense of humor.

Dish Served Hot Podcast Transcript–Episode 45

[Podcast theme song plays, sung by creator, host, and star Mandy Thorne]

MANDY THORNE: Get ready, Thornies, because today's episode is OFF THE WALL. I mean, I will never forget this one, for as long as I live, because it is just . . . Well, you'll see. Y'all will see.

So without further ado-do, please welcome my guest for today, Fiona—so named because she transformed her ogre of a situation into a royal dream!

FIONA: Hiya, Mandy! As I told you in my email, I am just so chuffed to be here today! You are such an inspiration to me—my absolute hero—and I owe everything in my life to you.

MANDY: Well, isn't that a nice way to get this started? Happy to help, Fiona, always. My Thornies are everything to me. Everything.

So tell me what happened. What horrible event made you need me?

FIONA: [disgusted noise] I almost don't want to talk about it even though it all ended so well for me.

MANDY: I support you, Fiona. We all do. We're on your side.

FIONA: Well, my ne'er-do-well boyfriend at the time had been just-enough-do-well that I thought we had something real. I mean, it was serious. I was all in—living together, dreaming about a ring. We had a dog together, for Christ's sake.

MANDY: Well, something must've made you like him. Nothing to be ashamed of.

FIONA: I mean, he was passionate? But maybe too passionate. And smart, though he didn't apply it to the important things. Not that anything was ever his fault—he didn't get the promotion because they were too dumb to see his potential, and he couldn't have done anything wrong when they were the ones who didn't make it clear what they wanted . . . Ew. Saying all that aloud, I should've seen the signs sooner. What was I thinking?

MANDY: Well, clearly whatever happened next was enough to make you look at him in a different light. So what happened? What did he do?

FIONA: [sigh] I stopped by my friend's house on her birthday to surprise her with her favorite cake—red velvet from this little bakery near my work. Sad that I still remember that, right? Her car was in the driveway, but she wasn't answering the door. So I called out her name, then went to the back to see if she was outside, and there he was! My boyfriend, climbing out her bedroom window in just his boxers! I was so shocked I froze! And he just keeps going, fucking Spider-Man, climbing down the side of the house, more athletic than I've ever seen him in my life. Once he hit the ground, he just started sprinting, barefoot, without a backward glance. I don't even know if he saw me.

MANDY: So what did you do?

FIONA: I stood there for I don't even know how long. Felt like a lifetime, though it was probably just a few minutes.

MANDY: Did you eat the cake? I would've smashed my face in it and started munching.

FIONA: I don't even remember what I did with it. Probably dropped it straight to the ground.

MANDY: So then what? Did you confront your friend?

FIONA: I didn't. I don't know why. I was just . . . so shocked. I mean, I hadn't seen this coming at all. Maybe I felt stupid? Maybe it hadn't sunk in yet and I was half convinced I didn't see what I saw?

MANDY: So what did you do?

FIONA: I went home. I don't even remember getting in the car or driving. I just remember suddenly being at our front door. [pause] *Our.* How insane is that? How could I not see who he really was when we lived together? Then I remembered. I remembered, Mandy.

MANDY: What?

FIONA: You! I remembered *Dish Served Hot*! And how so many of the guests on this show say the same exact thing! I mean, it's like you said earlier—obviously we were with that person for a reason. We didn't know until we knew. And this has happened to others. I wasn't alone. [breath] I wasn't *alone*. Even though I felt completely alone. Not only had I been tricked by the person I trusted most, but I didn't have any friends! Not real ones anyway, they can all rot in hell. Turns out he was sleeping with more than one so-called friend, and even the ones he wasn't sleeping with knew about the others. But, thanks to your other guests, I realized I wasn't stupid. How could I be when so many others had gone through the same thing? And so your show made me realize—it's him, not me. I didn't do anything wrong.

So then I started thinking, what now? What would Mandy do?

MANDY: I'm honored.

FIONA: I'm honored to get to tell you this now. So what would you do, Mandy, now that I've got you here?

MANDY: Y'all know what I would do! I'd get revenge!

FIONA: Exactly! I would've never thought of it otherwise—it's pretty out of character for me—but then the thought was just so delicious I could already taste it. I mean, fuck, Mandy! Before, I felt like I was drowning, and then the idea of revenge was the buoy floating along that saved my ass! And suddenly I felt calm, in control, and sane.

MANDY: So what did you do?

FIONA: I walked into the house and said, "Hi, hon," as I normally would.

MANDY: [laughing] You didn't!

FIONA: I did!

MANDY: And what did he do?

FIONA: He fucking said, "Hey, babe," right back! Pretended nothing had happened! He was clothed now, wearing socks—probably 'cause his feet were torn up from running home—not a drop of sweat on his face!

MANDY: Then?

FIONA: Then I took my time. I had the utmost patience. I let him think all was well, we were well, and then—*bam!* Fucking knife to the throat.

MANDY: What did you do???

FIONA: I still can't believe how perfectly it all came together. There was just so much planning but [squeal] it all paid off.

MANDY: What was the final masterpiece?

FIONA: I orchestrated it so that he walked in on me . . . having sex with his dad.

MANDY: WHAT?!

[beat]

MANDY: Seriously? You did that?

FIONA: You bet your ass I did. He sleeps with my friends, I sleep with his dad. Isn't revenge all about upping the ante, serving an extra bitter dose of medicine?

MANDY: If there were a *Dish Served Hot* trophy, you would get it, my friend.

FIONA: Oooh, what would that look like? A golden oven mitt? Trivet?

MANDY: [laughs] Clever gal. I love it! And unto you I do declare, the golden oven mitt.

FIONA: Thanks, Mandy! I have to say, I think I earned it!

MANDY: No kidding! [pause] And how was Daddy?

FIONA: Fucking fire!

MANDY: No kidding?

FIONA: What can I say? Revenge is sweet.

MANDY: There you have it! An example of *Dish Served Hot* changing the world for the better.

FIONA: Thanks, Mandy. Take it from me, Thornies. If you're on the fence, *do it*!

MANDY: Do what—revenge or our exes' fathers?

FIONA: [laughing] Both! Two birds, one huge fucking stone! And I chose those words on purpose.

MANDY: Huge fucking stone? [laughs] Go Daddy.

FIONA: I'm so glad I didn't just ghost the fucker like I was originally thinking of doing.

MANDY: Don't just ghost, folks, go for the throat—or the huge fucking stone, whatever the case may be!

CHAPTER 54

"What it mean to ghost—put on sheet and say *boo*?"

Thank god that was what my mom was focusing on after we listened to the episode instead of the *many* other worse topics she could've picked.

She turned to Mandy next. "That you on there? Wah, so impressive. I not know this type of show, but you do so well. Like TV, but better, because screen is bad for eyes. I not let Yushan watch until she go to college—she so mad, but so important!"

I closed my protected-from-TV-for-too-long eyes and willed this to stop. Luckily, there were more important matters to discuss.

"Ms. Thorne, do you by chance—" Adrian started, but Mandy was already on it.

"I have Fiona's contact info. Not her real name, but if that email address is still active . . ."

And just like that, we were cooking with CH_4 (origin: marketing slogan for gas stoves).

• • • •

Fiona—really Cordelia—responded quickly, inviting us over to chat while calling Mandy a queen and hero and savior because Mandy's head just wasn't big enough.

But not all of us needed to go.

"I have to be there—I'm the queen and hero and savior," Mandy argued.

Like I said, just enormous.

"Ms. Thorne, this is official business."

"Why do Kat and Olivia get to go?"

"Kat—Ms. Hu—is a CSI-in-training and Ms. McCarthy is a consultant on this case."

"I should also consult!" Mandy exclaimed. "Who knows more about all this than me?"

"Ms. Thorne, you are a target. You must remain here."

Adrian didn't say it, but Mandy was also a suspect and a liability and the list went on and on.

"No, Yushan. Too dangerous. And you." She turned her honed Mom-glare onto Adrian. "How you okay with this?"

"Mom, I'll be fine. This is part of my job now."

"I go," my mother said. "No one protect my Yushan like I do."

This was much too chaotic. We had to end it. Solve it. And immediately.

Before anyone could respond, Adrian's burner phone chimed with a text.

"It's Cyber," he said. "The IP address of Cordelia's original email to Mandy led to an apartment that had been leased at that time to a Cordelia Lewis and a Hubert Ombra."

"Hubert Ombra," Olivia said. "Think that's Spider-Man?"

"Likely, given that she talked about living with her boyfriend on the podcast. Coincidence that his initials are HO?" I couldn't help adding.

"I should be going!" Mandy said, actually stomping her foot. "No one knows more than me about Cordelia and HO—or maybe he should henceforth be known as Hubes since it rhymes with—"

"You're not going," Olivia interrupted.

Mandy turned and ran out of the motel room. Queen, hero, savior—and child, apparently.

Sighing, I followed.

"Kat, thank god you knew I was trying to get you alone."

I hadn't, but she didn't need to know that.

Mandy pulled us into the crammed space between the side of the building and the ice machine. "We have to get justice for Jocelyn."

"Of course."

Mandy shook her head. "You don't get it—*we* have to. I only trust you now. Which is why I'm telling you, in confidence, that I did something. It wasn't bad, not really—well, I had to, okay? I . . . stole evidence. Off Jocelyn's body."

I couldn't help a gasp, and Mandy shushed me.

"Why didn't you tell us sooner?" I asked.

"I don't trust Ricky. I overheard him on the phone at the safe house talking to someone, saying he couldn't talk now, and to stop calling him, and that he was done."

Shit. That could have several interpretations, but none of them were good.

"Kat, please, if an opportunity presents itself—"

At that moment, Adrian, Ricky, and Olivia appeared.

"Ms. Thorne—"

"I'm not going, don't worry your broody little head," Mandy said with an eye roll. Just before she went back into the motel, she gave me a pleading look.

Neutron, pH7, helium—I kept my face neutral. Then I considered her words the entire drive, not sure what to do with them.

By the time we arrived, all I'd concluded was that I was going to put the case and the truth first. At this point, it was all I could do.

• • • •

Cordelia Lewis lived in a gorgeous mansion sitting on at least an acre of land. It wasn't a Mandy Thorne–level mansion, but as we pulled through a fancy gate, I couldn't help gawking.

After we rang the doorbell, a stunning petite blonde in her late twenties opened the door, clad in an incredibly high-cut bathing suit. She welcomed us in, and instead of leading us to the swimming pool, she brought us to the couch, where a tray of fresh-squeezed lemonade was waiting.

"I was hoping Mandy Thorne would be coming," Cordelia said, disappointed. "I mean, I'm happy to help, but also, I thought I'd get to meet the woman who changed my life."

"May I ask how she did that, Ms. Lewis?" Adrian said.

"Please, call me Mrs. Ombra."

"Ombra?" Olivia repeated.

"As in Hubert Ombra?" I asked.

"Do you know him?" Cordelia said with a smile.

"Isn't he the one who cheated on you and climbed out the window?" How did we get this so wrong?

"That was Hubert Ombra Junior," Cordelia said. "I married Hubert Ombra *Senior.*"

My jaw physically dropped.

She hadn't just slept with the dad, then.

Cordelia flashed her enormous engagement ring and diamond-encrusted wedding band. "We had a gorgeous dream wedding followed by a honeymoon around the world. I'm still in the process of getting my name changed."

Too many questions ran through my head.

Is this part of the revenge, too?

How the hell did Hubert Junior react to that?

I glanced around and spotted a giant framed photo of Cordelia and her new husband canoodling on their wedding day, with Hubert Senior catching her in a kiss, his face buried in her cheek. She looked surprised and absolutely delighted even though this was clearly staged. I wondered how many tries that took, eight? Hubert Senior appeared in his sixties and did not *look* "fucking fire," but of course that didn't mean anything. Though it did make one wonder just how much this was about revenge.

"And Mr. Ombra Senior is . . . ?" Adrian asked.

"At work. He owns his own business. He's very successful, a self-made man. They don't make them like that anymore, do they!"

Adrian jotted a quick note, then continued. "May I ask about your relationship?"

"Of course. I'm not ashamed of anything. As you already know, I was dating Hubert Junior, and when he cheated on me, I slept with his dad. It's not a secret. I shouted it from the rooftops. And I don't regret it. Of course, I couldn't have predicted that I would fall in love and become Mrs. Ombra—especially given that the thought of becoming Mrs. Ombra the *other* way makes me want to vomit, but life is so funny, isn't it? Sometimes you just gotta laugh."

"Have you heard from your ex-boyfriend—" Adrian began.

"*Stepson*," Cordelia corrected. "I never want to think of him as my ex now, not after this." She gestured to her wedding band. "I mean, that would just be weird!"

Yes, *that* was what was weird.

Adrian didn't even blink as he corrected himself. "Have you heard from your stepson recently?"

"No. He did try to win me back at one point, but can you blame him? I of course told him to drop dead."

"How did he react to . . ." Adrian gestured in a vague circle.

"How do you think, sugar? He got his pom-poms out and cheered. Did a little celebration dance for us. It was the cancan."

"Mrs. Ombra—"

"He was furious, of course! He'd lost me! I moved straight out of our shared apartment and into this house! Well, almost directly. I spent a week at my parents' while my Hubey broke the news to his then-wife."

"Wait, so his parents got divorced . . ." I couldn't bring myself to say it.

"What, hon?"

Olivia could bring herself to, though. "So you broke his parents up?"

"Not intentionally. But true love is true love. They weren't happy. And they weren't in love anymore. In some ways, shouldn't Hubert Junior be glad? Isn't it better that his father and I are actually soulmates instead of this just being petty revenge?"

I still wasn't sure that wasn't all this was—revenge.

"This wasn't even about Hubert Junior," Cordelia continued. "Well, not in the end. The marriage wasn't about him. The sex might've been, but that's just me and Hubey's meet-cute, you know? A hilarious doozy of a meet-cute. One for the ages. Maybe I should contact Mandy and go on *Dish Served Hot* again. Hubert Junior probably won't be happy about being the first one featured on the show twice, but, again, this isn't about him. The second episode would be about how the podcast helped me find true love. How the most beautiful flower blossomed from the ugliest of situations."

Thank god she hadn't used *rainbows* and *storms* as her metaphor, or I'd have been offended.

"Did your stepson ever take any retribution out on you or your husband?" Adrian asked.

"I mean, he did follow me for a while, coming around here right after I first moved in. But my Hubey took care of it. He felt terrible that his own son was doing this. Embarrassed, really. But in his defense, he wasn't around much back when Hubert Junior was growing up—he was too busy working in order to provide a good home. But his hard work paid off, and now it'll be so much better for this next one." She cradled her belly.

I thought she had already dropped the maximum number of bombs during this visit, but I was dead wrong. I had not expected her to be expecting.

Olivia recovered first. "Congratulations. When are you due?"

"Six months! A girl. Hubey can't wait!"

I forced a smile.

"Again, this is all because of Mandy!" Cordelia said. "Oh, I'm just so darned disappointed she isn't here."

"Do you have any idea where your stepson is or how to contact him?" Adrian asked. "We've been having a hard time tracking him down." Cyber had called on our drive here to say they couldn't locate an address or phone number.

"Ew, no. As far as we're concerned, he's dead to us. I don't want him popping our happy bubble. What's this about, anyway? Is he in trouble?"

"Unfortunately, we are not at liberty to discuss details at this moment." Adrian stood. "Thank you for your hospitality today, Mrs. Ombra. If you or your husband hear from your stepson, can you please let me know?" He handed her a card.

The rest of us stood, including Cordelia.

"I know what I did was . . . unorthodox. I wouldn't call it bad, though, not really. How can it be bad when it led to true love? We had to follow our hearts."

Her words reminded me of what Mandy had said to me right before we left, and given everything we'd discovered here today, I suddenly had an idea.

Catching Olivia's eyes, I quickly and subtly tugged on my

hair. And luckily, we could communicate without talking. We were able to do so back when Ray had us in his clutches, and now we were more in sync than ever.

As Adrian and Ricky shook Cordelia's hand, Olivia went to the foyer, appearing like she was getting ready to leave, but instead of grabbing her own coat, she plucked two hats off the adjacent wall hooks. A second later, they were back in place.

By the time Adrian, Ricky, Cordelia, and I entered the foyer, Olivia was already one foot out the door.

It wasn't by the book, but we had to try. I told myself it was okay since I was in CSI training, but I knew better.

I just hoped Adrian would understand.

CHAPTER 55

After we left Cordelia's, Olivia and I couldn't find a moment alone because, horror of horrors, we had to stay at the motel for our safety.

"I'll leave you all to it," Ricky said, heading toward the door. "I'll be fine at my place."

Alarm bells rung in my head. *I don't trust Ricky*, Mandy had said. And this was the second time he'd tried to get out of staying with us.

"We're still working the case," Adrian stated, pulling out the chair next to him.

Ricky inched over and dropped into it, but my resolve was hardening. Maybe Mandy was right.

Which meant, maybe I'd done the right thing back at Cordelia's.

"Are we, uh, sure we're safe here?" Mandy asked, gesturing much too obviously to Ricky.

At that exact moment, Adrian's burner phone rang.

"They found us!" Mandy wailed.

"Aiyah!" my mother gasped.

It couldn't be, could it?

Adrian held a calm hand up. "It's the prison."

"Prison!" my mother yelled.

Adrian glanced at Olivia and me, and we both jumped up.

"Oh, uh, right. Just a . . . contact about the case, Mom," I said nonchalantly. Then Olivia and I hurried to the other room with Adrian while Ricky stayed behind with Mandy and my mom.

After Adrian accepted the call, a familiar, heartwarming voice said over speakerphone, "Is everything okay? Both of my girls' phones are off, and I had a damn hard time getting this number!"

"Hi, Elle!" Olivia said brightly.

"We're okay," I added. Suddenly, our motel safe house situation didn't seem so bad in light of what Elle was dealing with. "Just taking extra precautions."

"You keeping an eye on them, McTree and McCandy?"

"Ricky's not with us right now," I said, hoping he was in the other room keeping my mom from asking too many questions.

"Why the hell not? Liv, what're you waiting for—"

"Did you come across something?" Olivia cut in.

There was a brief pause. Then Elle said, "You know, if I were seeing you in person, there would be hell to pay for you not taking full advantage of—"

"I hear you," Olivia said quietly. "I'm . . . doing the best I can."

"No rush. I get it. I can't tell you how many people have written me love letters, and I just can't right now. Or maybe ever." After another pause, Elle's voice became cheery again. "So! I do have something for you. I've been digging as promised—talking to my new pen pals who despise the show and Mandy—and I learned there were pissed-off victims of Thornie revenge putting feelers out on the dark web in search of other angry victims. Could be related to your case? I'll forward you the messages."

"Thanks, Elle, that's super helpful," I said.

"Oops, there's my time. Fucking prison, huh? Stay safe! Take care of each other. Climb some trees. For me."

She hung up before we could say goodbye.

Things were beginning to come together in my mind. But before I could click any pieces into place, my mother burst into the room, with Mandy on her heels. Ricky followed behind helplessly, not sure what to do.

"You friends with a killer? You all date same man? Yushan!"

Goddamnit.

"Mrs. Hu—" Adrian started, but my mother whirled on him.

"And you! You think my daughter capable of killing? What wrong with you? And you with her now?"

And of course, fucking Mandy was standing there eating literal popcorn. After she'd just shaken the can of worms like a soda pop and let them explode.

"Mom—"

"You bad for my Yushan!" my mother yelled, pointing an angry finger first at Adrian, then Olivia. "Yushan, after all this over, I take you home. You need reset! Everyone here bad influence."

My mother stormed into the other room, Mandy following close behind. Ricky stayed with us this time, and as much as I didn't want to leave my mother alone with Mandy, there was a murder to solve.

"Show me the messages," I said.

"Kat, are you okay—" Adrian started to ask.

"I'm fine. The messages?"

He obliged, and Ricky, Olivia, and I leaned in.

Forwarded Messages from Elle

March 25

@DishServedNot: Has anyone else been fucked over by this show? If so, I'd love to talk!

April 13

@IHateDishServedHot: Has Mandy Thorne fucked over anyone else's life? DM me!

May 6

@MandyThorneIsTheDevil: Can we talk about how this show needs to be over? Anyone else an innocent victim of Dish Served Hot revenge?

May 8

@DownWithMandy: Hey @MandyThorneIsTheDevil, I agree. Dish Served Hot needs to be served some revenge of its own.

@MandyThorneIsTheDevil: Did that bitch hurt you, too?

@DownWithMandy: Let's talk.

"I already sent these to Cyber—" Adrian said, but he was interrupted by his phone buzzing.

Ricky's buzzed at the same time.

"It's them," Ricky said. "They found that the IP address of the first message matches the one Cordelia emailed Mandy from. Shit, we should talk to them."

As they sat down to contact Cyber, Olivia quietly pulled me into the bathroom and closed the door behind us. Then she pulled me into a hug.

"Sorry about your mom, Kat."

I sighed into her shoulder. "I did this to myself. I didn't expect it to explode in my face quite like this, but I did add the Mentos to the Diet Coke."

We pulled apart and she smiled. "Which causes an explosion because the rough surface on the Mentos promotes carbon dioxide formation."

"You remembered." I was touched. I'd told her that back at the York Beach bar-slash-arcade after we'd first met Elle.

"I really did always want to know that," she said. Then she reached into her pocket to retrieve the hairs she'd lifted back at Cordelia's. "So is there a reason you requested these?" She'd understood correctly that I was asking for DNA samples by tugging on my hair.

"I have to tell you something," I said.

Olivia leaned closer.

"And we have to keep it from Adrian and Ricky."

"Done," she said immediately.

"And we might have to break the law an eensie bit."

She grinned. "Extra done. What's the plan?"

"The next time the boys go into the department . . ."

CHAPTER 56

I was doing this to protect Adrian and his career.

I was doing this to protect Olivia, my mom, Mandy, and maybe even Elle.

I was doing this to protect myself.

No matter what I said, I didn't feel good about what I was about to do. What *we* were about to do. The most ragtag, oddball Murder Club in the history of the universe.

"You have . . . unlock pick? Wait, *pick*, as in pick your nose?"

"It's called a *lock*pick," Mandy clarified for my mom.

"But you use to unlock, not lock—make no sense!"

"You're right—your name is better," Mandy said, and my mom smiled smugly.

For someone who was judging me for being friends with Elle and Olivia, my mother had quite the nerve. And I, for one, did not like the friendship forming between her and Mandy—who, for the record, was the worst influence of all.

"I don't know why we needed them to come along," I whispered to Olivia. We were in her car, parked outside the police station. None of them were coming in with me—I was the only one officially allowed to be inside at this hour—so I didn't see why we couldn't have left them at the motel with the undercover agents out front. But no, Olivia had insisted we sneak them out the back window with us.

"You never know when they might be useful," she said again. She left the second part out in case they overheard. *And you never know what they might get up to left to their own devices.*

That part I understood, and I certainly felt better having Olivia with them. But I needed to focus right now, and the two people in the back seat were the biggest distractions I'd ever met.

"What're you going to do if you bump into Adrian or Ricky?" Olivia asked me. They were currently on duty.

"I have a cover story ready," I said.

"Do you want to talk anything through?"

I shook my head. "I have to go now." *Before I lose my nerve* went unsaid.

"You got this," Olivia said, and I believed her.

But then my mom added, "Yes, you got," and Mandy begged, "Please don't mess anything up."

This was not the Ex-Girlfriend Murder Club.

• • • •

This was also not the Mortal Enemy Murder Club.

Right now, this was just me. Dead of night, wearing my usual lab attire, but with a very different purpose than when I normally arrived for work. And while I never would've even agreed to this plan a year ago let alone thought it up, I wished I could channel Olivia's and Elle's confidence as I walked through the front doors.

The pink cupcakes were resurfacing. The physical representation, in food, of my inability to lie and, apparently, pull off an illegal scheme.

Yes, you got, I tried to repeat in my head instead of what my mother had said after the cupcake incident, which was that this trait of mine would be the death of me.

I kept my head down and walked quickly enough not to

be easily spotted, but not so quickly as to draw attention. And I hoped to god that the same anonymity that usually saddened me would benefit me now, especially as I swiped into the lab and retrieved my (un)lockpicks.

A lot of the machinery I needed was secured, and though I knew how to access a few of them, there were some I had to channel Double-Oh-livia's skills for.

After I gathered the necessary equipment, I retrieved the hairs from my pocket. Then I went to work, nose to the grindstone (origin: knife sharpening, where workers had to lean very close to the grindstone to apply steady pressure). Soon, I reached that state of rote, methodical Zen where I became one with the process. Where my years of studying and practicing kicked in and activated muscle memory. And this plus the fact that I was fighting to save others, including people I cared about, reminded me why I wanted to be in this crime lab in the first place.

And maybe I was finally starting to feel like I belonged.

"What're you doing here?" a deep voice boomed out, and I jumped in fear.

This was worse than Adrian walking in on me.

I swallowed hard, then turned around. "Hi, Gerard."

"I *said*, what're you doing here?"

"I . . ."

This was the person I should have planned for, but I hadn't. I'd been so worried about Adrian and Ricky I forgot who the real threat was.

"If you don't tell me within the next three seconds why you're in here, I'm going to have you arrested for—"

And then the perfect excuse came to me. I was here practicing. I'd obtained DNA samples from friends and was running them to test my proficiency. I had taken his advice and was getting serious, focusing on the science, making sure I could hone my skills to be the best at analyzing data and filling in the blanks, just like he wanted. I was using every tool except emotion.

But instead, what I blurted out was, "You're wrong, you know."

"Excuse me?"

"You're wrong. I think emotion is a crucial part to being a scientist, and most importantly, a human." And in that moment, I made a pivotal decision. I didn't want to find a way to stop caring, even if that meant there'd be more danger in my future. As Adrian, Olivia, and Elle had all said to me at different points, my heart was a vital part of who I am.

I squared my shoulders as I continued my declaration to the man who'd made me doubt myself for the worst reasons. "I'm here because I want to help people. I want to make a difference. And why is that a bad thing? Why is it bad to be inspired, driven, passionate about what I do? Why can't I care about the victims I'm trying to get justice for? I think that makes me a better scientist, not worse." Though that same argument was why I was here breaking the law for a case I was emotionally and physically involved in, but he didn't need to know that. In fact, he *couldn't* know that.

Gerard was glaring at me, eyes narrowed, arms crossed. "*You* are not passionate. *You* mistake careless emotion for passion. All you are is reckless and completely unfit to do this job. You are only here because you got in bed with the right person, and after your nepotism hire, all you've been doing is hiding behind him while you do and say the bare minimum."

"I—"

Is *that* what he'd been so mad about this whole time? I couldn't win. I was hated in my last job because when I did talk, I said the wrong things, and here, I was hated because I didn't say enough.

"This job is about life and death," he continued. "If you don't have the right intentions, people *die*. People *get away with murder.* You tried to let a murderer go once already. I'm not going to let you do that again."

"Is that what's been up your trousers this whole time?" a deep honey-and-molasses voice said. (Leave it to him to formalize *up your butt*, which extends from *bug up your butt*.)

Adrian's commanding presence filled the space between Gerard and me. "Kathryn Hu understands the stakes of this job better than anyone else. And her actions are why we were able to close that last case. *That* is why she was the top candidate for this position. She received this job *despite* her connection to me. If anything, her case had to be that much stronger to push past the complaints that would surely arise from her coming here, as you have proven. And she had to get approval from the captain." No one had to mention that she wasn't a fan of me. "Not only did her credentials speak for themselves, but Ms. Hu is more driven and passionate than the rest of us combined, which is why she's going to make—and already is—an exceptional forensic scientist. It's also why she's here so late, after hours, trying to solve this case before anyone else gets hurt."

Gerard's eyes took in Adrian's stoic face, then my nervous frown, before dropping down to the microcentrifuge tubes in my gloved hands. And I saw when he registered what was actually going on. His arms dropped from his chest to his sides as he took a step toward us. "Is this an authorized after-hours lab visit?"

Adrian didn't miss a beat. "I can supervise her. You can go."

Of course Mr. By-the-Book would never outright lie, even in a situation like this. His weapon of choice instead was carefully selected words.

But Gerard was able to see right through them. And shockingly, this seemed to turn the tide. "Nice to see someone finally standing up to you," Gerard said to Adrian with a smirk. "Because *you're* the one with something up that-which-goes-*inside* your trousers."

Gerard reached a hand out, and I flinched away instinctively, only to feel a brief pat on the back. "You know, I had been holding off on submitting your training hours, but keep this up, and maybe you'll get your certification after all."

That was why it had been held up? I should have known. But I hadn't realized Gerard held that much power.

Gerard sauntered out of the lab, whistling. And I didn't even have time to recover from the whiplash of what had just happened, because there was another roller coaster just around the corner.

Adrian's eyes remained on the door through which Gerard had just exited as he said, "If I'd known Gerard was just questioning your commitment to the job, I would've straightened that out sooner." He ticked his chin toward the DNA sequencer that was humming along. "How did you get DNA to test?"

"Um . . ." It was time, wasn't it? "Olivia might've grabbed some DNA samples from Cordelia's place. It just felt important, with Eugene pointing us to episode forty-five, to them. And . . ." The next part was even worse, believe it or not. "Um, Mandy might have grabbed some hair out of Jocelyn's fist when she lunged for the body. The *killer's* hair. And she said she only trusted me with it."

Adrian closed his eyes as if it were suddenly too much work to keep them open. "When did you learn about that?"

"What Mandy did? Not long ago. Just before we went to Cordelia's."

He didn't say anything. For once, I wasn't sure what he was thinking.

"Adrian . . ." I started, but I didn't know what to say. I'd kept things from him—and not just what Mandy had confided in me—and I was in here now breaking the law.

He opened his eyes. And the hurt in them sent a pang through me.

"I don't know how else I can show you that I know you, trust you," he said. "I just wish you would return that to me. That you could find a way to trust me, and also trust yourself, that you know me. You don't have to keep so much from me all the time."

Instead of internalizing his words, I blurted out the defense that was on the tip of my tongue. "If I had told you, you would've wanted me to do it by the book."

"We would've figured out a way to do that together. You know how important that is to me. Just like I know how important it is to you to solve this."

"But you love when I take things into my own hands! When I break the rules. The perfect mole, remember?"

Adrian looked disappointed, which was worse than angry. "I love when you're confident and trust the intelligence you have in spades, yes . . . but I wish you could also love and respect every part of me."

I *do*, I wanted to say. I loved that Adrian was morally straight, honest, and by the book almost to a fault. But I understood why it wasn't coming across that way.

Adrian sighed. "Let me know when you're ready to be a team."

"I'm ready! I have been this whole time!" I yelled. But he was already gone. And I knew those words were untrue and empty in light of my actions.

CHAPTER 57

As soon as Adrian left the lab, the DNA comparisons and cross-referencing to CODIS finished, with a photo, fingerprints, and lines of text appearing on the screen.

The text? Surprising. The photo? It hit me like alkali metal hitting water (i.e., explosive). It hit me like seeing Elle's photograph in Mrs. Watson's album.

I didn't even have time to feel guilty about doing this behind Adrian's back. Because everything was clicking together.

It wasn't what I had been thinking, not exactly. There was a piece I'd been missing. But now . . .

Everything made sense. Well, almost everything, but I'd address that later.

I printed the results out.

Now, I just had to fix what I'd unintentionally broken. Then, we could finally end this.

• • • •

"I know who did it," I said breathlessly as soon as Adrian returned to the lab.

I'd texted him to come back, and though only a few minutes had passed since he was last here, it felt like years inside my head. Because I now understood what he'd been saying.

His words had also made me realize: Why was it so easy

for me to be fearless when it was about others? I broke into the lab without much thought, but I somehow couldn't apply that to the important parts of my own life. So here I was, finally being fearless.

"I know who did it," I repeated, "but you were also right. About me, you, us, everything. And I'm sorry."

His eyes softened. But he was still just watching me. Waiting. Letting me talk.

"This whole time, I kept thinking I had to make you trust me, but the real problem was me. You already trusted me! And it was exactly like you said—I wasn't letting myself trust *you*. And the truth is . . . I didn't know how. I was scared and it was too hard after what happened with . . . him. Tucker."

But just because Tucker hurt me didn't mean Adrian would. And as much as I believed otherwise, I deserved to be loved. But I had to *let* myself be loved.

"I'm ready to be a team," I said. "I finally grasp what that means. I'm sorry I didn't get here the best way, but moving forward, I'm ready."

The left side of his mouth curved up. Then he grunted. Deep, subtle, and with rounded edges. Meaning, all was forgiven. And he was ready to be a team, too. He had been all along.

"So what's the plan?" he asked.

I loved that he knew I already had one. And most importantly, that he would be a part of it.

• • • •

When I returned to the car where Olivia, Mandy, and my mom were still waiting, they were all surprised to see Adrian beside me.

"Uh, is everything okay?" Olivia asked as she peeked over at Adrian while exiting the driver's seat.

"Better than ever," I said, thrilled that I meant it.

But I was just referring to my romantic relationship. Adrian, apparently, had a bone to pick, which I guess made sense.

He opened the door to the back seat. "Ms. Thorne—"

"Aren't we on a first-name basis by now?" Mandy asked as she exited the car. "I mean, jeez. How long before you started calling her Kat?"

"Cat? Where is there cat?" my mother asked, following Mandy out of the car to stand outside with the rest of us.

"Ms. Thorne. I need to hear the details from when you irresponsibly and illegally stole evidence from the crime scene."

Mandy turned to glare daggers at me. "How could you, Kat?"

"*Ms. Thorne.*" The gravity of Adrian's voice finally hit a nerve in Mandy, and she broke down.

"I didn't know what I was doing, okay? It was a moment of panic, you understand. I mean, can we be held accountable for things we do when we're overcome by shock, grief, and fear? I think not!" She covered her face with her hands.

Adrian remained calm as he said, "I am just looking for the details."

Mandy sniffed a few times (and I briefly wondered if she was acting). "Well, I always told Jocelyn, if anyone comes for you, *DNA first*—scratch him, get some hair or skin cells, make him bleed. And she did. So when I saw the hair in her fist, I just grabbed it. On instinct. It felt too important to just leave there. And the person I trust most is me, so I figured, I should hold onto it, no? Don't I have Jocelyn's best interest at heart? I mean, I hear y'all calling her *the body* or *the victim*. She has a name! I was going to use my contacts, hand the DNA over to a PI unconnected to the case, but then I was scared to leave the group. And then enough time passed that I couldn't tell you about it, and then I was hindering the investigation!

So when we had a suspect and you were going to see them, I just thought—"

"You'd ask Kat to risk her career and neck for you?" Adrian couldn't help finishing.

Mandy hung her head. "Yes."

That was not the reaction I expected from her.

"I'm sorry."

I didn't expect her to say that, either.

"So you ran the DNA?" Olivia asked me.

I nodded, a thrum of excitement and fear running through me. "I know who did it."

"Hu done it," Olivia said, and I knew she was using my last name.

"Aiyah, you know already?" my mom exclaimed. "How you do it?"

For the first time, when I gave my mom an overview of DNA extraction, PCR, and comparing DNA profiles, her eyes did not glaze over. She did not bring up dermatology.

"Aiyah, Yushan." I had no idea what words were coming next, but the answer was no words. She reached a hand out and cupped my cheek. A gesture she hadn't done since I was a child. A gesture that said so much—love, pride, support—that it was hard to want anything else, though I still craved to hear her say the actual words out loud. But I knew she wouldn't.

Before, I would have thought about what was missing, but now, I zeroed in on what I did have (military origin of "zeroing" or adjusting sighting mechanisms).

I leaned into her hand and closed my eyes. A second later, it was over, but I took a mental picture of the moment to carry with me.

"For the record," Mandy said, "Kat was the only one I trusted with the DNA because . . . well, I hate to tell you this, Detective Broody, but your partner is shady."

Adrian sighed. "Unfortunately, you may not be wrong."

Mandy's eyes bugged out in surprise. "What? What did you find out?"

Instead of answering, Adrian turned to Olivia. "Can you come with Kat and me?"

Adrian and I had followed up with what I'd found, and that was why we'd come to the car in the first place.

"Mandy, can you and my mom go back to the safe house?" I asked.

Mandy pouted. "Why don't we get to come?"

"It's better this way, trust me." For so many reasons.

Olivia tossed the keys to Mandy, and then she, Adrian, and I hurried away, ignoring Mandy's protests.

We were so close to the finish line. I could see it.

I just hoped we could all get there in one piece, including our hearts.

CHAPTER 58

"We need to talk," I said as soon as Adrian, Olivia, and I arrived at Ricky's desk inside the precinct.

"Sure thing," he said, closing the folder in front of him. "What'd you find?"

"You, unfortunately," Olivia said as she slapped the DNA results onto the desk in front of him.

"What—" Ricky started, but he trailed off when he saw what was on there. "Wait. Does this mean—? Oh, shit. Wait, but that's . . . This doesn't make sense."

Olivia waited for him to put it all together, then tapped her finger on the printout where we wanted him to focus.

Ricky's face paled.

He wasn't the person in the photo, but his name had come up in connection to the suspect.

"You were the killer's arresting officer in a previous case when you were still at another precinct," I said. "So after seeing that, we looked into you further, and we learned that you requested your transfer here *and* asked the captain to be partnered with Birch."

I glanced at Adrian, whose arms were crossed over his chest, his steely gaze locked on Ricky. I would not want to be on the other end of that.

"It's not what you think," Ricky finally said.

"It's too many coincidences," Olivia said, not able to hold it in anymore. She'd been betrayed too many times by the men she was interested in, and she needed to get to the bottom of this. "Why the focus on Adrian? Why haven't you wanted to stay with us? Why, after you got here and partnered with Birch, does your first case not only involve all of us personally, but you also have a preexisting connection to the killer?"

Ricky was shaking his head. "You're getting this all wrong. It's just a coincidence I happened to be the arresting officer on the previous case—and it was for stalking, not murder."

I noticed how he'd only addressed that one piece. "Well, then, what about the rest of it? Why did you target Adrian?"

Ricky squirmed in his seat. "I would never do anything to hurt you two or Adrian."

"That's not what we asked," Olivia said.

Ricky didn't respond.

Olivia turned to me. "Why do I always attract the red flags? I should've known from the beginning—"

"I was friends with your previous partner," Ricky blurted to Adrian. He must've been referring to the partner who had turned dirty, betrayed Adrian, and ran off. "Charlie and I grew up together. Neighbors, with nothing and no one but each other, you know what I mean? We'd hide from our home situation in the supply closet of a gas station down the street where we could watch the TV through a crack in the door. It was my introduction to cartoons. And we'd say we were the Ninja Turtles, escaping into the sewers, which, yes, were filled with shit, but it was still better than the shit that our lives were. That kind of thing, it bonds you. And we wanted to be like them. Heroes. Making the world better and helping people who were in bad situations and needed out. But we took different paths. I didn't know what he'd gotten himself into, I swear, and that's not how I operate."

There was a beat of silence. This wasn't what I'd been expecting, and from Olivia's face, the same was true for her.

"Yet you *were* involved," Adrian said, more of a statement than a question.

Now it was Ricky's turn to be surprised. "What do you mean?"

"You knew where my bathroom was even though I hadn't invited you over before. Did you break into my place with Charlie to destroy evidence?"

"Not exactly. I didn't know what was going on when he brought me there or even whose place it was. He said he needed help, and I believed him, so I helped. I didn't realize what I'd done until after he ran. And by then, it was too late."

Adrian's arms finally uncrossed. "Why didn't you tell me?"

"I didn't want you to think of me differently. I was going to tell you, I swear, but after you got a chance to know me, the real me, without all this clouding your judgment. But it seems you already knew some of it."

"Who've you been talking to on the phone?" I asked.

"I tried to find Charlie after it all happened—to make him come in. I called his contacts. And now they won't leave me alone. They want to track him down, too, but for other reasons. It's . . . a mess. That's why I sought Adrian out in the first place. Because I knew he had been looking, and I wanted to help. I thought maybe together, we could finally do it—bring him in."

"So you not wanting to stay with us at Adrian's and the safe house—" I started to ask.

"I felt guilty. I was hiding a piece of me from Birch, and I didn't think I should be allowed in—not fully—until everything was out in the open." He turned to Adrian. "I promise you, I'm on your side. If you want to, we'll get him, together. But if you don't want to be partners anymore, I understand. And I'll still help you."

"You really knew nothing about this?" Adrian said, gesturing to the printout.

"Absolutely not. I remember that initial arrest—we helped the stalking victim file a temporary restraining order—and I had no idea this was the same perp as our current case. I swear it, on everything I hold dear in my life—which now is all of you, if I'm being honest." Ricky couldn't meet our eyes as he said the last part, which made it all the more endearing. "I'm sorry about the lies. If you let me, I'll help you wrap this one up. I promise I have your backs."

After a beat, during which Ricky was sweating and Olivia and I held our breaths, Adrian went over and clapped Ricky on the shoulder. Then, he grunted.

"What does that mean?" Ricky asked.

"It means you're officially stuck with us," I answered.

Ricky grinned, relieved.

"Don't get too excited yet," Olivia said. "The next part of the plan is going to be a fine kettle of worms."

I couldn't help smiling at the malaphor.

"Buckle up," I told Ricky. "We need to set a trap."

CHAPTER 59

"I knew you'd call again sooner or later. Can't get me out of your mind?"

How was it possible for Asher to be this pathetic and cocky at the same time?

We'd asked him to meet at the same diner as before, but this time, after Olivia and I walked up to the booth he was already in, Adrian and Ricky followed, badges flashing.

Upon seeing them, Asher jumped up, his feet landing on the upholstered seat, and he dove over the back into the adjacent booth—spilling fries, ketchup, and salad in the process—only to run straight into Adrian.

Seeing my man grab him by the elbows and restrain him easily made me have the sudden urge to leap over the booth at him myself, but I, erm, restrained myself.

"Apologies," Adrian said to the group with a dip of the head. "We'll get you more food to replace what spilled—on me, of course. Excuse us."

He guided Asher by the arm back into the original booth and we all shoved in around him.

I had to say, I did get a guilty pleasure from seeing the piece-of-trash blackmailer pissing himself. But trapping him in that booth also gave me pure guilt (and a little shell shock) from Ray and his non-barista goon trapping me and Olivia in one, so I ended his misery. "Relax, Asher, we're not here about that."

"Though we might be someday," Adrian said nonchalantly as he signaled to the waitress about food for the adjacent booth. The contrast couldn't be bigger—he was making sure the innocent bystanders were taken care of while he was also threatening a criminal. I couldn't think of anything more attractive.

Olivia, however, didn't seem to be feeling the guilty part of the pleasure. "We're here for a worse reason," she taunted, a smirk playing on her lips. "We know who killed Eugene."

All the blood drained from Asher's face. "I didn't do it! I swear! I mean, I'll admit it, I'm not squeaky clean, but, holy shit." He started emptying his pockets of his phone, keys, earbuds, lint. "Look through it all—I didn't kill anyone!"

Olivia leaned toward him across the booth. "Okay, Asher. We'll believe you."

"You will?"

She nodded. "If you help us."

Asher hesitated. "What do you need me to do?"

We had a trap to set, and we needed a very particular worm to do it.

CHAPTER 60

A few hours later, we were ready.

"Are you sure about this?"

Well, almost ready. Adrian, of course, was hesitant to put us in danger.

"Maybe we should rethink this." As was Ricky, apparently.

"We'll be careful," I said. "We know the risks and we're prepared."

"It's a solid plan," Olivia added, and since I'd come up with it, I obviously agreed.

"We can't stay in this motel for the rest of our lives," I said. "So are we ready to end this?"

"Cowabunga," Olivia said, her eyes on Ricky, who in turn looked like he'd fallen in love on the spot.

With a boyish grin, he added, "Jinkies."

Olivia's eyes now mirrored his.

Adrian still looked hesitant, so I went over and grabbed his hand. "Let's do this. Together."

His eyes softened. But before he could respond, my mom came up, separated our hands, and stood between us. "Together."

"Hey, don't forget about me!" Mandy exclaimed, popping in between my mom and me and grabbing our hands with gross sticky fingers covered in (I hope) M&M residue.

Like I said, we had to get out of this motel.

All eyes were on Adrian, who finally grunted.

Everyone turned to me.

"He's in," I said.

"Now, that's a grunt I can finally get behind," Olivia said. We shared a smile.

To catching a murderer, I thought, remembering that first toast with Olivia and Elle. And we had succeeded, technically, so maybe we could do it again.

Except we've swapped out a Murder Club member for wild cards, I couldn't help thinking.

But we had no choice.

Kathryn's First Law of Life, for better or for worse: Because there's no luck in the world, you have to make everything happen for yourself, one step at a time.

CHAPTER 61

We had spent hours and hours running for our lives while trying to put the pieces together. And it all came down to this.

"Why does it have to be here?" I asked, failing to suppress a shiver as I stepped into the coffee shop.

But I already knew the answer to that. The boys had picked this coffee shop because it had been seized when Ray Underwood went to jail for a slew of charges, meaning it was empty, with no risk of civilians entering.

Olivia came over and hugged me. "It'll be over before you know it."

Adrian and Ricky were currently securing the perimeter. It was just Olivia and me, which somehow felt fitting.

Mandy and my mom had been livid when we forced them to stay behind. But Mandy made the situation too volatile—the killer wanted revenge on her, after all—and my mom would only be in the way.

"I help! I help!" she'd exclaimed, and my heart had hurt. But I knew I couldn't focus if she were in danger, so we'd insisted. They were in the motel under police protection, far away from here.

"You ready?" Olivia asked me.

"With you, always."

She beamed. “Lasses and asses,” she said, pointing to me, then smacking her tush.

“Lasses and asses,” I said, repeating the gesture.

We were about to start a reaction, and one of the reagents was an unknown, but we’d done what we could. Time to see what product we’d get.

I retrieved Asher’s phone and sent a text to the killer.

CHAPTER 62

Fifteen minutes later, our expected guest walked into the coffee shop.

"Wyatt, hey," Olivia said nonchalantly.

"Good to see you again," I added.

"Do I know you?" he asked politely.

Technically we hadn't talked to each other at the boba café—Olivia and I had merely eavesdropped on his conversation with his ex, Isla—but he knew damn well who we were.

"We're the ones you've been tracking using my Helicopter Mom," I said just as nonchalantly as Olivia had greeted him. We'd originally suspected he'd been using the tracker Mandy had put on Olivia's car, but then my mom's arrival pointed us in the right direction. The Helicopter Mom was cheaply made and, as we'd found out the hard way, easy to hack. And we were dealing with Wyatt, who had learned a thing or two from his cybersecurity-specialist ex. How paradoxical that one gift from my mom had saved me while another put me in danger, though we did manage to turn the latter around in our favor.

"I don't know what you're talking about. What's a Helicopter Mom?" Wyatt's head swiveled left and right. "And where's Asher?"

"He's wherever the Helicopter Mom is. I turned that back on and gave it to him so you'd think we were elsewhere."

Wyatt held both hands up. "Look, I don't know what this is, but I'm out, okay? Whatever it is you're thinking, you're wrong. I thought I was meeting my boy Asher, but since he's not here . . ."

Everything about him was a lie, wasn't it? Including calling Asher, his blackmailer, his "boy."

Wyatt had one foot already out the door, but then I said, "We have what you want."

He paused.

I kept going. "What you wanted from Jocelyn. And didn't get. Mandy had it."

He turned back around to face us. "What is it you think I want?"

"I know all about you," I said, taking a step backward. Olivia and I were standing behind the last booth, ten feet away from Wyatt. "And I actually liked you when I first saw you, when you talked about how you were an *embarrassment*. But you don't belong with a group of pandas. You belong with a group of feral cats. Because you're a destruction. Destroying everyone and everything in your path. And at first, I thought you'd used a malapropism at the boba café, saying you could care less, but now I know you're like me. You're into words and meanings and you choose them carefully. So you meant exactly what you said to Isla that day—you truly *could* care less about Mandy Thorne and Dish Gets Served. Because you care so fucking much it led to murder."

I leaned my elbows on the back of the booth in front of me. "I don't think it started out that way, though. I think you got in over your head. I think what happened was, you hated Mandy. Blamed her for the *Dish Served Hot* revenge enacted on you. So you went on message boards trying to find other people who hated her, too. Who might also want to serve the dish right back to her. And there you found Eugene—or should

I say, MandyThorneIsTheDevil found DownWithMandy. And Eugene completely understood your anger. He even understood the show inspiring his ex's revenge. Together, you started planning. Eugene had stolen ethylene glycol from his former lab and told you about it so you could use it on Mandy together, but then things started spiraling out of control. Eugene was threatening Mandy, becoming unhinged, deviating off script, doing everything but staying anonymous. I'm guessing you came to the Dish Gets Served meeting to keep an eye on him—and probably panicked when your ex Isla showed up and spotted you. But you played it cool—A-plus acting, by the way—and got her to leave you alone, but everything else was falling apart. Eugene was going up to everyone and their mothers asking them to team up to get revenge, and you realized you had to do something. Eugene had given you the ethylene glycol, you knew how he liked his coffee, and you even knew it would work extra fast on him because he'd complained to you about how Mandy ruined his life and caused his kidney disease. And he trusted you, making it extra easy."

I tilted my head at him. "But it backfired, didn't it? You didn't predict the poison would make him agitated, disoriented, even angrier. And when Eugene screamed at Mandy in front of that huge crowd, you thought you were screwed. But then you realized there was a golden opportunity here. To kill two birds with one stone—and I unfortunately mean that quite literally. Mandy was *there*. And you could both silence Eugene *and* blame it on her. That must have felt like the heavens—or hells—aligning." (Origin: ancient astrological beliefs linked to celestial alignments of planets and stars.)

"Eugene had told you about the knife, so when you saw it in Mandy's purse, you knew exactly where it had come from and whose fingerprints would be on it. It was the perfect way to not only get rid of Eugene quickly since the poison was taking too long and making him act out, but to have all the evidence point to Mandy. And then to be extra sure all roads led to her, you later planted the bottle of ethylene glycol in Mandy's pantry using the keys Eugene had swiped from Jocelyn—which you took from his pockets, along with everything else, while he was dying." Hence, Eugene's empty pockets.

"But there was something—some*one* you didn't account for," I said. "Jocelyn. You didn't know about her involvement." To be honest, we weren't completely sure about Jocelyn's motivations, but he didn't need to know that. "And that threw a wrench in your plan"—origin: industrial revolution, when throwing something into machinery would break it and cause delays—"and you had to get rid of the wrench."

This one had so many pieces, but my mother was right—my lists had helped me put everything together.

But Wyatt wasn't going down easily. He shook his head as he said, "I don't know who this Jocelyn person is; I'm telling you, you have it all wrong."

His acting was leaps and bounds (origin: sports) above Mandy Thorne's, and I forced myself to keep going despite the sliver of doubt surfacing in the back of my brain. "Your plan was good—brilliant, even—but perfect? No. Because Mandy hasn't been arrested yet. No matter our efforts."

Finally, he stilled, seemingly holding his breath for a second. "What do you mean?"

"Mandy asked us to help her, but we've had our own motivations here," I said.

Olivia nodded. "We've been wanting to take her down this whole time."

He contemplated our words, then asked, "Why do you hate Mandy?"

"We're the girls from the true crime season, Queens' Revenge," I told him. "We're the queens."

"Pleasure to meet you," Olivia said with a wink.

He already knew this, of course, which only made it more powerful for us to admit it directly to him.

"It took us a while to figure out if we were going to approach you," I said. "Because there was one thing that didn't make sense to us. Why? Why were you this angry at Mandy Thorne? Yes, it's mortifying for your sexts to go to your family, but while it's worthy of a group of pandas—embarrassing—it doesn't seem to be group-of-cats-level worthy of destroying other people's lives. So I kept asking myself, *why is Wyatt so angry?* And then I realized, you weren't."

Wyatt's face shifted from blank to curious. I was winning him over. He was impressed by what I'd figured out and was maybe, hopefully, starting to wonder what we could accomplish together.

So I explained, "*You*, Wyatt, weren't the angry one. Not just you. Because you're not actually Wyatt. Isn't that right, Hubert Ombra Junior?"

He didn't even blink. He was giving even Adrian a run for his money (origin: horse racing where the expected winner is challenged by another competitor).

He didn't respond, so I kept going. "The reason we had such a hard time locating anything about Hubert Ombra Junior after his breakup with Cordelia is because, after you were arrested and hit with a restraining order"—courtesy of Ricky and Hubert Ombra Senior—"you started going by Wyatt. Too embarrassing what happened with your *stepmom*? You wanted to start over."

While Ricky had never seen Wyatt in person or by photo, Olivia and I had never seen Hubert Ombra Junior. So we hadn't put together they were one and the same until his photo had appeared on the DNA analysis screen with his real name underneath and a 50 percent DNA match to Hubert Ombra Senior.

"And in your new relationship," I continued, "you thought being upfront was the better strategy after what happened with Cordelia, and you didn't understand why Isla reacted so poorly to wanting an open relationship or threesome, especially when you *communicated*. And what Isla didn't know was just how much it hurt you when she tricked you into sending dick pics to your *ex* and now stepmom, especially after they made Cordelia think you were trying to get back together with her. And *both* Cordelia and Isla said in their podcast episodes that they wouldn't have thought to get revenge if not for the show. So you blamed Mandy for everything."

"The first person to be on *Dish Served Hot* twice, what an accomplishment," Olivia said, clapping.

Wyatt/Hubert remained silent.

"Nothing, Hubert?" Olivia said. "We know that you're Hubert Ombra Junior. That's not hard to prove." Though it was what made it so hard to track down both Wyatt and Hubert Ombra Junior.

Hubert finally spoke. "It's not a crime to go by a different name."

"But it is a crime to stalk—which is why you're in the system and how we got you—and now you've gone and upped the ante: threatening others with Molotov cocktails, and, oh, let's not forget murder. Twice." Olivia held two fingers up.

He clammed up again.

"We're not here to turn you in," I told him. "We want to team up. *Actually* get Mandy. You need us. We have access that you don't."

Hubert took a step closer to us. "Sure, ladies, I'd love to." He paused. "But there is just one problem." The corners of his lips lifted in a smug smirk. "Your acting is as abysmal as Mandy Thorne's."

Okay, there was no need to hurl daggers—or really, swords—here. I thought we'd done a pretty good job, but maybe it was impossible to lie to an expert.

"Did you really think that would work?" He took another step closer, and Olivia and I both backed up instinctually. "Did you really think I'd believe that you two doe-eyed girls would want to hurt someone?"

"You'd be surprised," Olivia said, her doe eyes darkening.

But Hubert just laughed. We weren't going to convince him of this.

"Well," I said, changing tactics, "you chose your path. We really did mean it. But now we have to go forward with what we have."

"It doesn't sound like you have anything," he said.

"Both Jocelyn and Eugene made sure to point a finger at their murderer before they passed."

"Then, great," Hubert said. "That person should already be in jail."

Cheeky bastard. "Jocelyn was right when she told you that you'd never get your hands on it."

This made him pause. It was the only leverage we had, and I had to use it correctly.

His eyes searched mine. Then he stated, "You don't have it."

"So that's a risk you're willing to take?" I taunted.

Jocelyn died to make sure he didn't get his hands on it. And he cared so much that he chose to search for it instead of cleaning up the crime scene—which, unbeknownst to him, contained strands of his hairs in the victim's hand—only to be interrupted by our arrival, causing him to flee. The ironic part of this—*actual* irony—is that he had thrown the Molotov cocktail through Adrian's window to distract and threaten us so we wouldn't go to Jocelyn's where he'd be taking care of that loose end. But he hadn't known about her threatening notes and couldn't have predicted that it actually sent us directly to the very place he was trying to keep us away from.

Hubert sized me up, a challenge, and I took it, trading glowers back and forth until he reached a decision. "You don't have it," he said with a sneer, cocky now.

"I do," I insisted, puffing my chest out to match his confidence.

"You don't."

"How can you be so sure?"

Olivia joined in, and together, the two of us kept pushing.

"Haven't you learned to stop underestimating us by now?"

"Your hubris will be the death of you."

"You don't know jack squat, Hubert."

I nudged Olivia's elbow. "I bet he *so* doesn't know jack squat that he doesn't know that *jack squat* is a malaphor. Or even what a malaphor is."

"Hubert thinks he's so smart, but his plan is falling apart right before his eyes because of us. Some plan."

Hubert had been simmering slowly until the last two insults pushed him over the edge, you-can't-handle-the-truth style. "If you had Eugene's phone, I'd already be in jail! So you don't. Fucking. Have it! And without it, you have nothing."

And scene. Here was the sinker, key, clincher, death blow. Just like I'd said earlier: His hubris was the death of him.

I glanced at Olivia and we shared a look of triumph.

"Thanks, Hubes," she said.

He looked confused and, for the first time, worried.

I couldn't contain my smile. "I never said it was Eugene's phone."

It was the last piece we needed. Our leading hypothesis was that Eugene and Hubert had been communicating via an app that only stored messages locally, and the only way to access them—and the damning evidence—was on the phone itself. (Which was also why the messages hadn't shown up in the records subpoenaed from Eugene's phone company.) We believed that Jocelyn took the phone from Eugene at the boba café—I remembered seeing the sexy firefighter bump into him, which was likely when she grabbed it—but we had no idea what Jocelyn had done with it. Hubert was likely as surprised as we had been when he hadn't found Eugene's phone on his dead body, and it wasn't until later that he figured out Jocelyn was the one in possession of it. And it was the last loose end Hubert needed to take care of.

Olivia's lips tilted up with the same smugness Hubert had worn just a few seconds ago. "The jig is up, Hubes." (Origin: sixteenth century slang definition of *jig* was a *trick*, *joke*, or *scheme*.) "You'll soon wish the worst thing that happened to you was sending nudes to your stepmom."

"She's. Not. My. Stepmom!"

With a roar, he charged at Olivia, taking her down to the floor.

"Where is it?" He scrabbled for Olivia's pockets.

Shit. This was trouble, but we'd prepared for it.

Olivia used her sleight of hand—one moment her hands were empty, and the next, a phone was there—and she flung it as hard as she could away from her and also me.

Hubert dove for it. As soon as he reached it, he smashed his heel down on it hard, sending shards flying.

But we were barely watching. We were hustling for the door. We had what we needed.

A shot rang out. A warning shot. From Hubert, who now had a gun in his hands.

"You got what you wanted," I said, hoping it was enough.

"Loose ends. You understand."

This had not been part of the plan.

He started to turn his gun toward me, and my life flashed before my eyes.

I should have let Adrian all the way in (no pun intended, but I guess that meaning worked, too). I should have told my mom the truth. I should have enjoyed all the little moments more. I should have realized just how good I had it.

"Put the gun down," said a calm and very sexy voice. Adrian appeared out of the shadows, his gun trained on Hubert.

Ricky emerged next. They had been waiting in the wings out of sight as per the plan, watching everything.

"You won't shoot me," Hubert said to Ricky and Adrian while continuing to keep his eyes and gun trained on Olivia and me. "You won't risk hitting your gal pals here." He was using our positions to his advantage, with him standing between us and the boys. "But I won't hesitate to shoot them both to clear the path out. You have three seconds to decide your next move, Detectives. And I think I have the upper hand here."

The door to the coffee shop opened. Hubert's head turned. In that split second, Adrian charged, taking Hubert down and sending his gun flying across the floor as their two bodies slid toward the front door.

Suddenly, a mop came down through the open door and whacked Hubert on the head—and maybe also caught Adrian in collateral damage. A second later, a tree branch joined in on the action, catching mostly Hubert but also Adrian.

Somehow, in the melee, Adrian managed to cuff Hubert. The mop and stick continued going until Adrian said, "It's okay, he's down."

Ricky grabbed Hubert's gun and engaged the safety.

The mop and stick dropped and in walked . . . my *father.* Followed by my mother.

I ran over to them. "What're you doing here?"

"Your baba was so worry when the Helicopter Mom get

turn off he come to Massachusetts. Then he call me. I tell him to come here. I already here because I follow you."

"Mom!"

"Why else you show me how to sneak out of motel if you not want me here? And no worry, we not come alone."

At that moment, Mandy came through the door. "Is it over?"

Upon seeing her, Hubert hauled himself up and charged toward her.

Except I was in the way.

Time seemed to slow. I clocked the threat, the trajectory, the danger. My brain screamed at my feet to move.

Suddenly, my body went flying.

But not because Hubert attacked me. Because *Mandy* had pushed me out of the way. She had a split second to make a decision, and instead of saving herself, she hadn't hesitated to shove me sideways. Only to become the sole target for Hubert. If I were still there, I would have taken the brunt of the impact, but now, Hubert rammed into Mandy head on, knocking her into the wall so hard it shook.

"Mandy!" I yelled as I came forward.

"I'm okay," she eked out.

Adrian reached Hubert a second before me, and together we took him down—completely in sync thanks to our self-defense sessions.

This time, Adrian also zip-tied Hubert's feet.

"Aiyah, Yushan!" my mother exclaimed. "So impressive!"

I waited for the disparaging part to come, but that seemed to be it.

Then she opened her mouth again. "You two a good match, work together so well."

That was the last thing I'd expected to hear.

"Good job. You protect her even better than cardboard Glen Power."

Or maybe *that* was the last thing I'd expected.

"Are you okay?" Adrian asked, his eyes raking over me.

"I am," I reassured him. I wanted to kiss him, but I couldn't, not in front of my parents, even if my mom did seem to like him better now.

"Ooooh!" Mandy said, and I turned.

To see Olivia and Ricky kissing.

"*Finally*," I said with a laugh.

Adrian and I shared a grin.

Then I remembered what it felt like just a few minutes ago when my world flashed before my eyes, and I thought, *To hell with it.*

I grabbed Adrian's shirt and pulled him to me. Our lips met more forcefully than I'd intended and I heard an "Aiyah!" and "What this?" from behind me, but I ignored them. And I kissed my boyfriend with all the passion and gratitude in the world.

Because as Elle said, these were the things that made life worth living. And I wanted to live.

"I'm in," I told him. "For all of it."

He leaned forward close to my ear. When he inhaled to speak, a shiver ran down my spine. "Even if I have a splotchy penis?"

Okay, now *that* was the last thing in the world I'd ever expected to hear. I laughed so hard my stomach hurt.

CHAPTER 63

"Thank you for coming to help," Adrian said to my parents at the station after we'd all given our statements.

"Aiyah, was nothing," my father said. "I learn gong-fu as kid—can you tell? Mop just like using staff. All come back to me so quick."

"Thanks for getting her the Helicopter Mom and Life Alert, too," Adrian said to my mother. He'd said he wanted to thank her for it one day, though I never thought it would be under these circumstances.

"You smart," my mom said. "See the value in my gifts. Though maybe I send less now." She turned to me and waggled her eyebrows. "He even better than Glen Power—not just cardboard one."

Gross. But also, thank all the gods. Though now that my mom would be sending fewer packages, maybe I would miss the laughs that came with them.

Olivia and Ricky joined us, holding hands. I gave her my own eyebrow waggle, which I expected her to ignore, but she winked back at me, warming my heart.

"So all over?" my father asked me. "You have killer?"

"I think we have him for Jocelyn's murder, but it will be harder to get him for Eugene's. It's good we have everything that just happened on video"—we were wired and there had been cameras set up in Ray's coffee shop—"and we got him to fall into our trap, admitting he was looking for Eugene's phone and then destroying the decoy. But the final decision will be up to the jury."

"If we could just find Eugene's phone, that would cinch it," Ricky said. (Origin: Spanish word *cincha* for a strap that secures a saddle to a horse.)

"I could even unlock it immediately," I said, thinking of the resin fingerprint I'd made from the one I'd pulled off his glass all those weeks ago.

"Why do you think Jocelyn took it?" Olivia asked. "And where do you think it is?" All our searches had come up empty.

"We may never know her exact involvement in all this," Adrian said. "But we'll keep looking."

I sighed. "I wish it were more of a done deal."

"These things rarely are," Adrian said. "You did good, though. You figured out how the pieces fit together, and we wouldn't have gotten this far or gotten him into custody without you."

"My Yushan, the best. Number one," my mother said.

And that was it. No additional disparaging comments. I wasn't sure I'd ever get used to this kind of praise from her. Was it possible for my heart to burst open?

"So is official yet?" my mother asked.

"Is what official?"

"We part of Murder Club?" She gestured to herself and my dad.

I chuckled. "You've both earned your spot."

Though I was never putting them in danger again. But maybe there was something to this. Hadn't I been wanting a new joint interest with them? And they had helped with both cases, even if the first one was unwittingly.

We'd need a new name, though.

My mother checked her watch. "I have to go. New job."

"What? What job?" I asked. When did this happen?

"Podcast. With your friend."

"Wait, *what*?"

But I didn't get a chance to follow up because the department receptionist called out, "Kathryn Hu, you have a package!"

I glanced at Adrian. "Do you think it could be? My certification?" Maybe Gerard had finally put my hours through.

"I hope so," Adrian said. "You deserve it."

I stood to go to reception.

"Oh my god," Olivia blurted, grabbing my arm. Her phone was vibrating.

"What?" I asked.

She showed me the screen.

She was getting a call from the governor's office.

"Do you think—did Mandy—"

Olivia and I shared a hopeful, excited look. Then I frantically motioned toward her phone.

"Hello?"

Kathryn's Thirteenth Law of Life: Sometimes you *can* make things happen for yourself, one step at a time, but it's better to do it as a team.

Through the Looking Glass

Three Days Ago

From the point of view of Jocelyn

How did I get into this mess? Not just this current predicament, but all of it! My entire life was a puddle of melted Jell-O, which was apt since that's how my Jell-O always turned out. The easiest thing to make and I couldn't even do it.

I came to Massachusetts dreaming of a sisterly bond with Mandy Thorne. The sibling I've always wanted—and more importantly, truly needed after losing my adoptive parents and finding out my birth mother was already dead. But in Mandy's presence, I couldn't get my mouth or limbs or brain to work, and I'd ended up her assistant of all things. And I was miserable. But I was near her. I was getting to know her. It wasn't quite enough, though.

How could I get her to notice me? How could I find a way to tell her who I was?

And that was when it hit me. How else but to play a prank on her? If I pranked the Queen of Revenge, she'd notice me. Respect me. See me as her sister.

It was perfect. Brilliant. Easy. Especially because someone—Eugene—had found me online and wanted to team up to prank her. So I agreed.

But when we met up, it was not at all what I thought it would be. His suggestions for pranks quickly escalated from silly and funny to downright sinister. Then he asked me for access to Mandy's home. And to bring in another person.

I tried to talk him down, but it only seemed to rile him up. Soon, he was calling Mandy terrible names, swearing, scaring me. I had to end it. So I told him I was out, this wasn't going to work, that I'd changed my mind.

He was angry, banging his fist on the table so hard it spilled my drink right into my lap. But a few seconds later, he seemed to defuse. He even thanked me for my time and got me more napkins. We parted ways amicably, and I was thankful it was over and I'd gotten out unscathed. But when I got home, I realized he'd stolen my keys! The trouble was just beginning.

I had to figure out what he was planning. And I had to fix it. I got myself into this, and I could get myself out. Mandy didn't have to know.

So at the Dish Gets Served meeting, when I saw him there, I took his phone. For once, my clumsiness had served me. In that moment, I had felt like Double-Oh-livia, who Mandy admired, though she'd never admit that. Maybe I could be cool and sly like Olivia and smart and scrappy like Kat. I don't know why Mandy needed them when she also had me. I just had to show her I could be like them, too.

But getting Eugene's phone only dug a deeper hole. Because what I saw on there was terrifying. Messages to an unidentified person about poison and how Mandy had to pay. A plan had been laid out to serve her the deadliest dish of all. But Eugene was also growing frantic and impatient, which was leading to fights with the mystery person, who warned him to stop attracting attention or else their plan wouldn't work. Eugene had agreed, but I knew from my end that he was escalating—threatening Mandy with first messages, then the knife.

I was beside myself, worried Eugene would make his move at the Dish Gets Served meeting. I had to stop him. But before I could do anything let alone go to the police, Eugene turned up dead.

It had to be the unidentified person. He took care of Eugene before anything could come out about their plans. And I thought, maybe it was over! He wouldn't come after Mandy now, would he?

And then he framed her for murder. *Perfect*, I'd thought. This was his revenge. He wouldn't actually harm her, and Mandy didn't do it, so she'd be able to get out of it.

But then he did it too well. *Everything* pointed to her. And Kat and Olivia were on my tail, too close, too suspicious, and I had to get them to back off. If I could keep myself out of it, I'd find a way to get Mandy out of this mess, I knew I could.

So I sent the notes. I just needed to buy myself some time.

Then the murderer contacted me. He said he knew I had Eugene's phone. Demanded I hand it over.

But I couldn't. That was the only proof we had of what the killer had done. The only proof of Mandy's innocence. But I also didn't want to turn it in and have eyes turning to me.

Everything was coming to a head. Time was running out.

Should I come clean? Go to the police?

Or . . . I could run.

But he wouldn't leave Mandy alone. I knew he wouldn't.

So I put a plan in place. One that would protect Mandy. But the only way to protect myself was to get the hell out of Dodge—origin, the TV Western *Gunsmoke* (see? I could be Kat).

But just as I was packing, I heard a noise outside.

He's here.

I had to run for it. But before I'd made it three steps, the back door banged open. Kicked in.

I wasn't going to make it to the front door in time. So I grabbed my Swiss Army knife out of my pocket and turned to face him.

"I don't have the phone."

"I tracked it here before it went offline," the murderer said.

I was out of options. I'd led myself here. Now I had to finish it.

I charged.

He dodged.

I swung a hand forward, slashing out with the knife, but he slammed his forearm onto my wrist and sent my only weapon flying.

I dove for it, but he grabbed me by my hair, pulling me back.

I scrambled, turning around and knocking his hand off. But he immediately wrapped it around my neck. His other hand followed.

I reached forward, fumbling for purchase on something, anything.

My fingers wrapped around his ear, slipped off. Then grasped his hair but slipped off again. But in the process, I managed to grab a few strands of hair.

If anyone comes for you, DNA first, I heard Mandy say in my head.

I focused my energy on keeping that fist closed, keeping the evidence clutched inside.

I thought of Mandy, of all the mistakes I'd made, of all the mistakes I still wanted to get to make. At least I'd just sent her to Kat, Olivia, Adrian, and Ricky before I started packing. They would keep her safe.

Stars swam in my vision.

As I looked into his eyes, I wondered if he'd meant for it to go this far. And in them, I saw a feeling I recognized. He was in too deep, just trying to claw his way out.

Just like me.

My last thought as I sank into darkness was, *Thank gods I mailed the phone to Kat.*

Dear Mama Hu Podcast Transcript–
Episode 1: *New Release*

[Podcast theme song plays, sung by
Mandy Thorne and Mama Hu]

MANDY THORNE: Welcome, welcome, my lovely Thornies, to the first episode of our soon-to-be award-winning podcast, *Dear Mama Hu*! Where Mama Hu, the mom hostess with the mostess, takes your questions and gives you the best advice!

Our first guest today is Lucille, who is in a tricky situation with her beau. Lucille, tell us what brings you on our show as our special inaugural guest!

LUCILLE: Hi, Mandy! Hi, Mama Hu! I'm so excited to be here today! But I am *not* excited to tell you what's been going on. I just met my partner's family, and it's a nightmare. Seriously, nightmare with capitals, italics, everything.

MAMA HU: Hi, Lucy, you have nightmare? I tell you how to fix. Warm tea one hour before bed, and put Salonpas on head—you know Salonpas? Best medicine. Cure everything. One patch, on forehead—*pah!* Instant sleep.

MANDY: Great, great, thanks, Mama Hu. So now that Lucille and all our lucky listeners know how to fall asleep instantly at night, what advice do you have about bad in-laws?

LUCILLE: Well, I'm not married yet, but yes, my partner's family—

MAMA HU: I tell you story. You learn from me. I marry for almost thirty year. You know how I pick? I tell you, I have so many option. All the men, they chase me. I very pretty, and successful, and I cook best scallion pancake in the world. Just ask my Yushan. She know. One of the men handsome like movie star *and* is doctor. Can you believe? Dream, yes? No! I learn after three months he eldest of *six*! Can you believe? Six! That too many brother and sister!

LUCILLE: Okay, and . . . ?

MAMA HU: And! You know what that mean! In Chinese culture, eldest must give red envelope to younger brother and sister at New Year! All that money, just run out the door! Nothing I can do! So I leave!

LUCILLE: Seriously? Just because—

MAMA HU: Exactly. So smart of me. And another one, he only child. So you know what that mean! His parents move in with us in future. No avoiding! So I also leave! So I tell you now. You leave. If in-law bad, your life bad. You get out now, before too late. But if you find good one—one who protect, who like you for you, then grab tight! My Yushan choose well. Better to wait—and aiyah, she wait so long! My hair white now, all her fault! But is okay because she wait for right man. You wait too, okay? Listen to Mama Hu! And as soon as you *do* find right one, then hurry! Marry and have babies! No time to lose!

MANDY: There you have it, straight from Mama Hu herself. You are worthy. You deserve love. You deserve the best. So wait for it.

LUCILLE: I don't think that's what—

MAMA HU: And until you find right man, buy Helicopter Mom!

MANDY: Oh, that's right! Mama Hu just reminded me, here's a word from our most generous sponsor, Helicopter Mom! A wonderful product, and not just for toddlers.

MAMA HU: That right! Helicopter Mom is best gift, for child, for single daughter, everyone! I wear right now! And at end of ad, discount! Cannot get better than that! So cheap! Buy for everyone you love!

MANDY: [mischievously] And even *don't* love. Wink, wink.

MAMA HU: Good, good. Is smart to keep tab on your mortal enemy!

* * * * *

ACKNOWLEDGMENTS

I am so grateful for the love and support this series has received. Thank you. To each and every one of you. For going on these adventures with this trio; for reviewing, posting, telling a friend. I am just so grateful. When I changed careers over a decade ago, I didn't even dare dream this big. Thank you for loving my characters. Thank you for your support and enthusiasm and joy. Thank you, thank you, for making it so I can do my dream job. Writing books filled with humor, shenanigans, and ride-or-die friendships brings me so much joy, and I hope in turn I was able to bring you some joy as well.

Kathleen Rushall—thank you for being the best agent from day one. I couldn't do this without you, and I am so lucky to work with you.

Leah Mol—thank you for your love and support for these characters and for continuing on this journey with me and them. Thank you for your brilliant editorial eye and always bringing out the best in the story, for your incredible attention to detail, and for always going the extra mile. The girls (and I) are in the best hands with you, and it is an honor and privilege to get to work with you.

Sophie James—there are no words for how grateful I am for your time and hard work on these books. I am blown away by how passionate, competent, kind, and responsive you are. Thank you for getting so much buzz for this series!

Ambur Hostyn—I am in awe of your creativity, talent, and enthusiasm. Thank you for always being so open to my ideas, for being so on top of everything, and for being so enthusiastic, kind, and passionate. You are an absolute joy to work with!

Thank you to Quinn Banting for yet another perfect cover. You are exceptional, and I am so grateful to you for bringing both books to life so beautifully.

Thank you to all the wonderful people at Park Row Books, MIRA, Harlequin, and HarperCollins who helped bring this book into the world: designer Renata DiBiase, copy editor Dana Francoeur, proofreader Elena Gritzan, production editor Katie McHale, as well as Ashley MacDonald, Heather Connor, and the larger marketing, publicity, and sales teams.

Kim Yau—thank you for all your enthusiasm and hard work through the years, and for always understanding my stories on another level. And thank you for helping me find the best home for this series.

Wendi McLendon-Covey, Sophia Lucchesi, Gladys Gonzalez, and Strong Beach Productions—I'm over the moon that we've partnered to bring these books to the screen. Thank you for your incredible passion, your wonderful vision, and all the time you've put in. I'm excited for what's to come!

Taryn Fagerness—thank you for your love and support for my projects, especially this series.

A huge thank-you to the wonderful booksellers, librarians, bookstores, and reviewers for your support. I am so grateful to each and every one of you. Special thanks to The Hive, The Gloss Book Club, Erin Woodward, Kathleen March, Illinois Reads, The Book Cellar, Suzy T, Anderson's Bookshop, Murder By The Book, Tropes & Trifles, Next Chapter Booksellers, Mysterious Galaxy Books, Old Firehouse Books, Silver Unicorn Books, Porter Square Books, Paul Swydan, Barnes & Noble Wicker Park, *The Shit About Writing Podcast*, *The Well-Read*

Podcast, Megan Bjerke, Mary Kole, Good Story Company, West Coast Booksters, *Reeding Podcast*, Crime Reads, Novel Suspects, Book Riot, Katherine Ouellette, WBUR, Book Trib, About the Authors TV, Jake Brown, Dru Ann Love, Deborah Kalb, Book Notions, Elise Dumpleton, TaiwaneseAmerican.org, Leona Chen, Goodreads editor Sharon, Barnes & Noble Oakbrook, and The Avid Pen.

Thank you to my fellow authors for your inspiration and support. Special thanks to Jilly Gagnon, Mia P. Manansala, Laurie Elizabeth Flynn, Bianca Marais, Mary Winn Heider, Lindy Ryan, Samira Ahmed, Lizzie Cooke, Anna Waggener, Kat Cho, Ronni Davis, Rena Barron, Kate Hannigan, and Jim Klise.

Mom and Dad, thank you for your support. I love you so much.

Waipo, thank you for your support from the very beginning. I will never forget your enthusiasm. I love you, and you are missed.

Anthony, I would not be where I am without your love and support. Thank you for reading every word (and many times), for brainstorming, for your brilliant ideas, for always believing, and for being the most fun, positive, and loving person I know. You are my everything.